THE UNKINDNESS
OF RAVENS

This is a work of fiction and any resemblance of characters to persons living or dead is purely coincidental.

Kids Can Press acknowledges the financial support of the Government of Ontario, through the Ontario Media Development Corporation's Ontario Book Initiative; the Ontario Arts Council; the Canada Council for the Arts; and the Government of Canada, through the CBF, for our publishing activity.

Published in Canada by
Kids Can Press Ltd.
25 Dockside Drive
Toronto, ON M5A 0B5

Published in the U.S. by
Kids Can Press Ltd.
2250 Military Road
Tonawanda, NY 14150

www.kidscanpress.com

Edited by Karen Li and Stacey Roderick
Designed by Rachel Di Salle and Marie Bartholomew

The hardcover edition of this book is smyth sewn casebound.
The paperback edition of this book is limp sewn with a drawn-on cover.
Manufactured in Shen Zhen, Guang Dong, P.R. China, in 4/2013 by Printplus Limited.

CM 13 0 9 8 7 6 5 4 3 2 1
CM PA 13 0 9 8 7 6 5 4 3 2 1

Library and Archives Canada Cataloguing in Publication

Torres, J., 1969 –
The unkindness of ravens / written by J. Torres ; illustrated by Faith Erin Hicks.

(Bigfoot Boy)
ISBN 978-1-55453-713-6 (bound) ISBN 978-1-55453-714-3 (pbk.)

I. Hicks, Faith Erin II. Title. III. Series: Bigfoot Boy

PN6733.T67U65 2013 j741.5'971 C2012-908288-0

Kids Can Press is a Corus™ Entertainment company

THE UNKINDNESS OF RAVENS

J. Torres and Faith Erin Hicks

Kids Can Press

For Titus, my little bigfoot.
Love, Da

For my brothers, who are now Bigfoot Men — F. E.H.

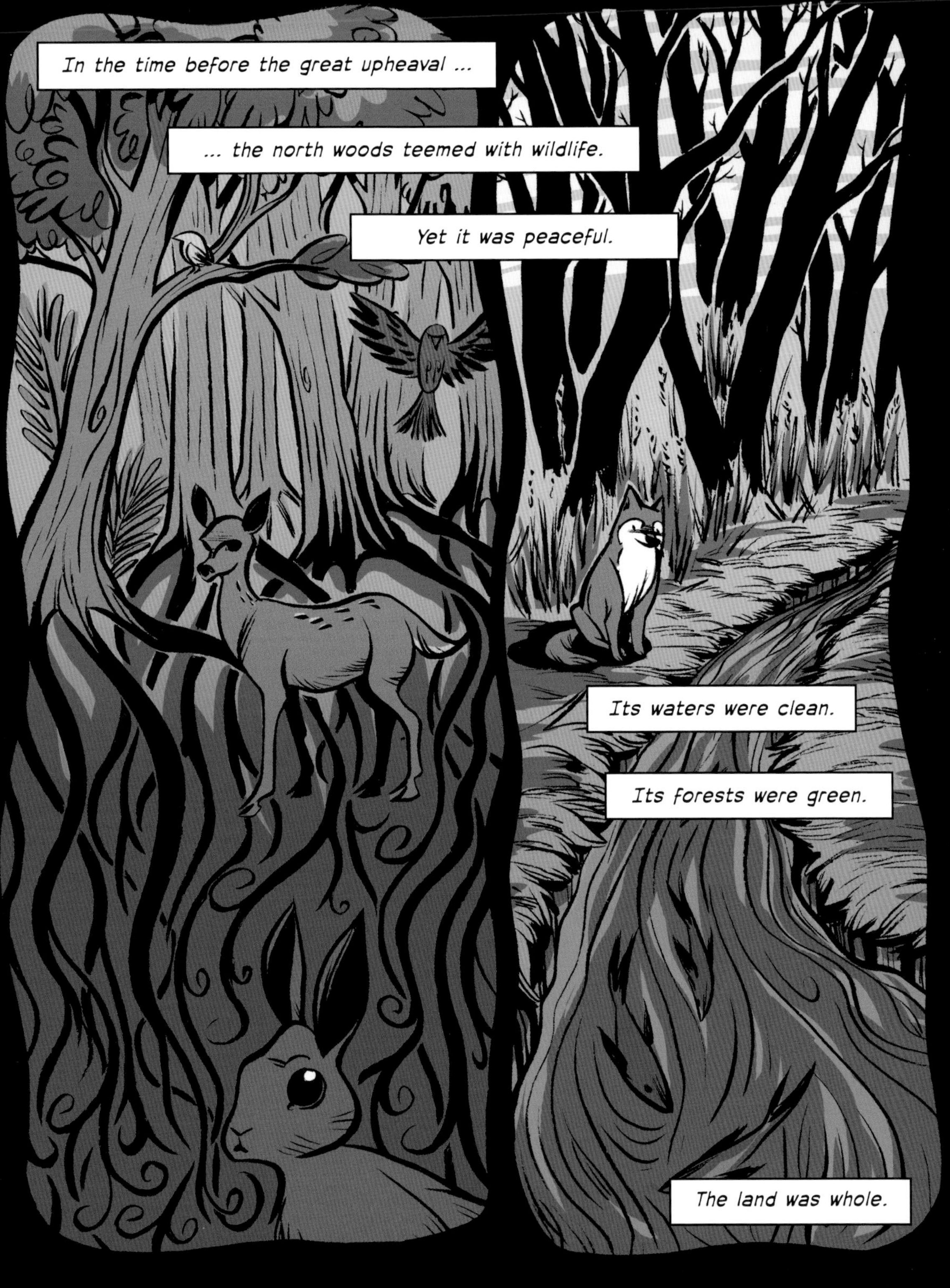
In the time before the great upheaval ...
... the north woods teemed with wildlife.
Yet it was peaceful.
Its waters were clean.
Its forests were green.
The land was whole.

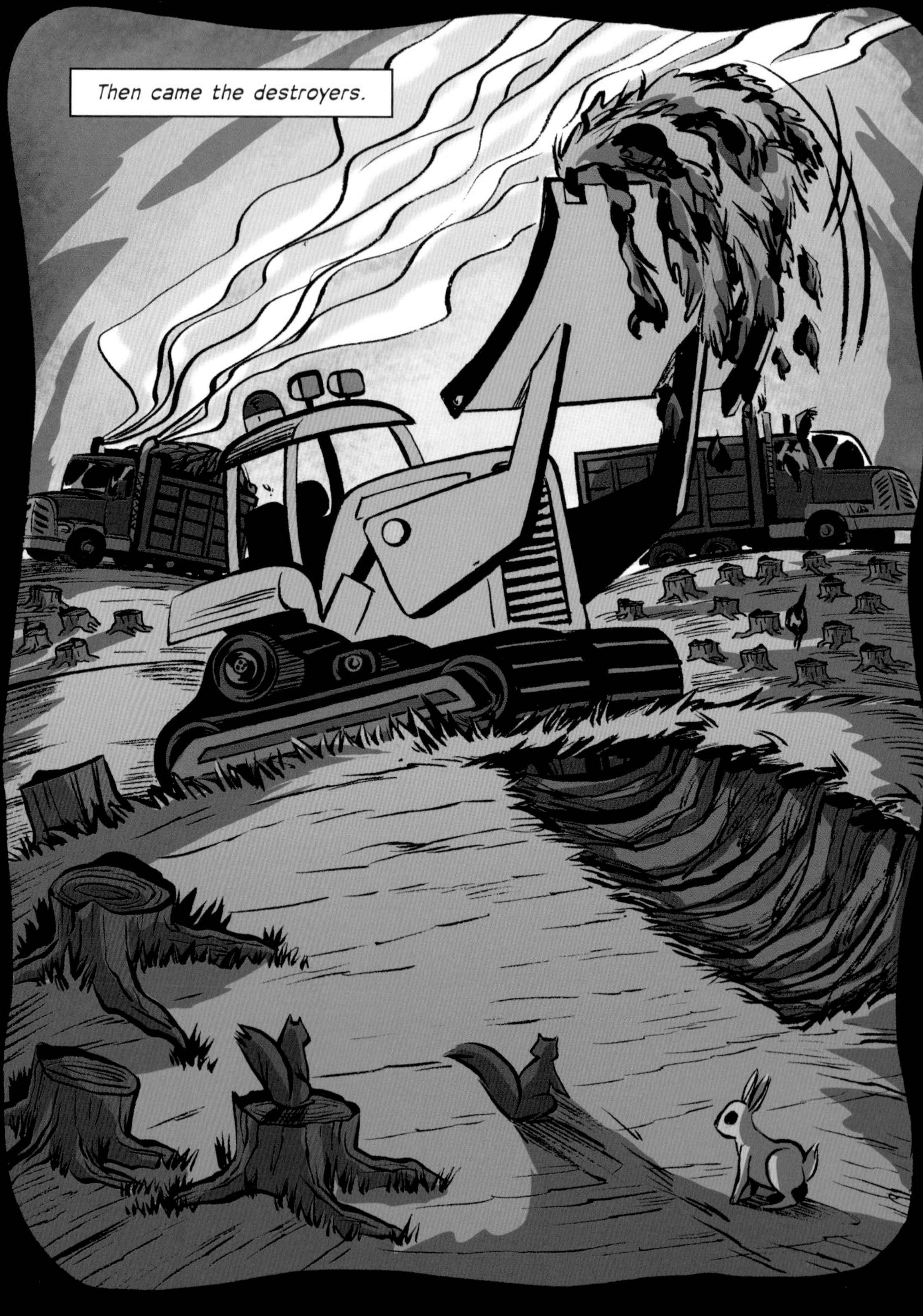
Then came the destroyers.

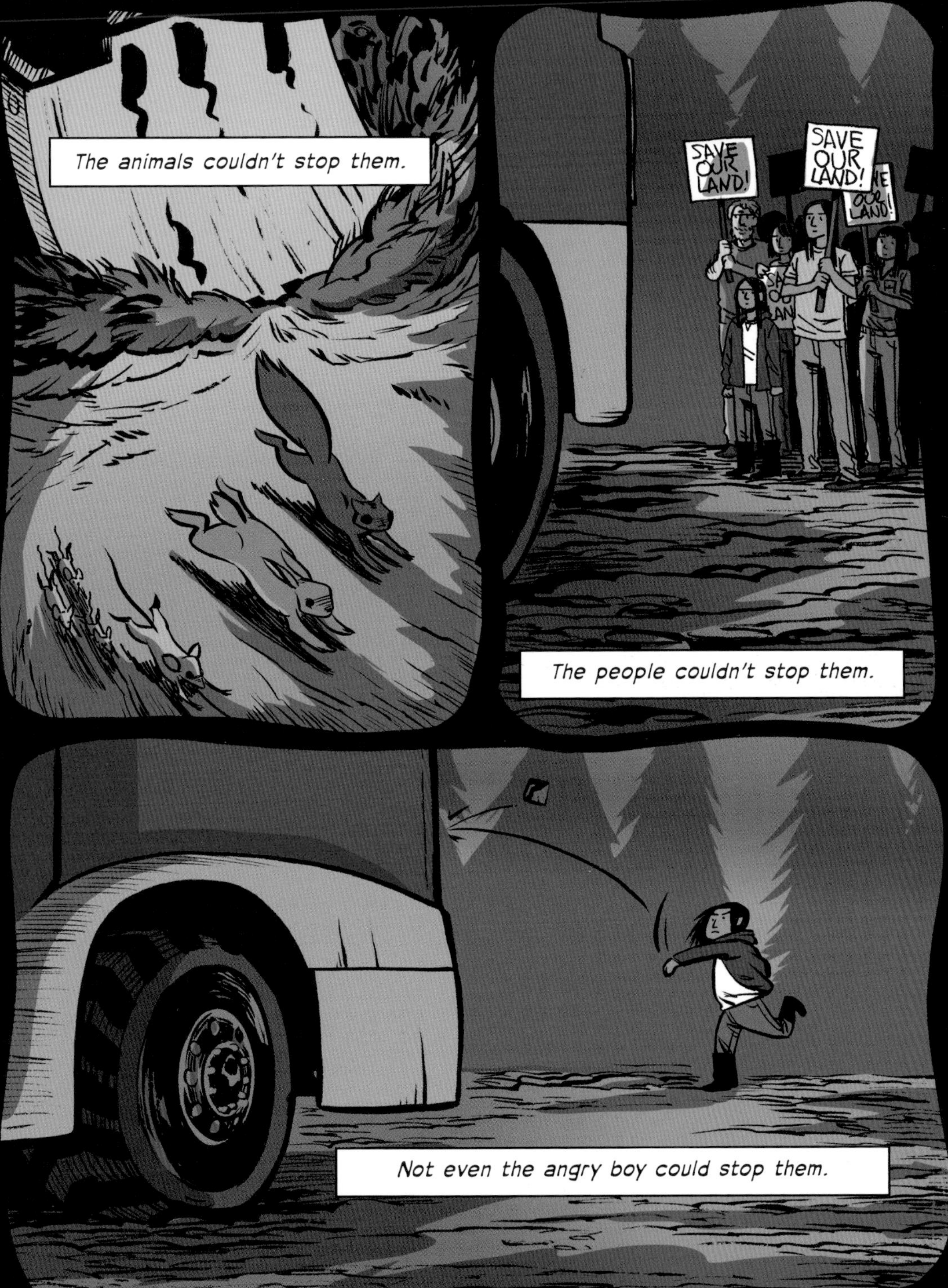
The animals couldn't stop them.
SAVE OUR LAND!
SAVE OUR LAND!
The people couldn't stop them.
Not even the angry boy could stop them.

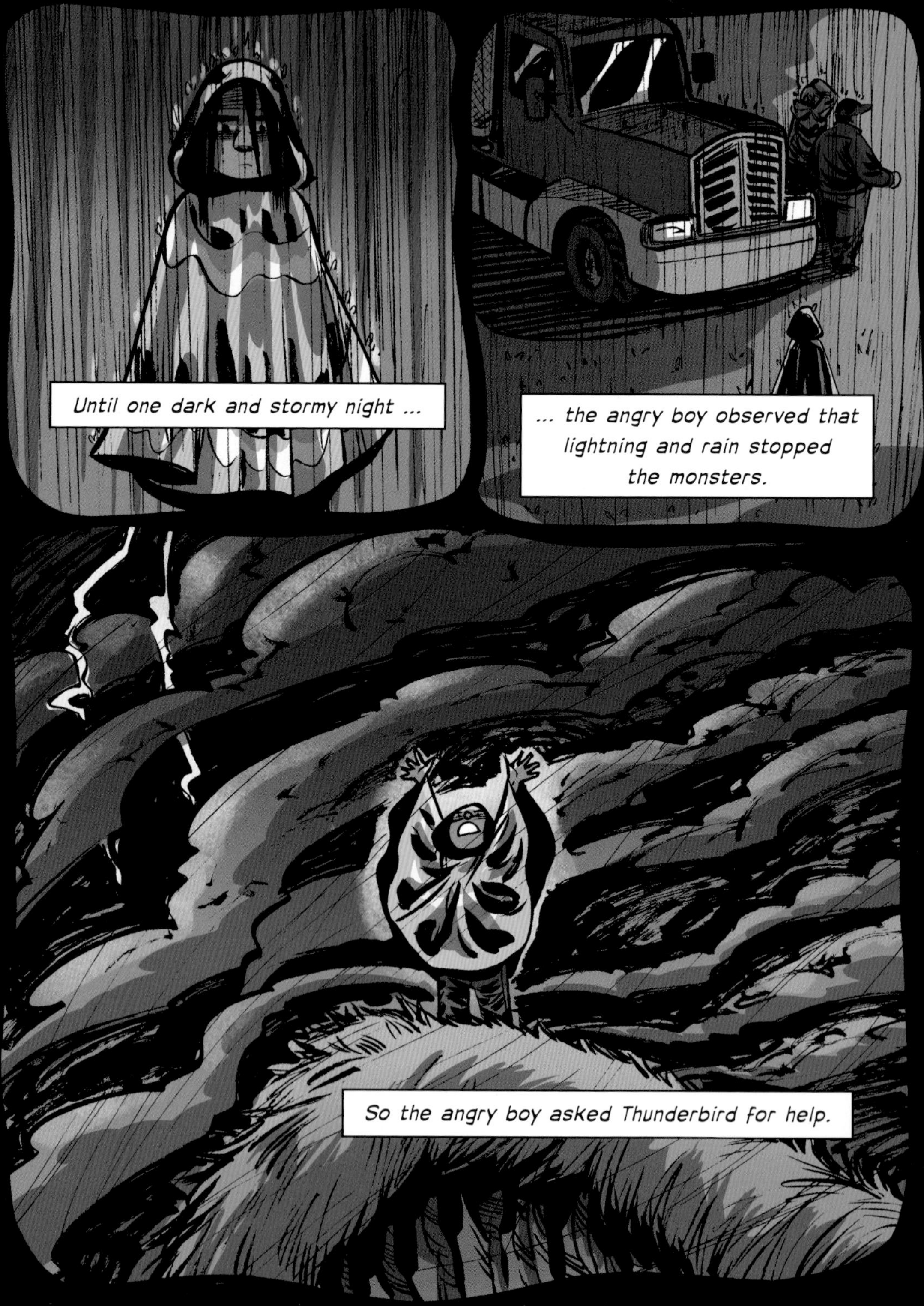
Until one dark and stormy night ...
... the angry boy observed that lightning and rain stopped the monsters.
So the angry boy asked Thunderbird for help.

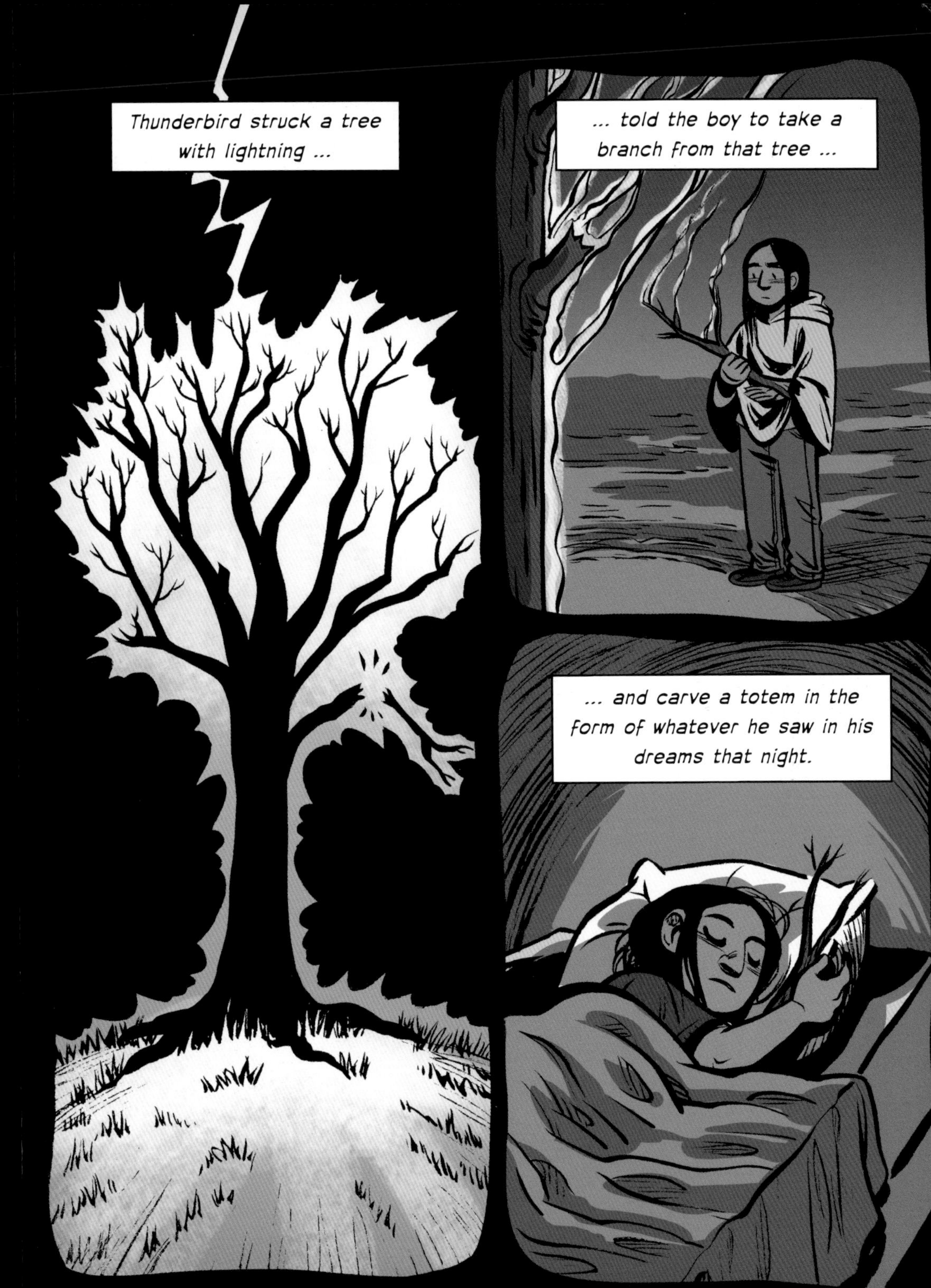
Thunderbird struck a tree with lightning ...
... told the boy to take a branch from that tree ...
... and carve a totem in the form of whatever he saw in his dreams that night.

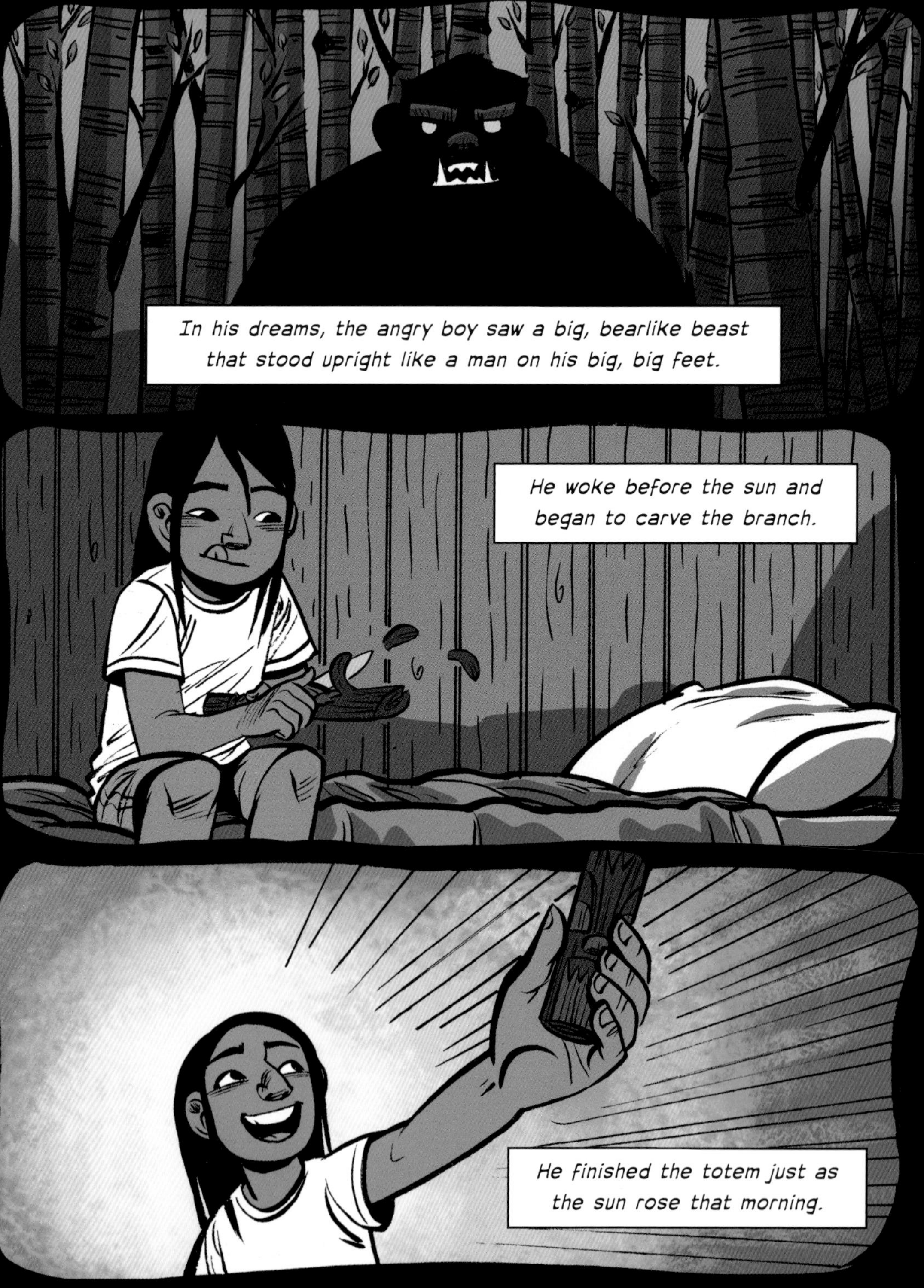
In his dreams, the angry boy saw a big, bearlike beast that stood upright like a man on his big, big feet.
He woke before the sun and began to carve the branch.
He finished the totem just as the sun rose that morning.

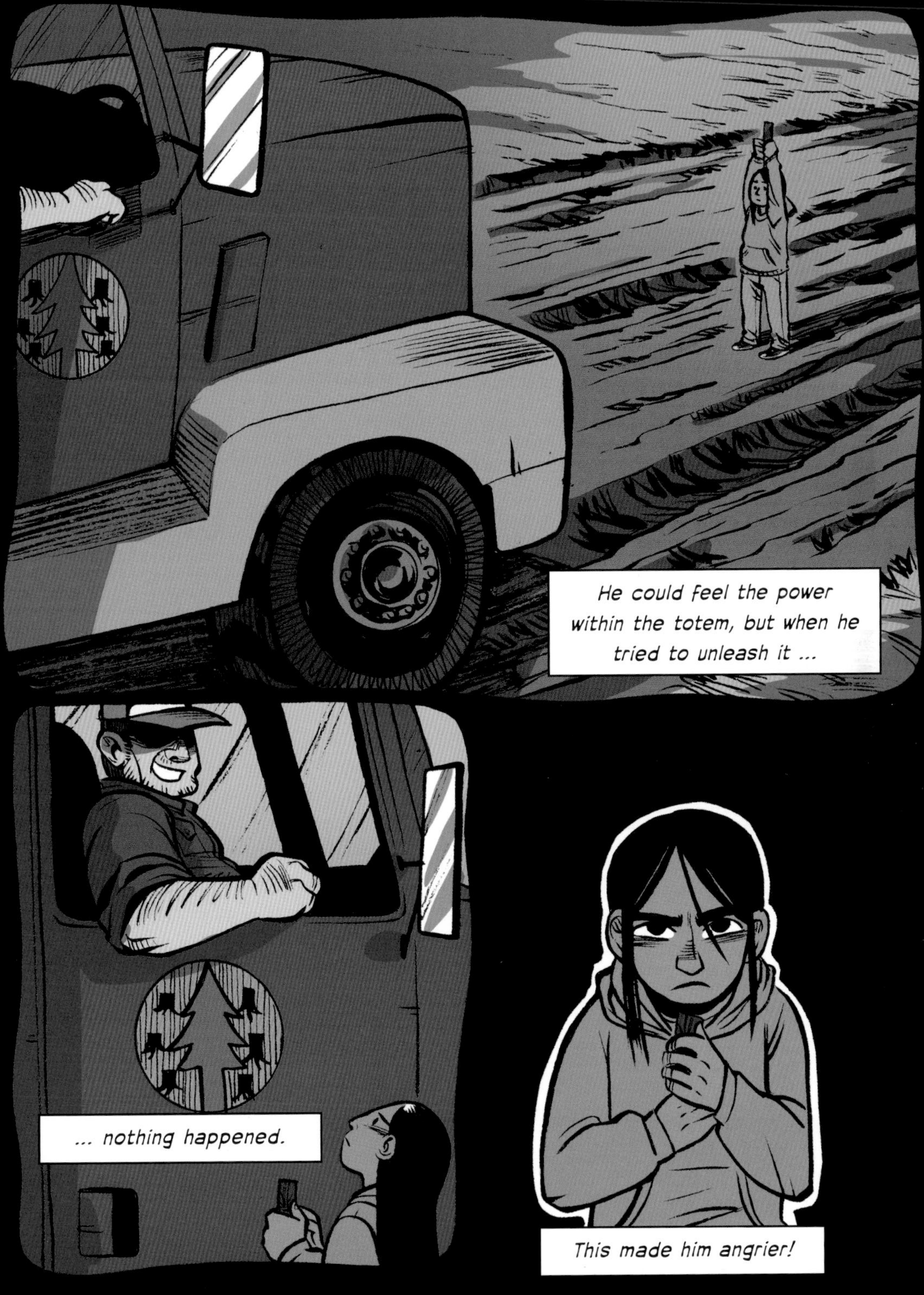
He could feel the power within the totem, but when he tried to unleash it ...
... nothing happened.
This made him angrier!

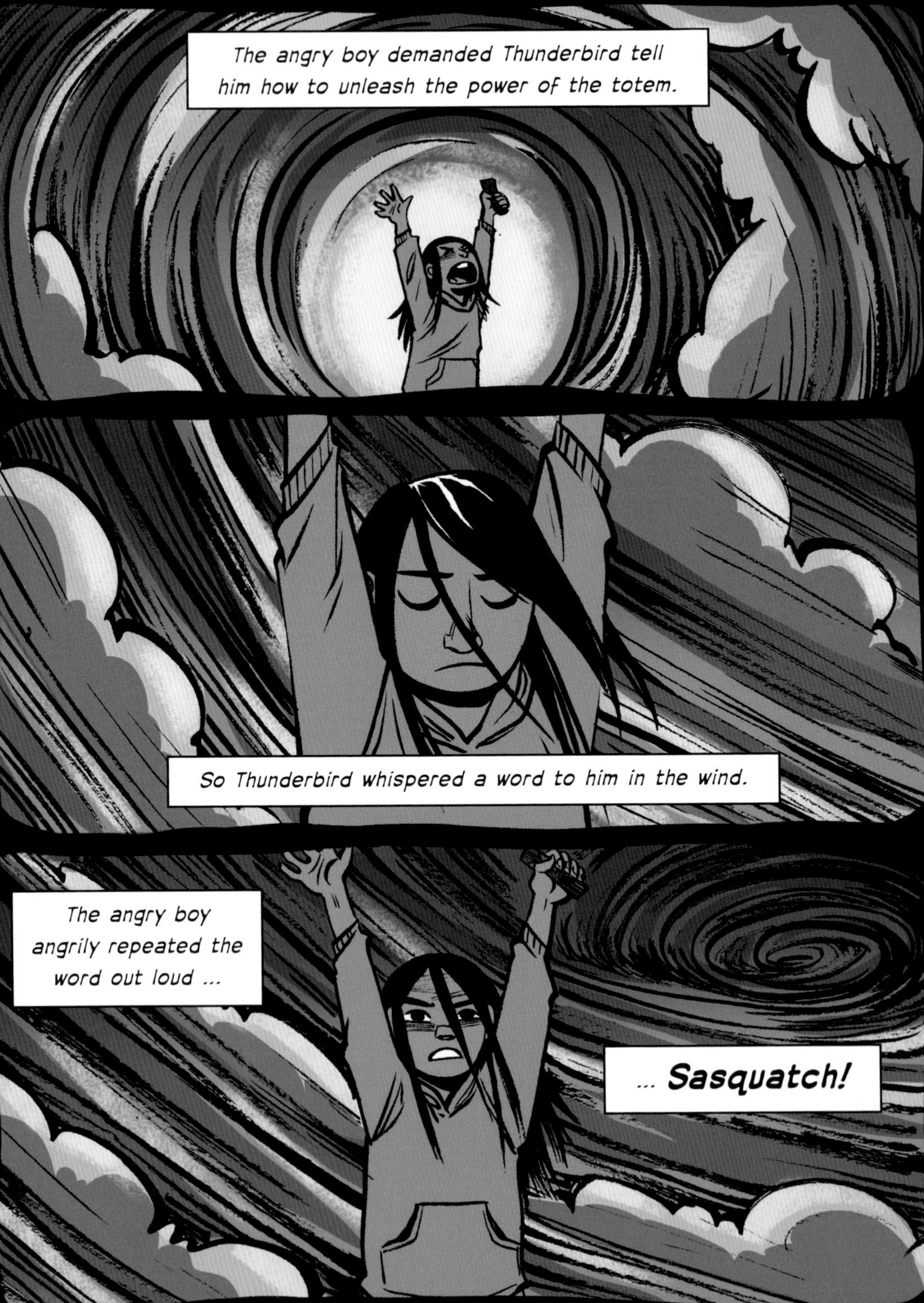
The angry boy demanded Thunderbird tell him how to unleash the power of the totem.
So Thunderbird whispered a word to him in the wind.
The angry boy angrily repeated the word out loud ...
... Sasquatch!

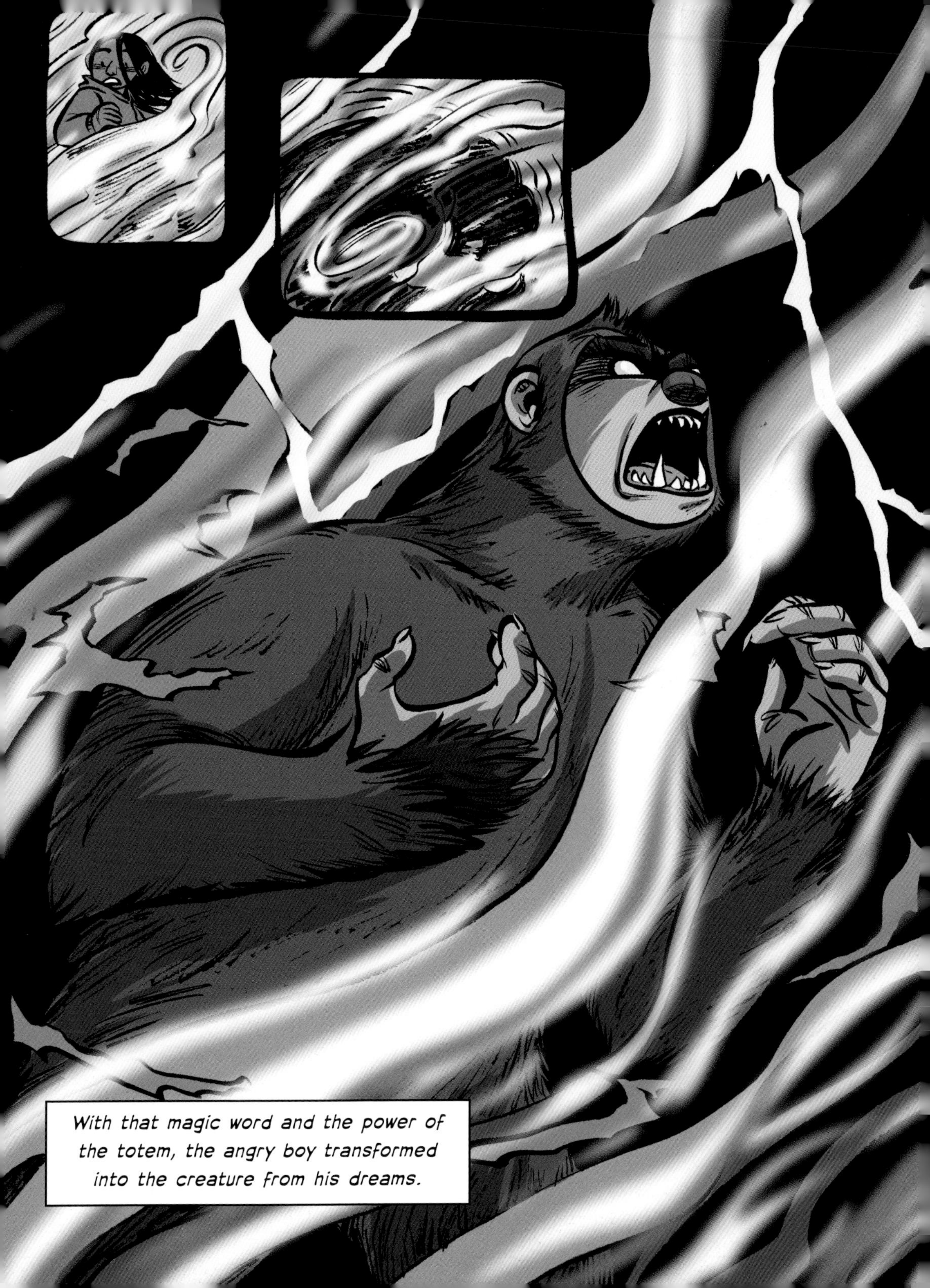
With that magic word and the power of the totem, the angry boy transformed into the creature from his dreams.

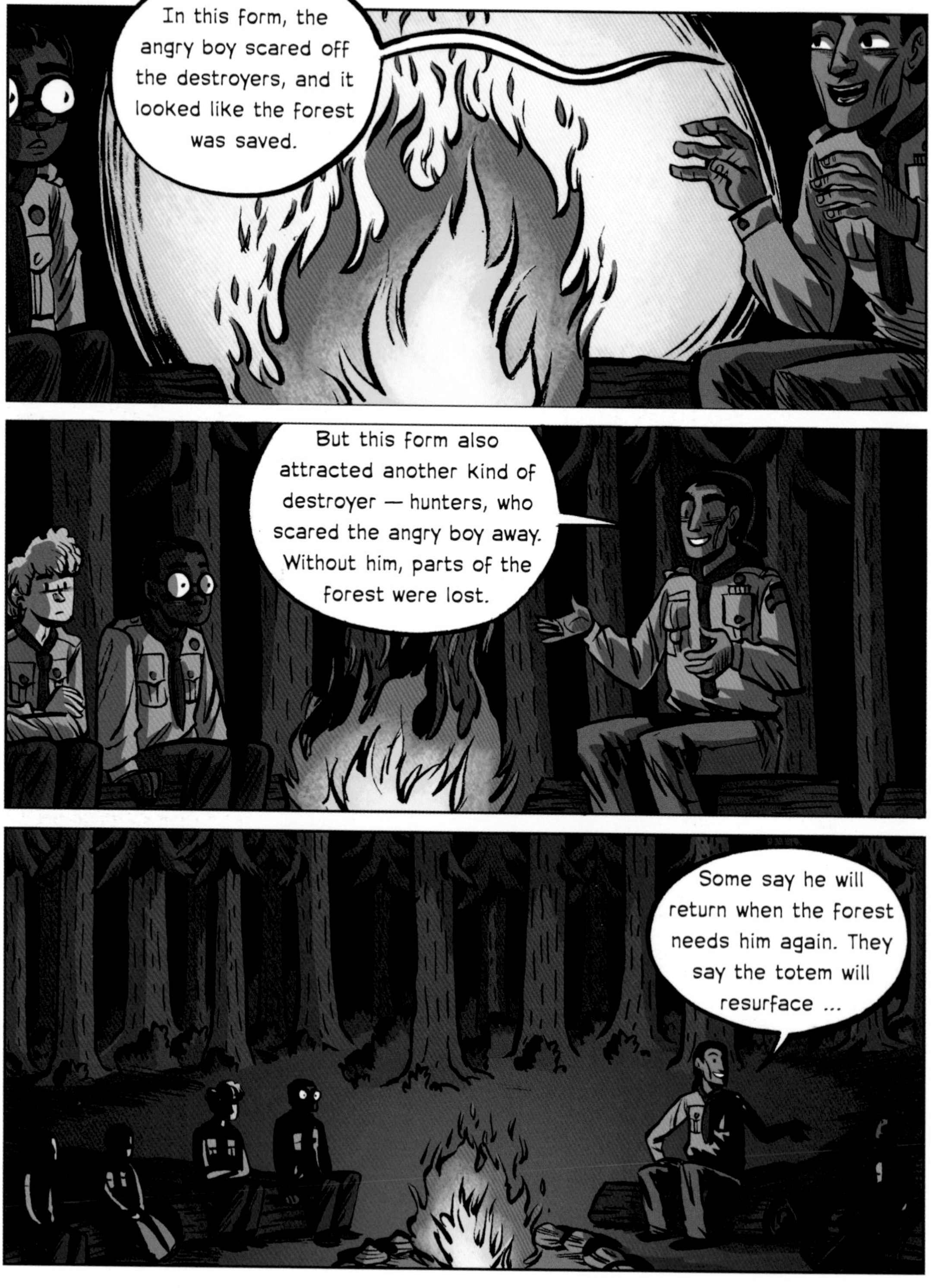
In this form, the angry boy scared off the destroyers, and it looked like the forest was saved.
But this form also attracted another kind of destroyer — hunters, who scared the angry boy away. Without him, parts of the forest were lost.
Some say he will return when the forest needs him again. They say the totem will resurface ...

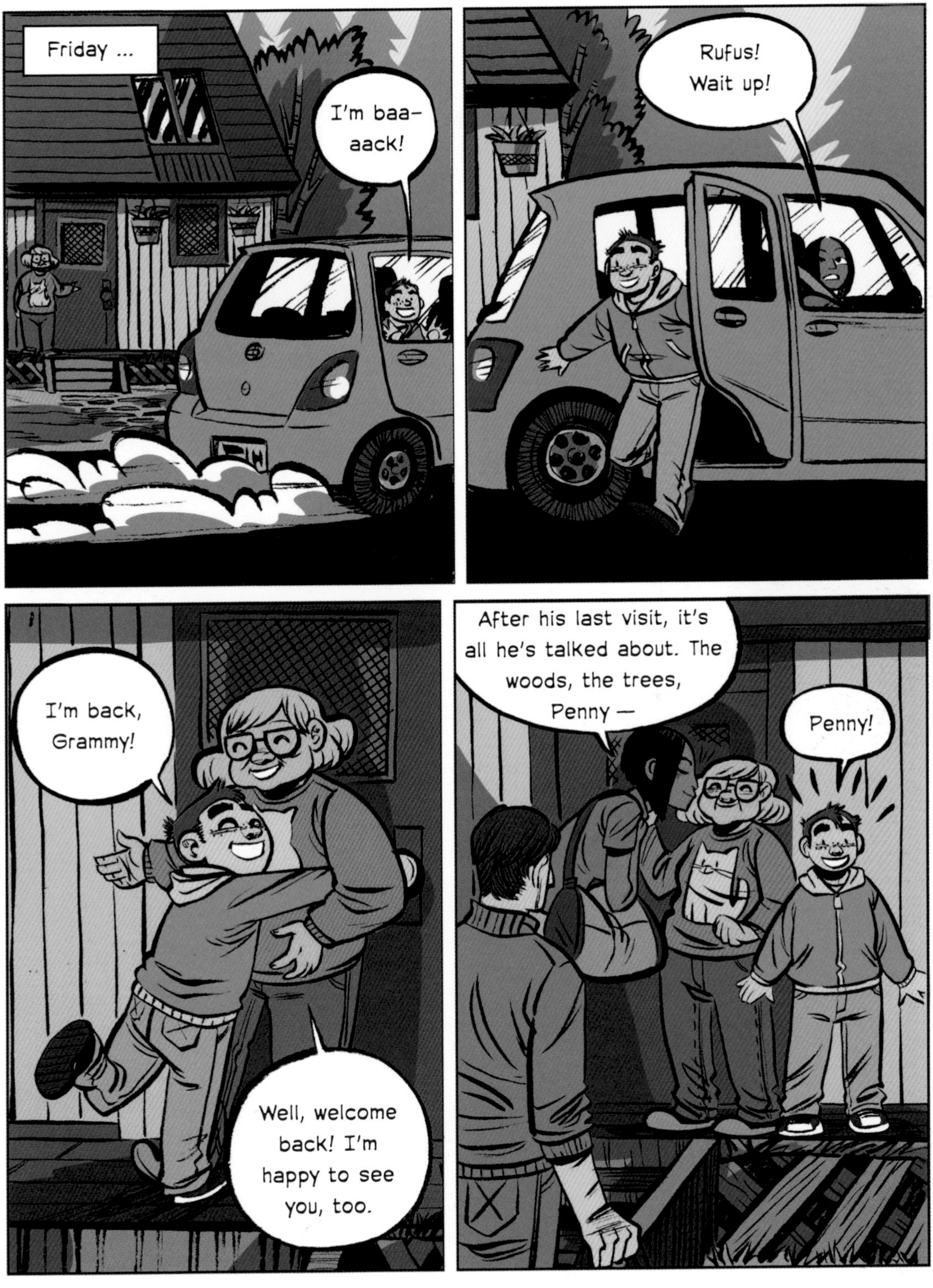
Friday ...
I'm baa-aack!
Rufus! Wait up!
I'm back, Grammy!
Well, welcome back! I'm happy to see you, too.
After his last visit, it's all he's talked about. The woods, the trees, Penny —
Penny!

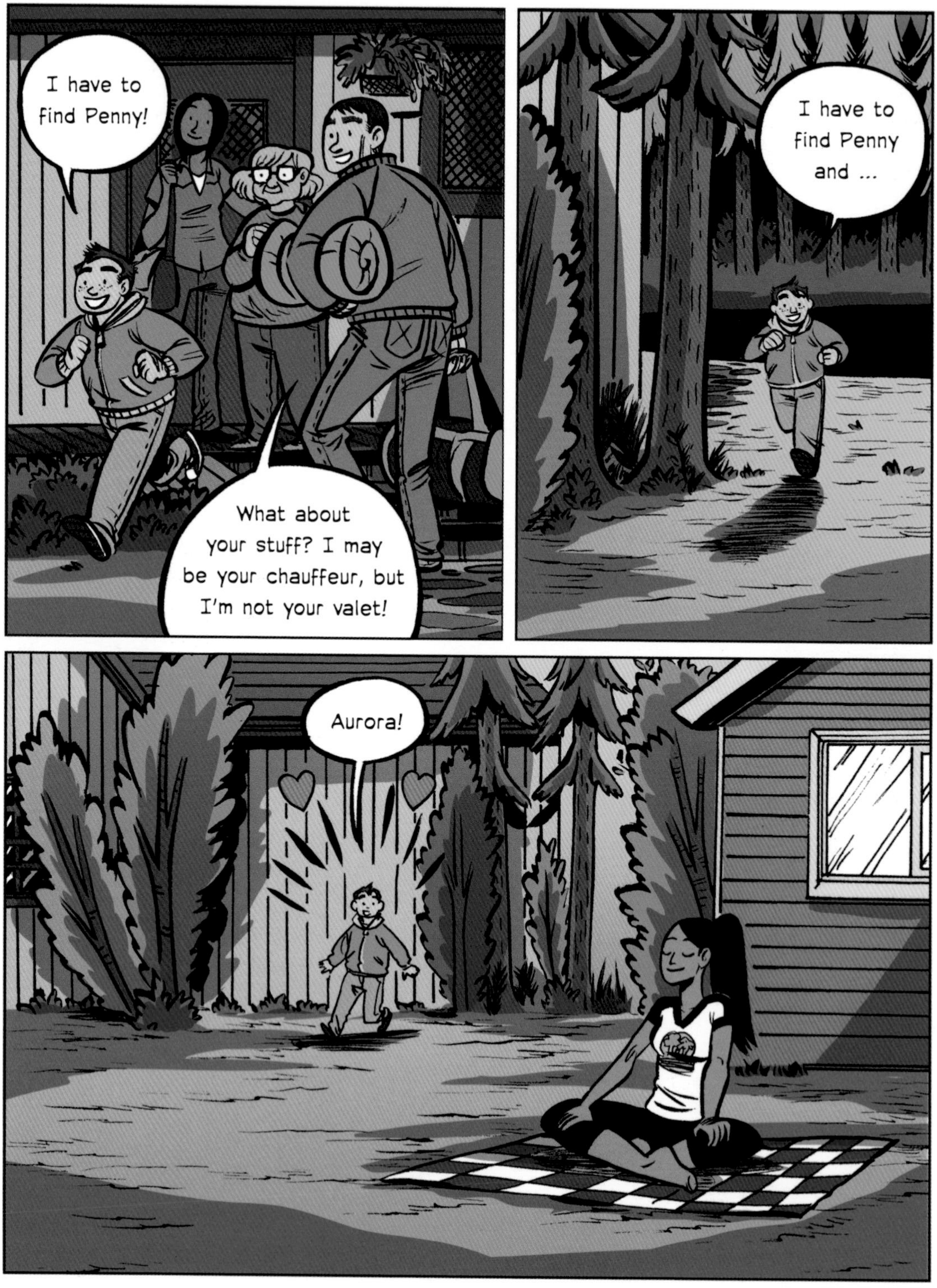
I have to find Penny!
What about your stuff? I may be your chauffeur, but I'm not your valet!
I have to find Penny and ...
Aurora!

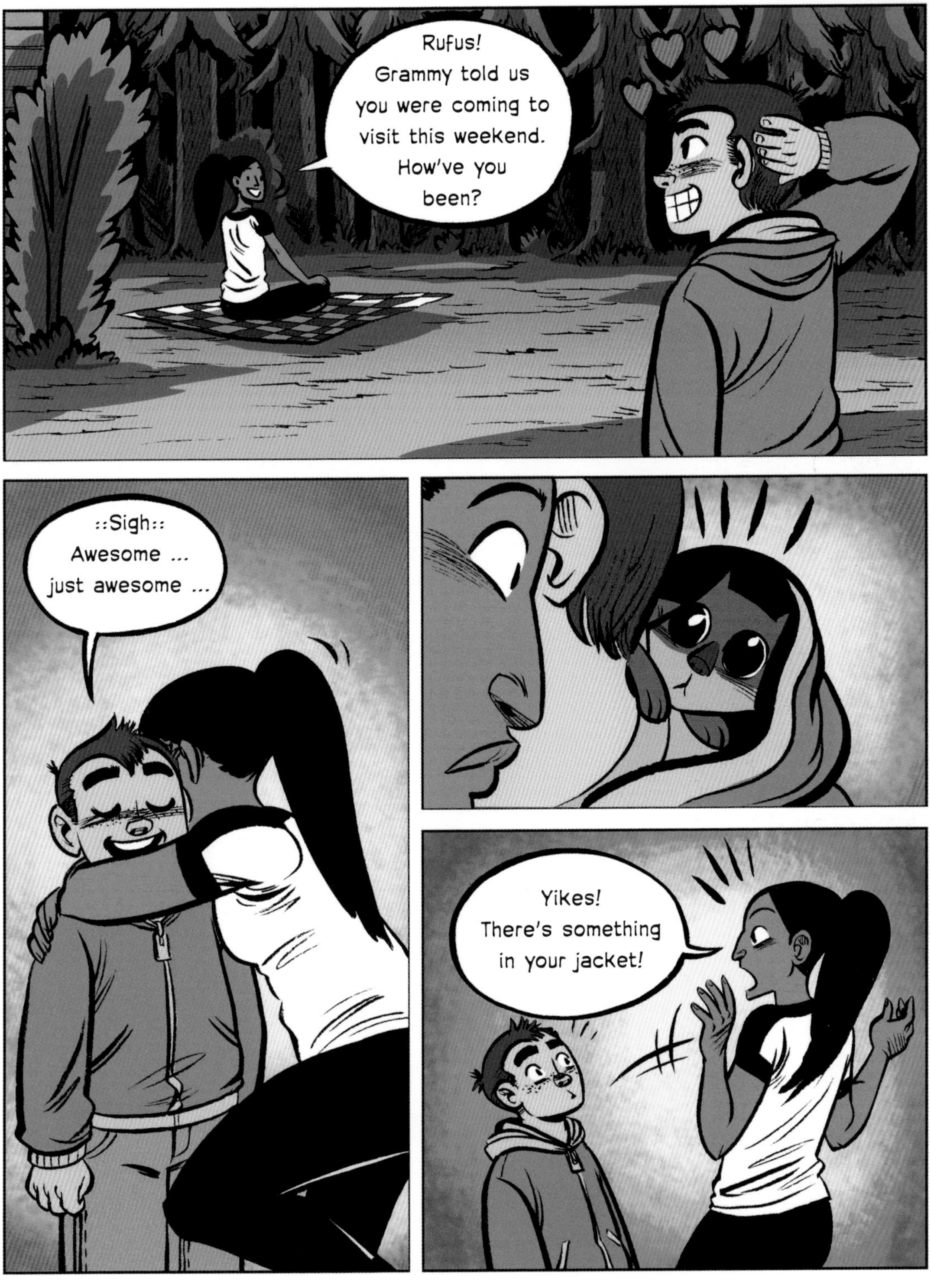
Rufus! Grammy told us you were coming to visit this weekend. How've you been?
::Sigh:: Awesome ... just awesome ...
Yikes! There's something in your jacket!

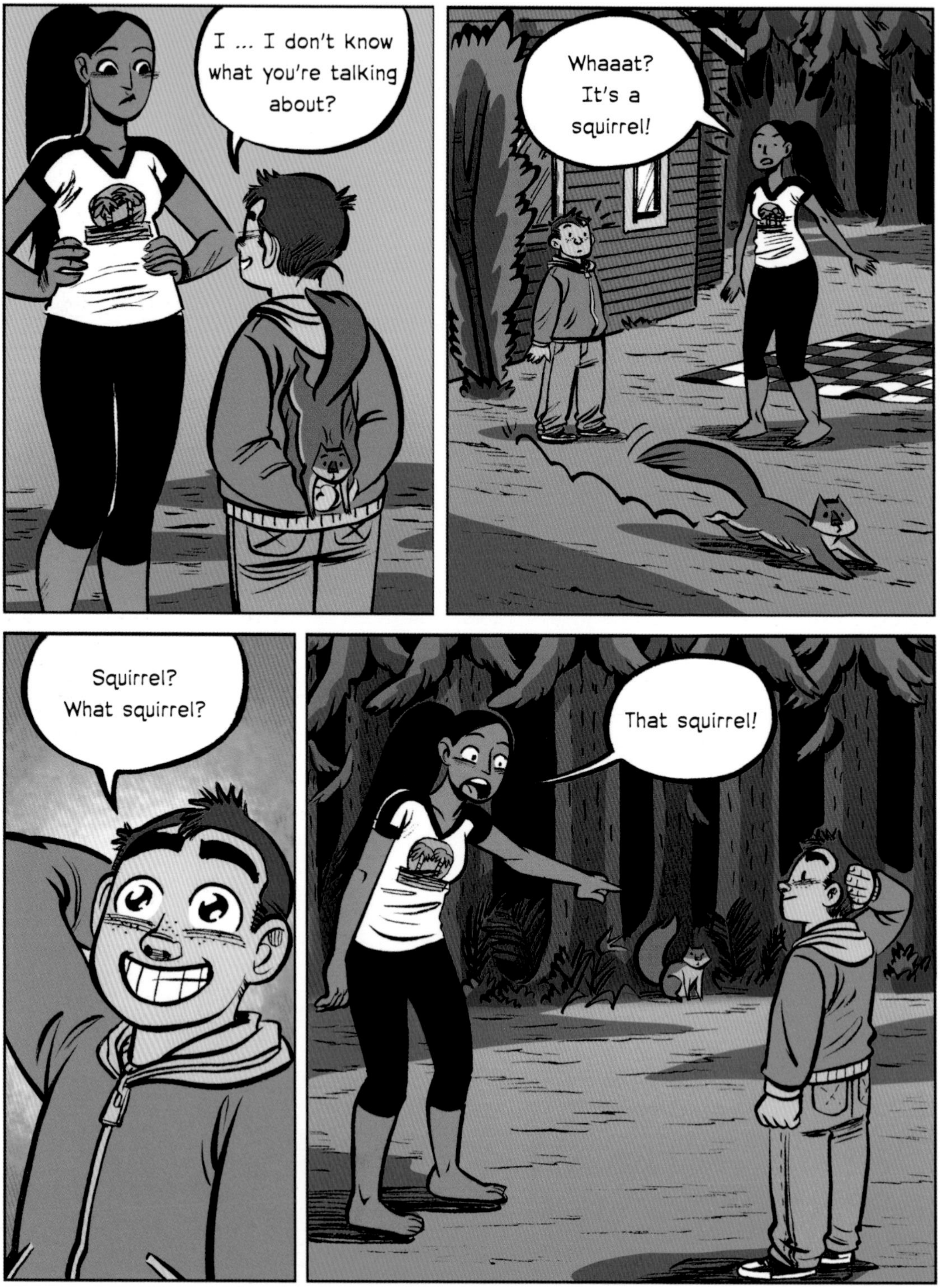
I ... I don't know what you're talking about?
Whaaat? It's a squirrel!
Squirrel? What squirrel?
That squirrel!

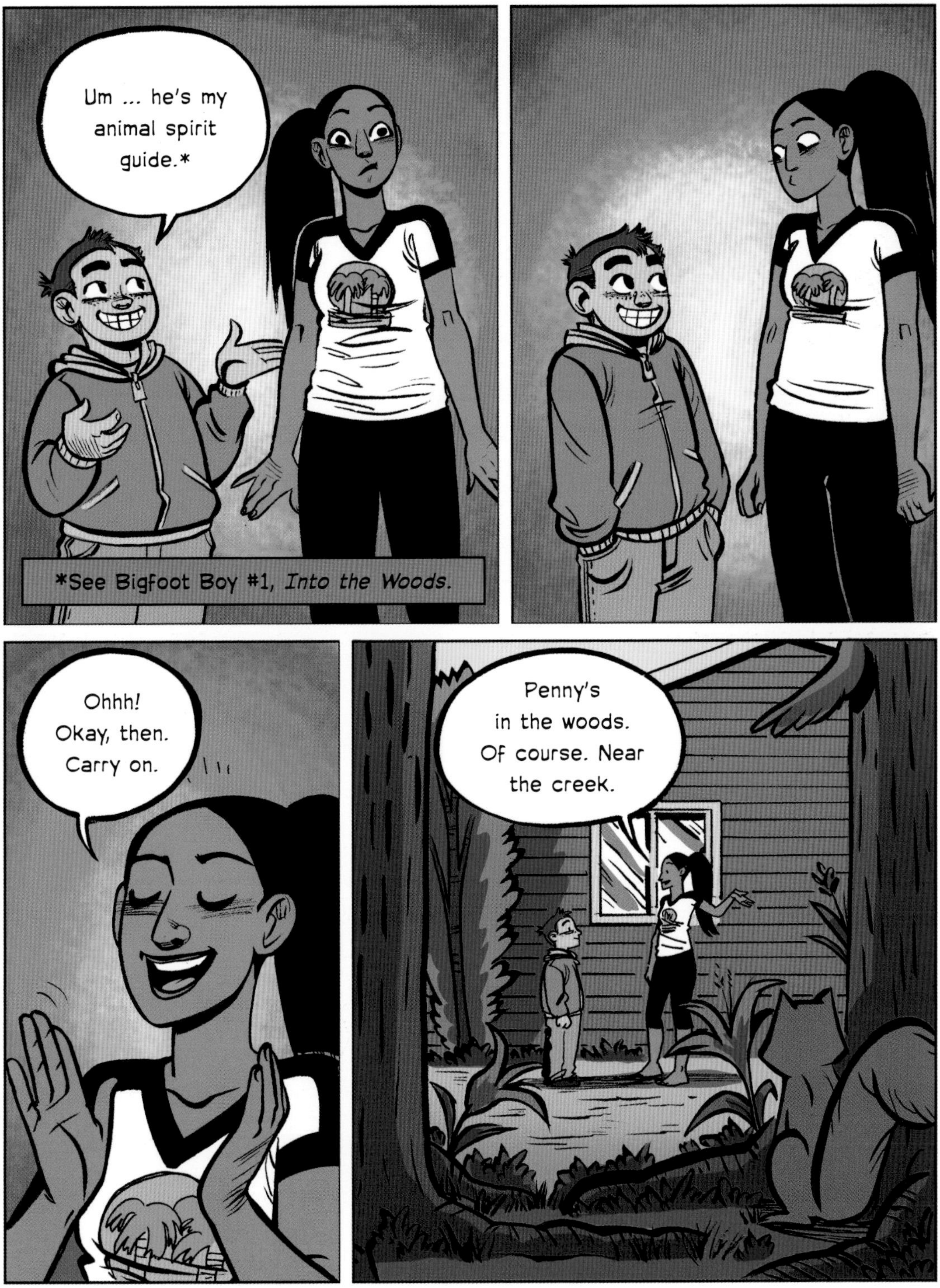
Um ... he's my animal spirit guide.*
*See Bigfoot Boy #1, Into the Woods.
Ohhh! Okay, then. Carry on.
Penny's in the woods. Of course. Near the creek.

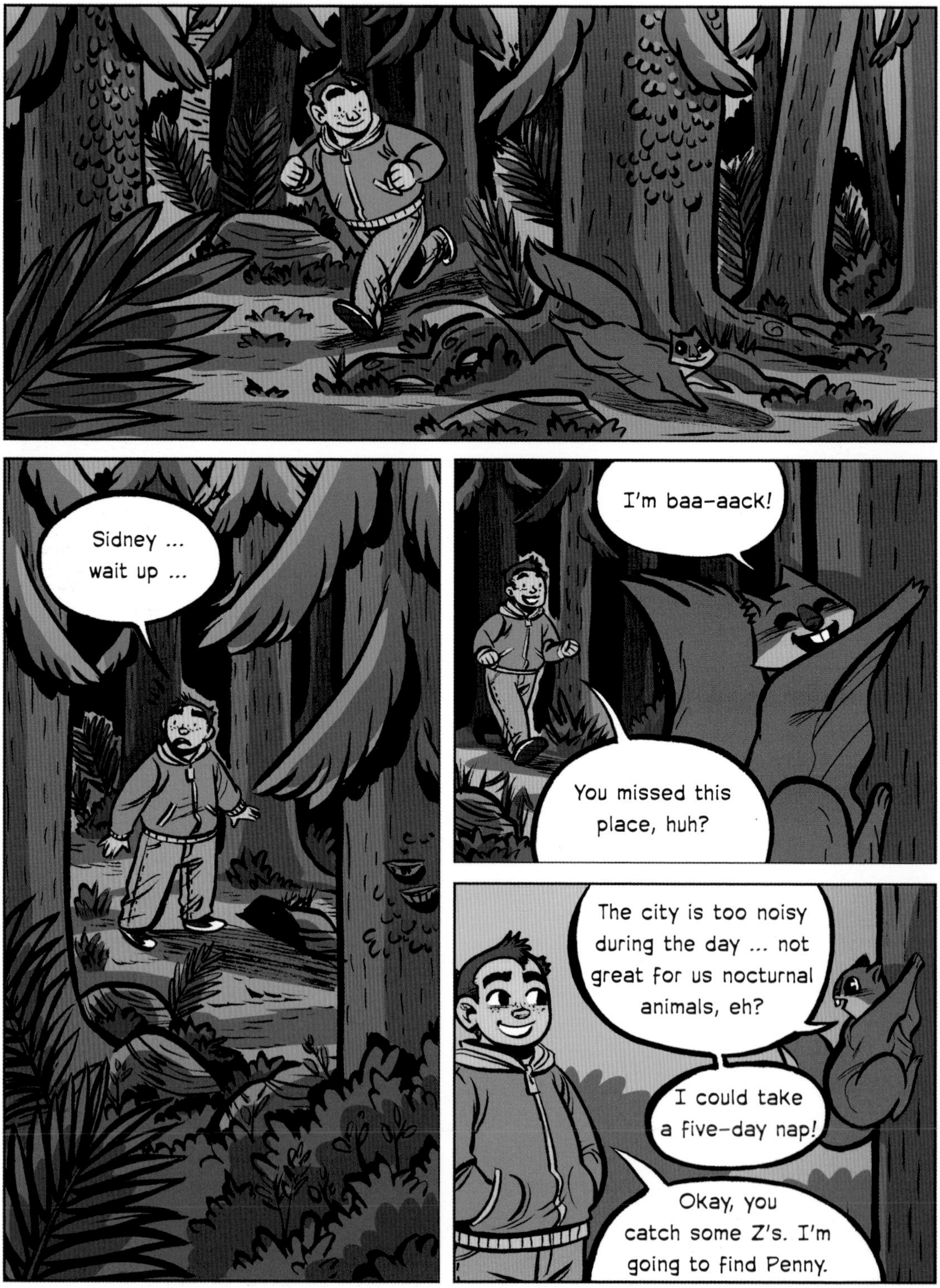
Sidney ...
wait up ...
I'm baa-aack!
You missed this place, huh?
The city is too noisy during the day ... not great for us nocturnal animals, eh?
I could take a five-day nap!
Okay, you catch some Z's. I'm going to find Penny.

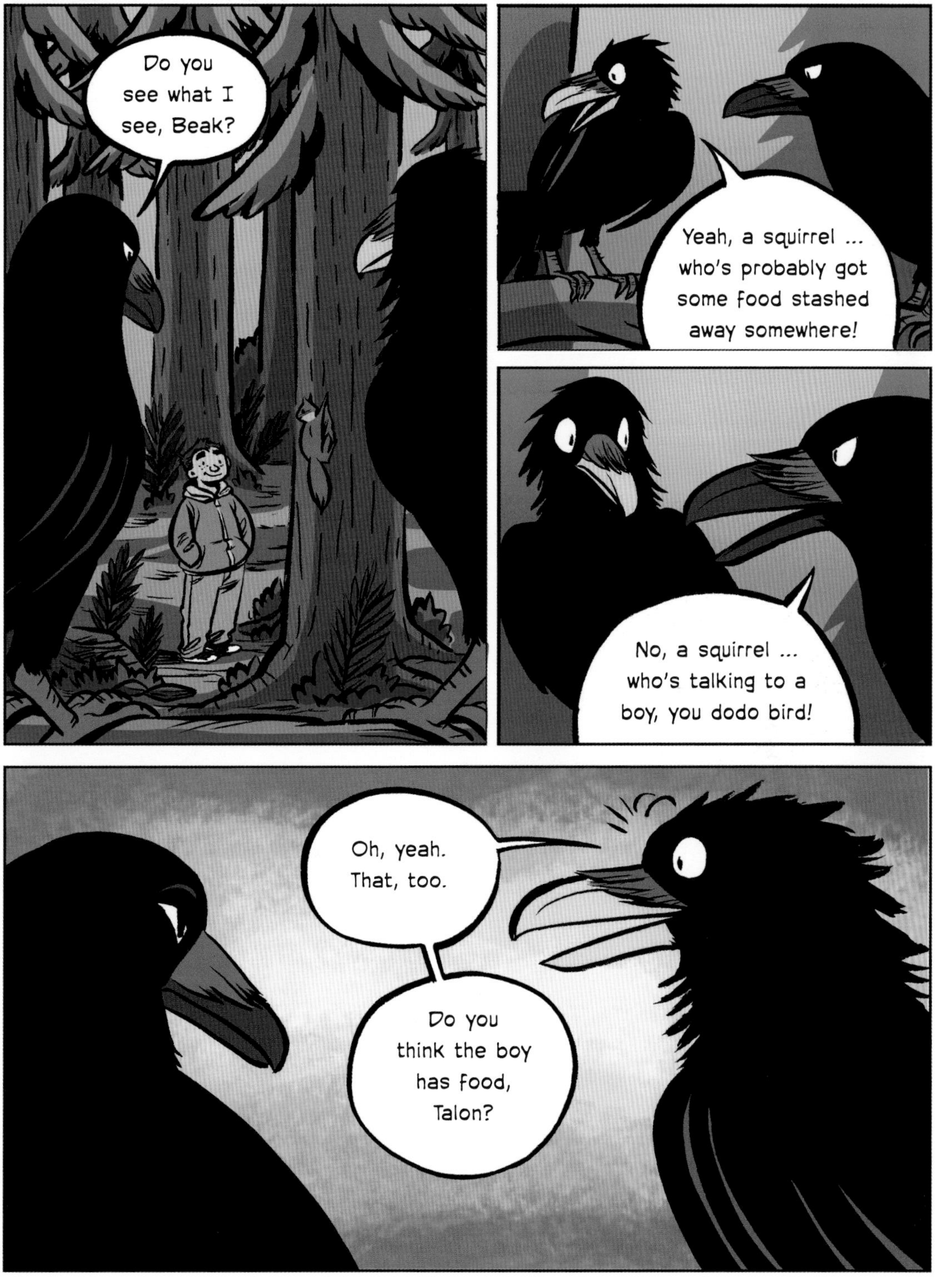
Do you see what I see, Beak?
Yeah, a squirrel ... who's probably got some food stashed away somewhere!
No, a squirrel ... who's talking to a boy, you dodo bird!
Oh, yeah. That, too.
Do you think the boy has food, Talon?

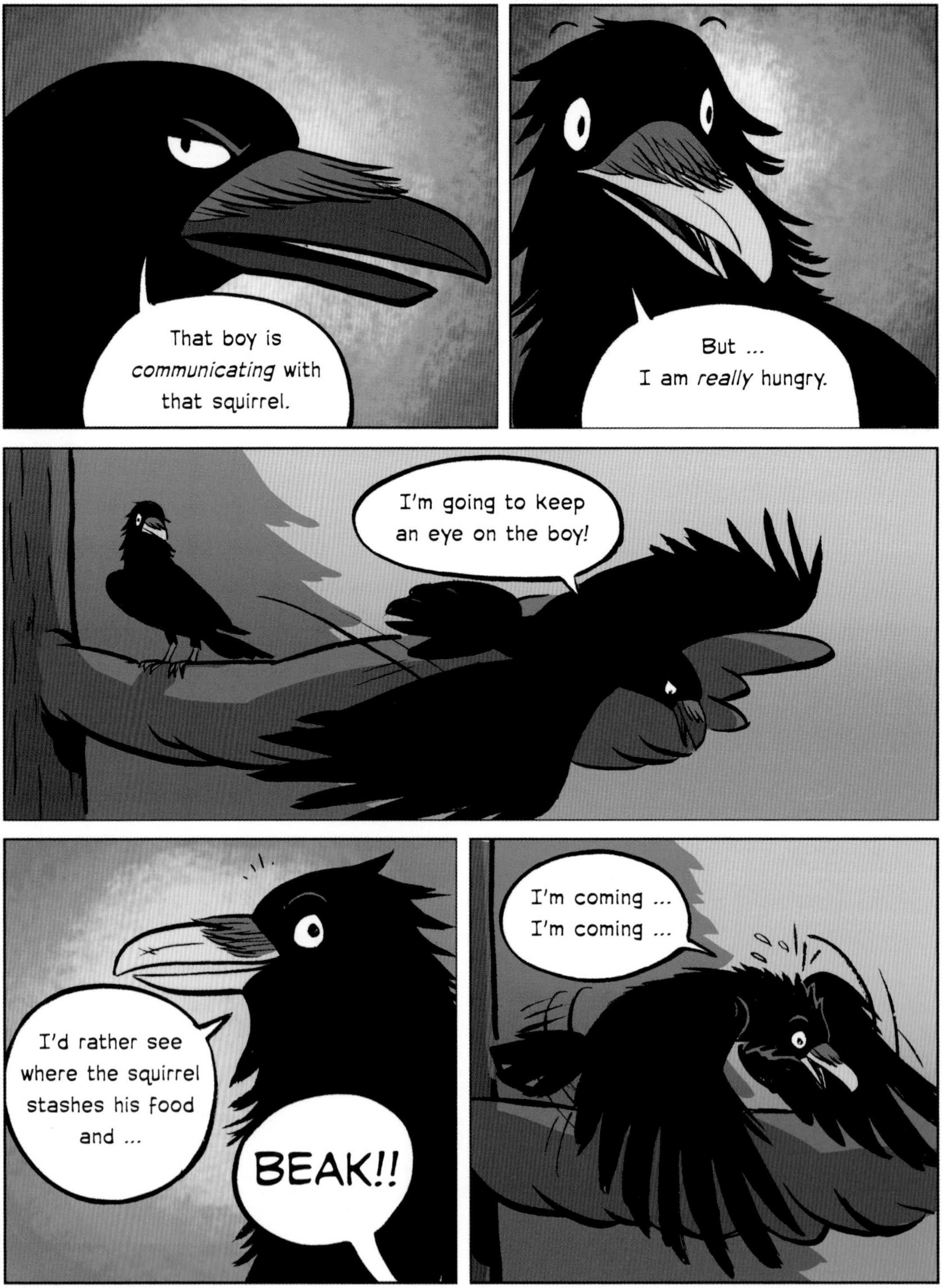
That boy is *communicating* with that squirrel.
But ... I am *really* hungry.
I'm going to keep an eye on the boy!
I'd rather see where the squirrel stashes his food and ...
BEAK!!
I'm coming ... I'm coming ...

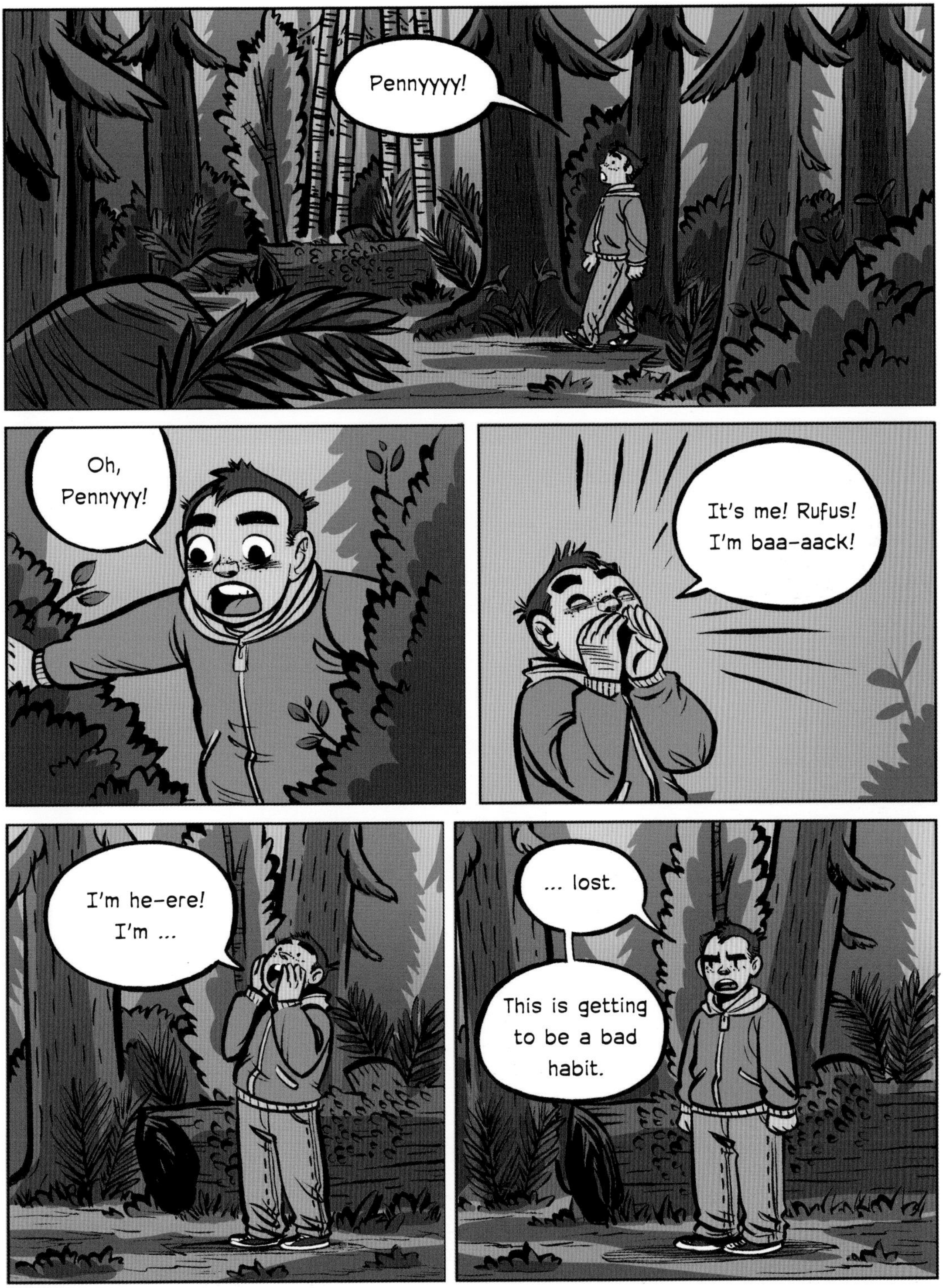
Pennyyyy!
Oh, Pennyyy!
It's me! Rufus! I'm baa-aack!
I'm he-ere! I'm ...
... lost.
This is getting to be a bad habit.

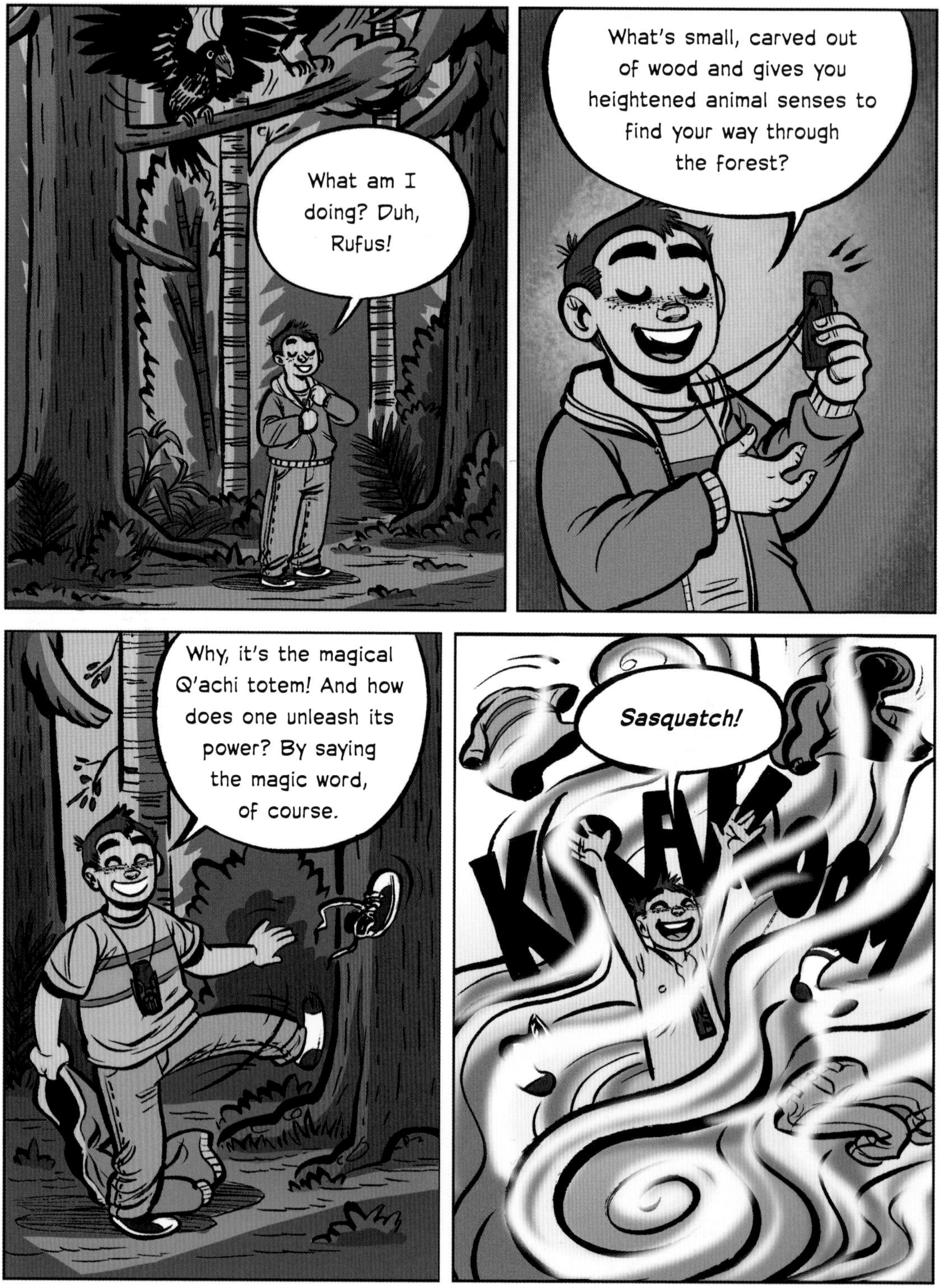
What am I doing? Duh, Rufus!
What's small, carved out of wood and gives you heightened animal senses to find your way through the forest?
Why, it's the magical Q'achi totem! And how does one unleash its power? By saying the magic word, of course.
Sasquatch!

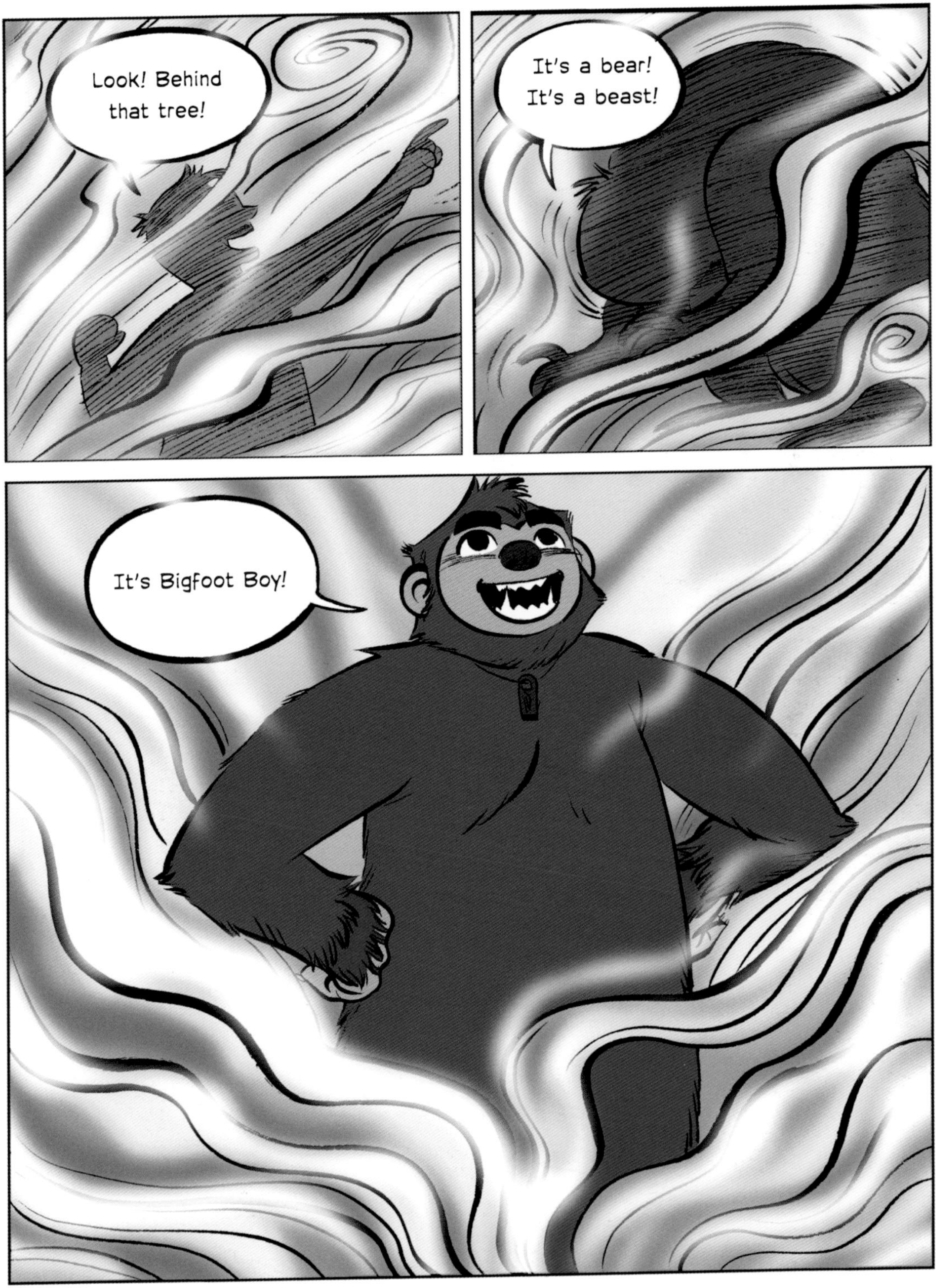
Look! Behind that tree!
It's a bear! It's a beast!
It's Bigfoot Boy!

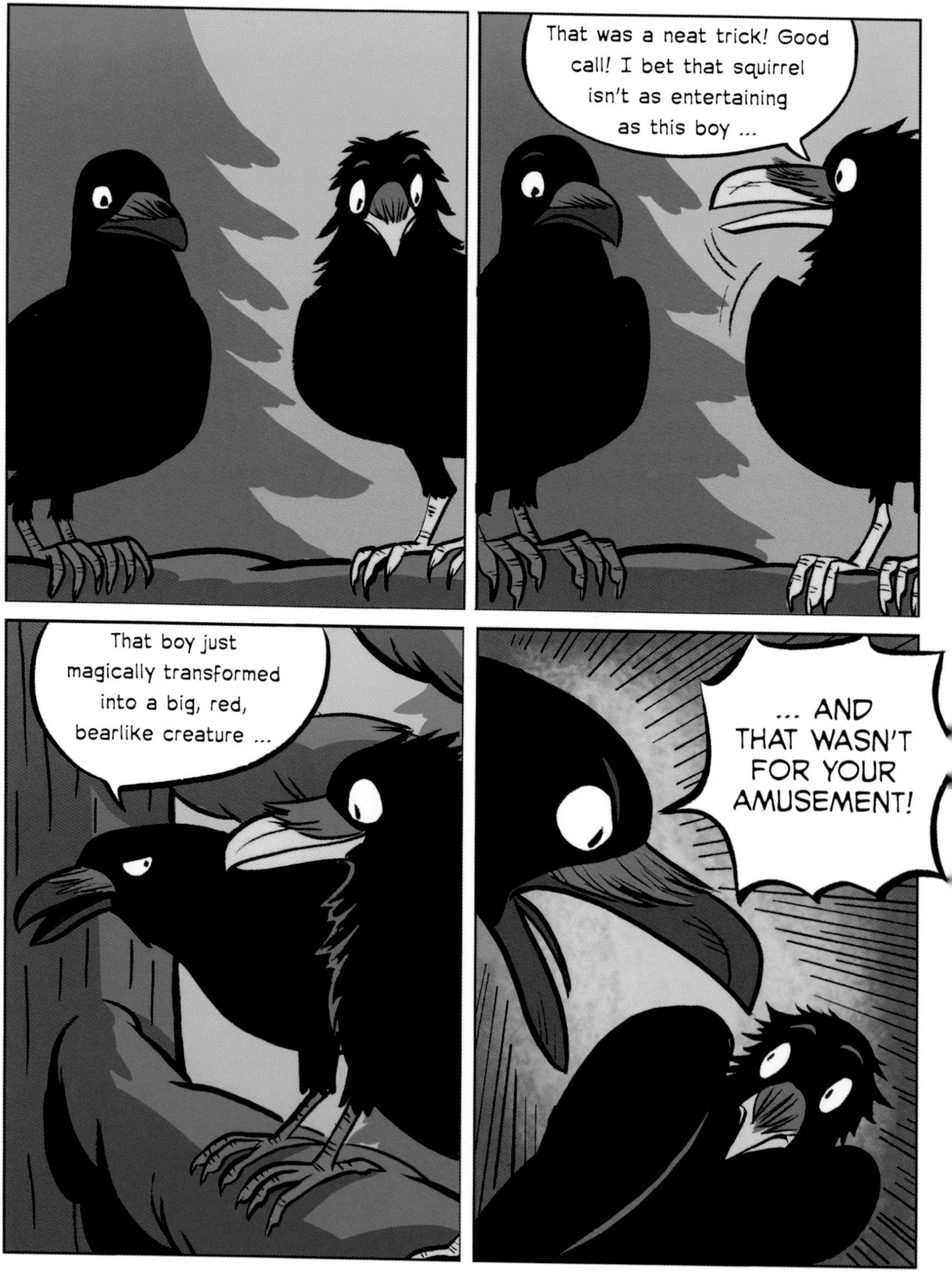
That was a neat trick! Good call! I bet that squirrel isn't as entertaining as this boy ...
That boy just magically transformed into a big, red, bearlike creature ...
... AND THAT WASN'T FOR YOUR AMUSEMENT!

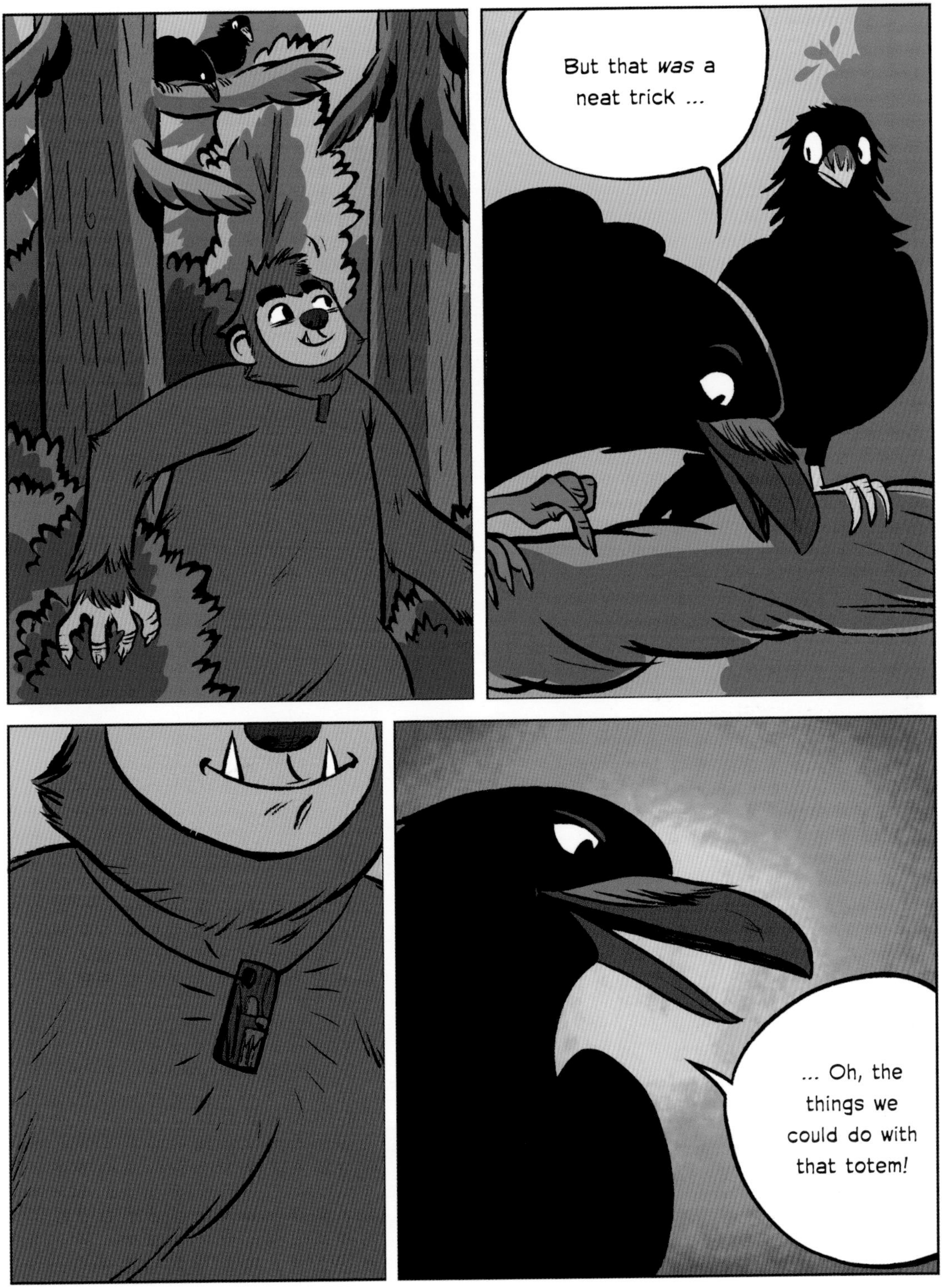
But that *was* a neat trick ...
... Oh, the things we could do with that totem!

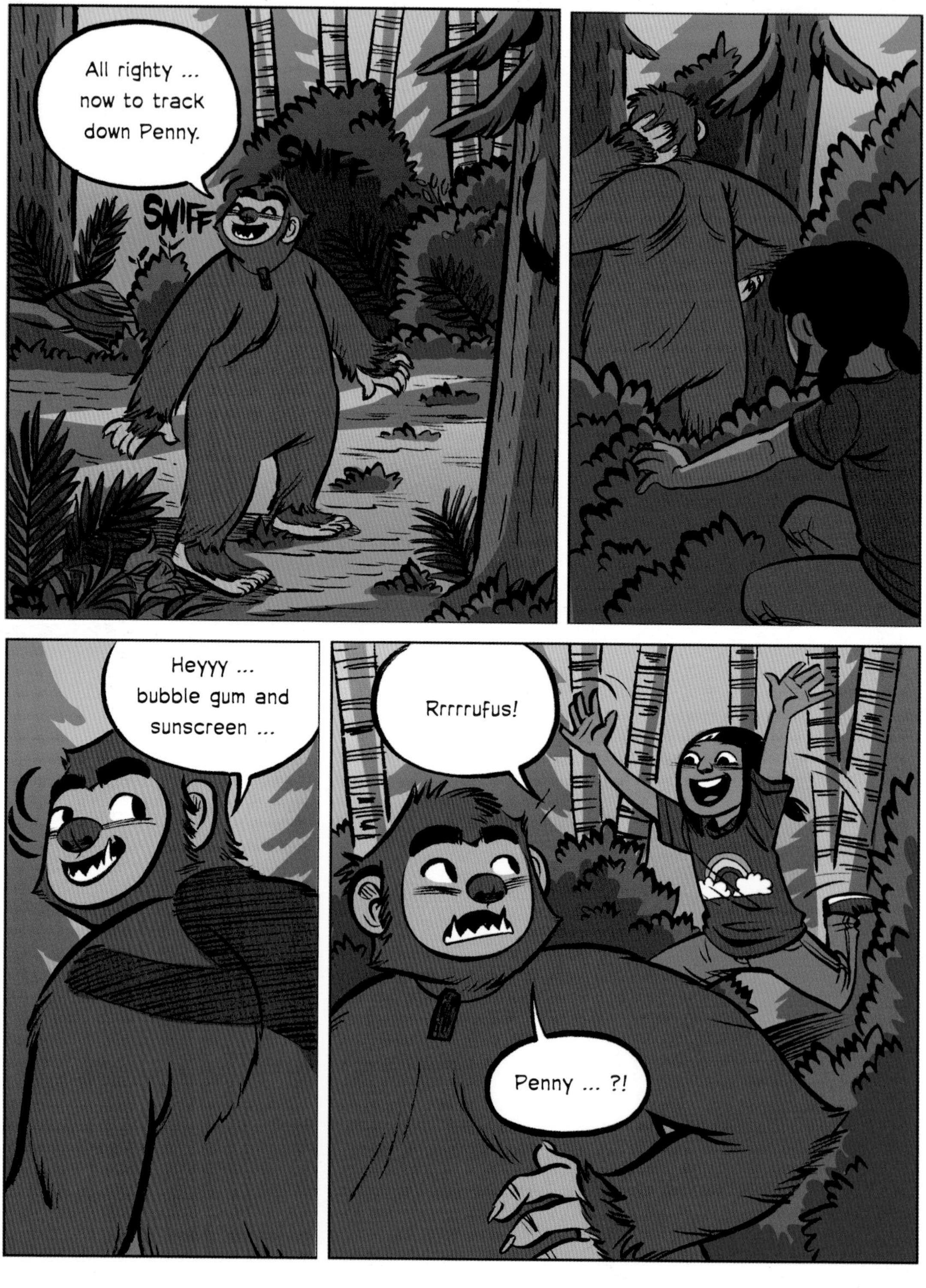
All righty ... now to track down Penny.
SNIFF
SNIFF
Heyyy ... bubble gum and sunscreen ...
Rrrrrufus!
Penny ... ?!

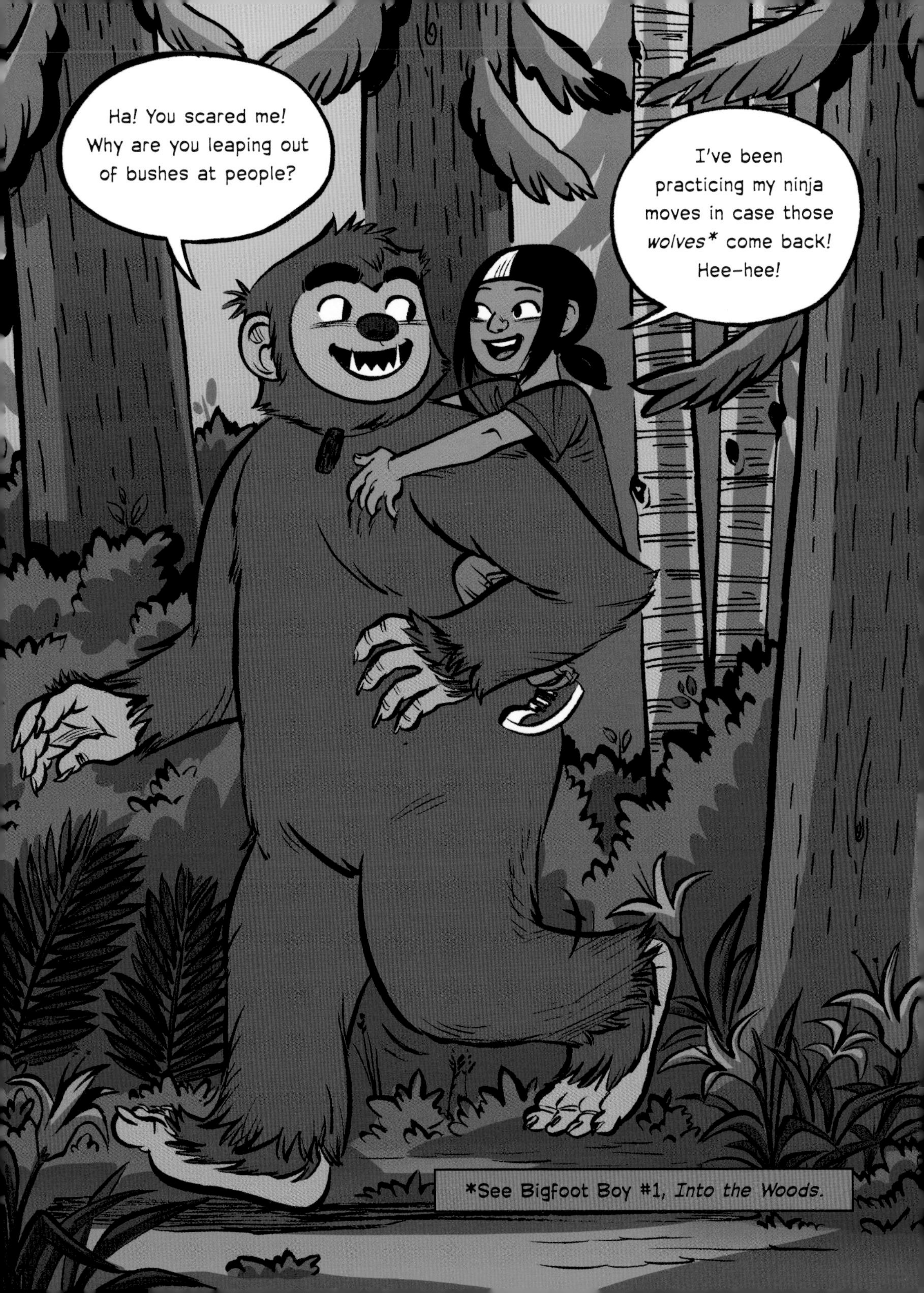
Ha! You scared me! Why are you leaping out of bushes at people?
I've been practicing my ninja moves in case those *wolves** come back! Hee-hee!
*See Bigfoot Boy #1, *Into the Woods.*

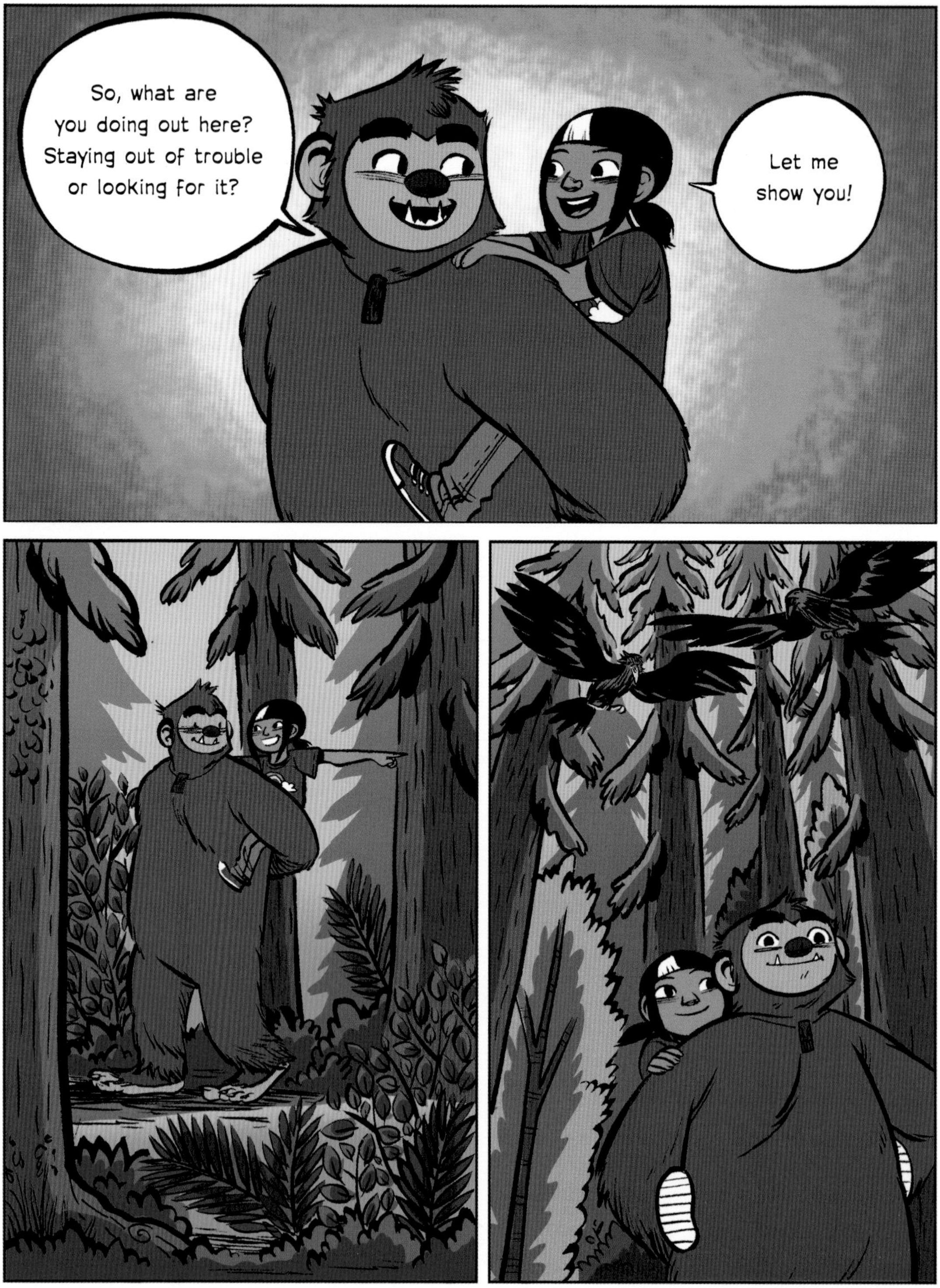
So, what are you doing out here? Staying out of trouble or looking for it?
Let me show you!

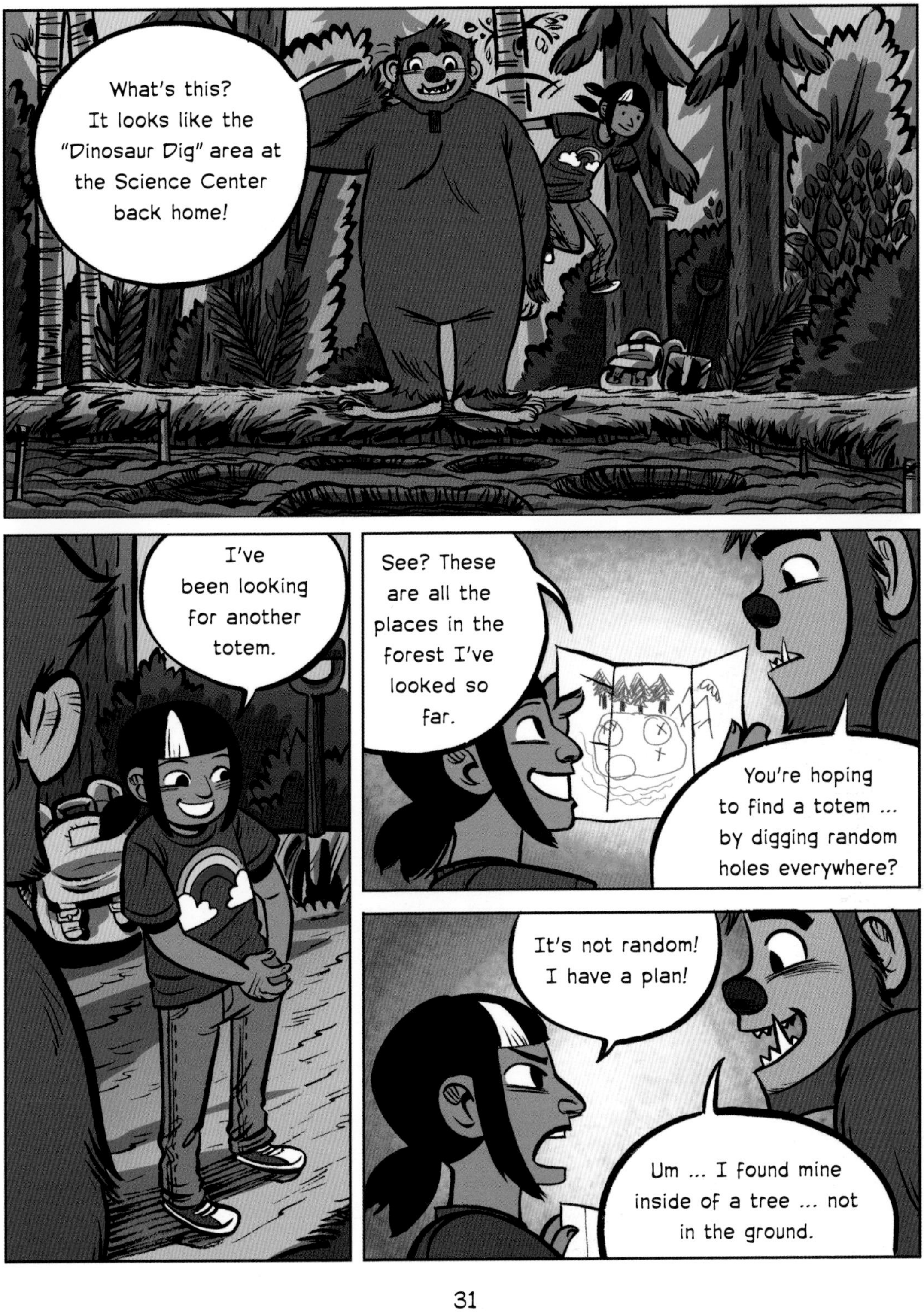
What's this? It looks like the "Dinosaur Dig" area at the Science Center back home!
I've been looking for another totem.
See? These are all the places in the forest I've looked so far.
You're hoping to find a totem ... by digging random holes everywhere?
It's not random! I have a plan!
Um ... I found mine inside of a tree ... not in the ground.

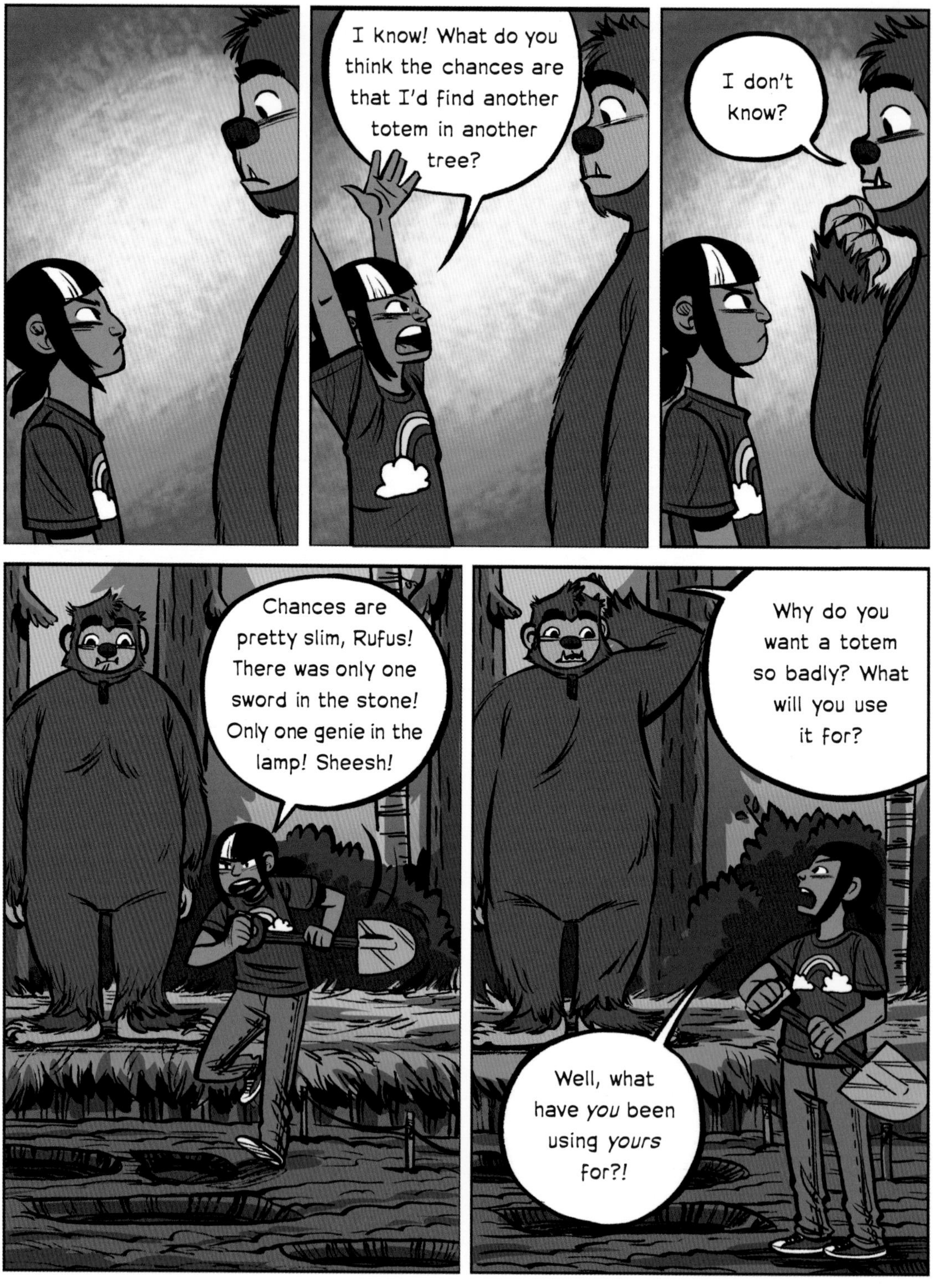
I know! What do you think the chances are that I'd find another totem in another tree?
I don't know?
Chances are pretty slim, Rufus! There was only one sword in the stone! Only one genie in the lamp! Sheesh!
Why do you want a totem so badly? What will you use it for?
Well, what have *you* been using *yours* for?!

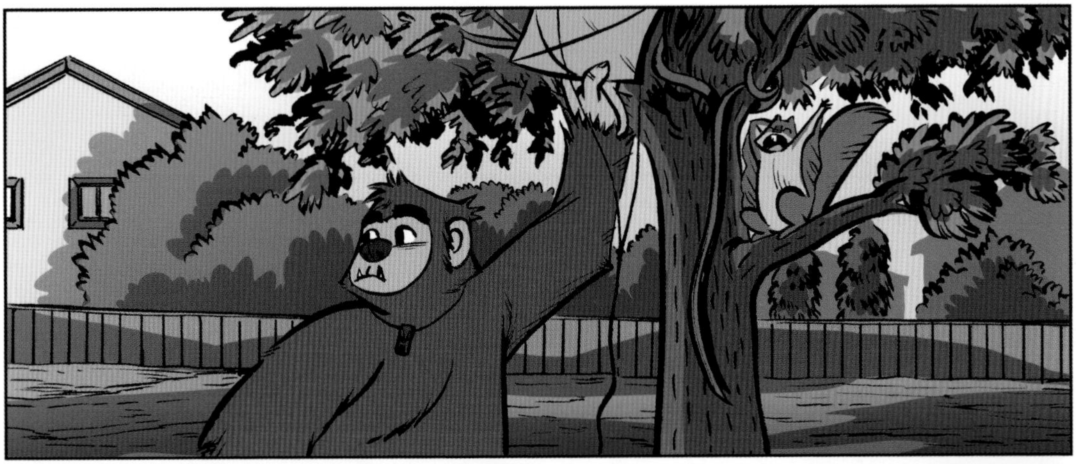

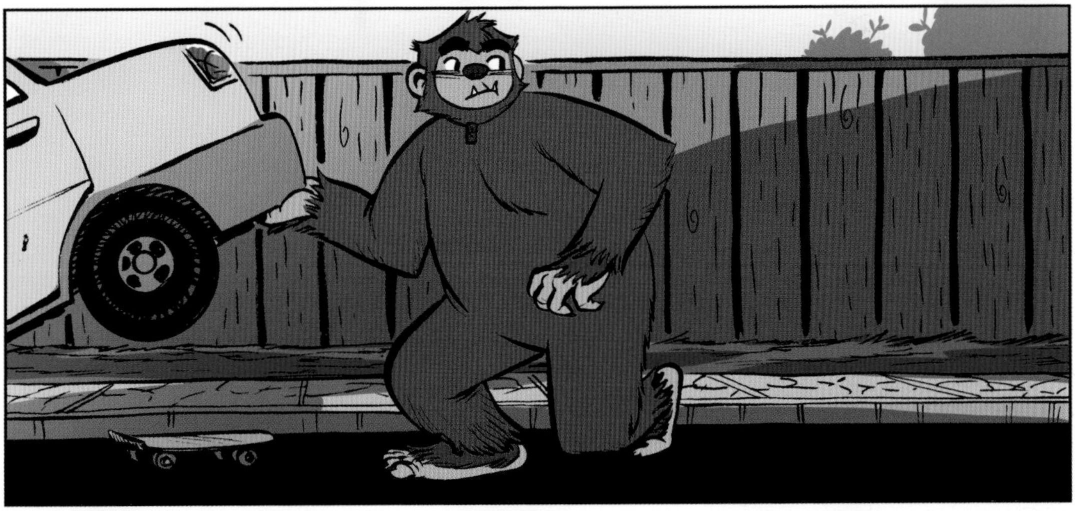

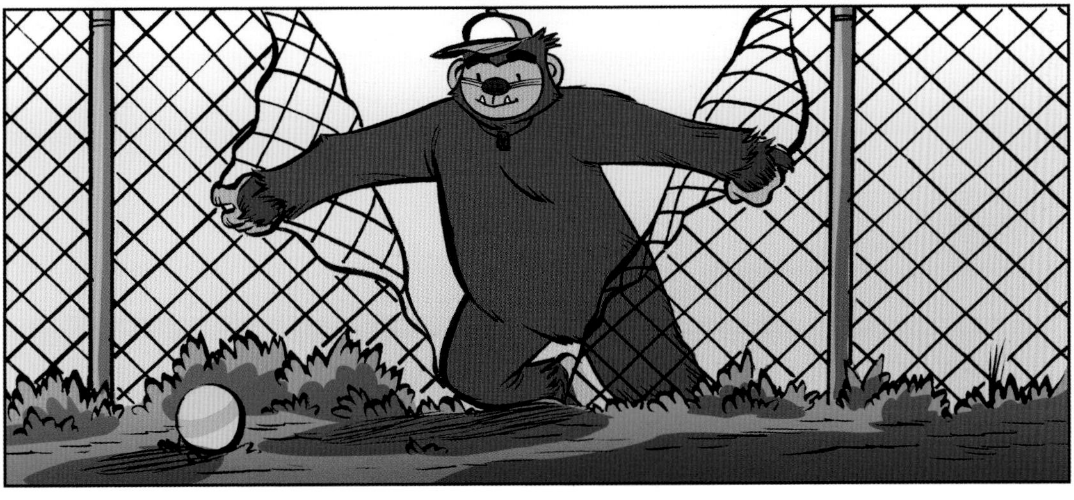

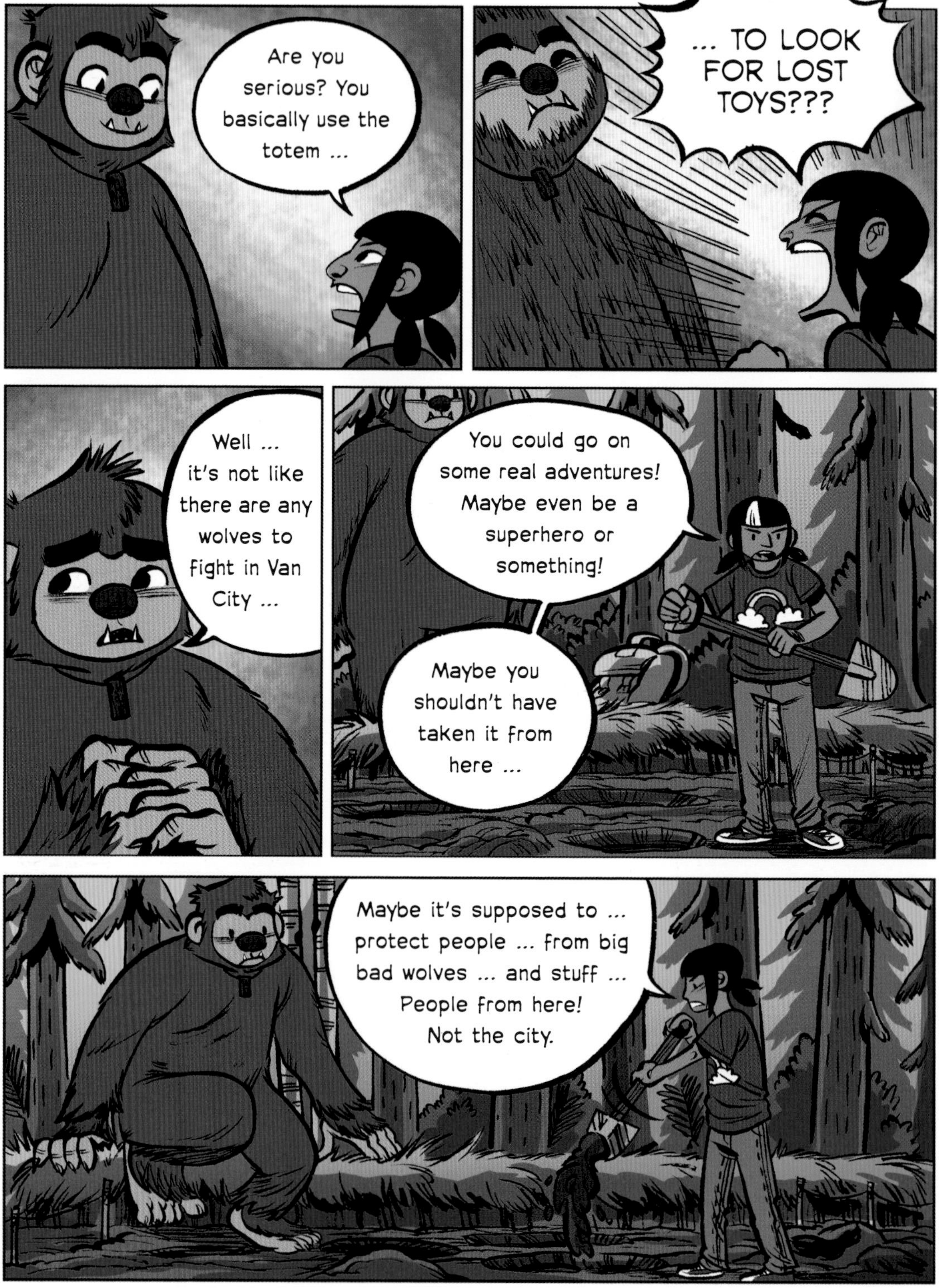
Are you serious? You basically use the totem ...
... TO LOOK FOR LOST TOYS???
Well ... it's not like there are any wolves to fight in Van City ...
You could go on some real adventures! Maybe even be a superhero or something!
Maybe you shouldn't have taken it from here ...
Maybe it's supposed to ... protect people ... from big bad wolves ... and stuff ... People from here! Not the city.

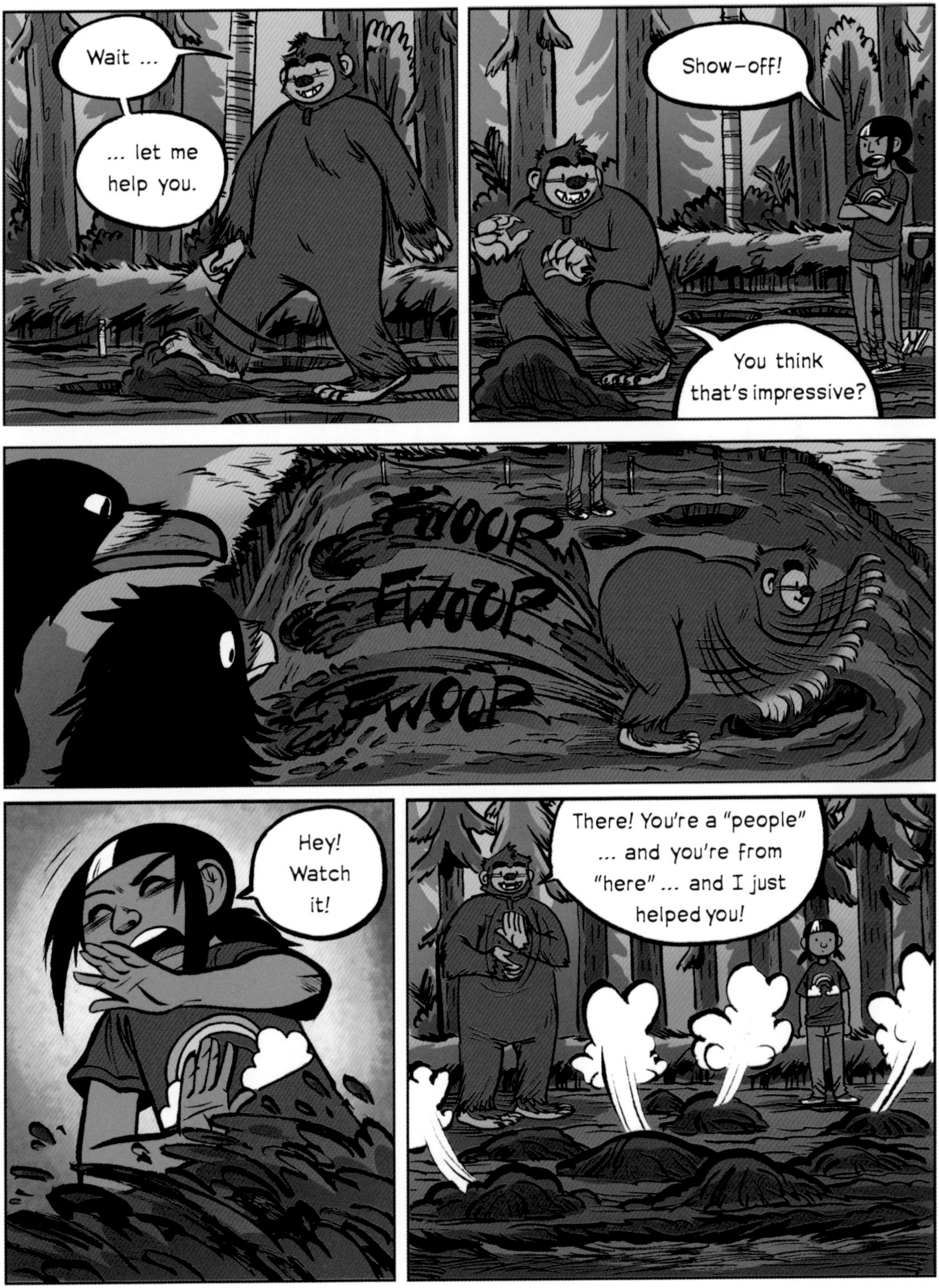
Wait ...
... let me help you.
Show-off!
You think that's impressive?
FWOOP
FWOOP
FWOOP
Hey! Watch it!
There! You're a "people" ... and you're from "here" ... and I just helped you!

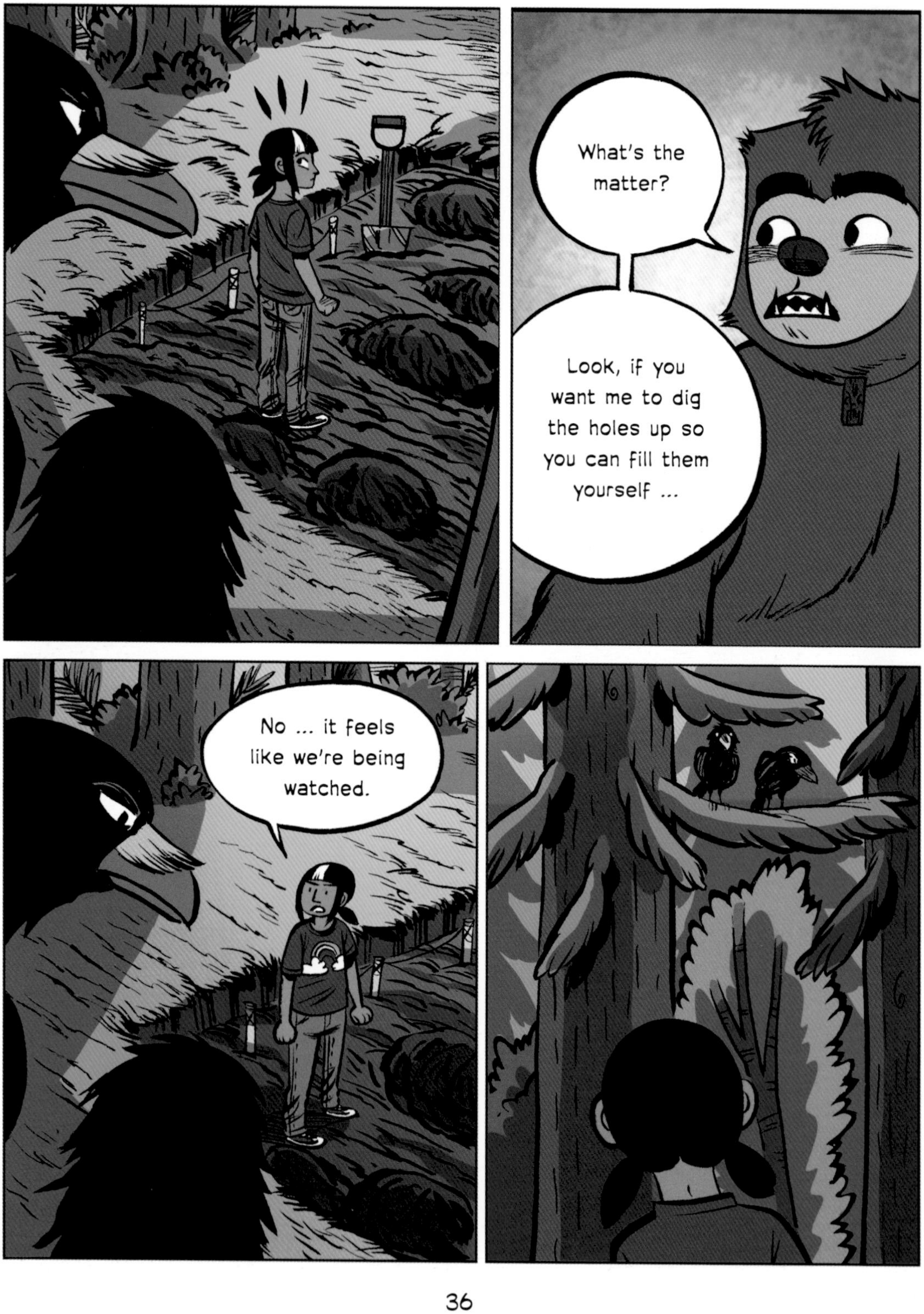
What's the matter?
Look, if you want me to dig the holes up so you can fill them yourself ...
No ... it feels like we're being watched.

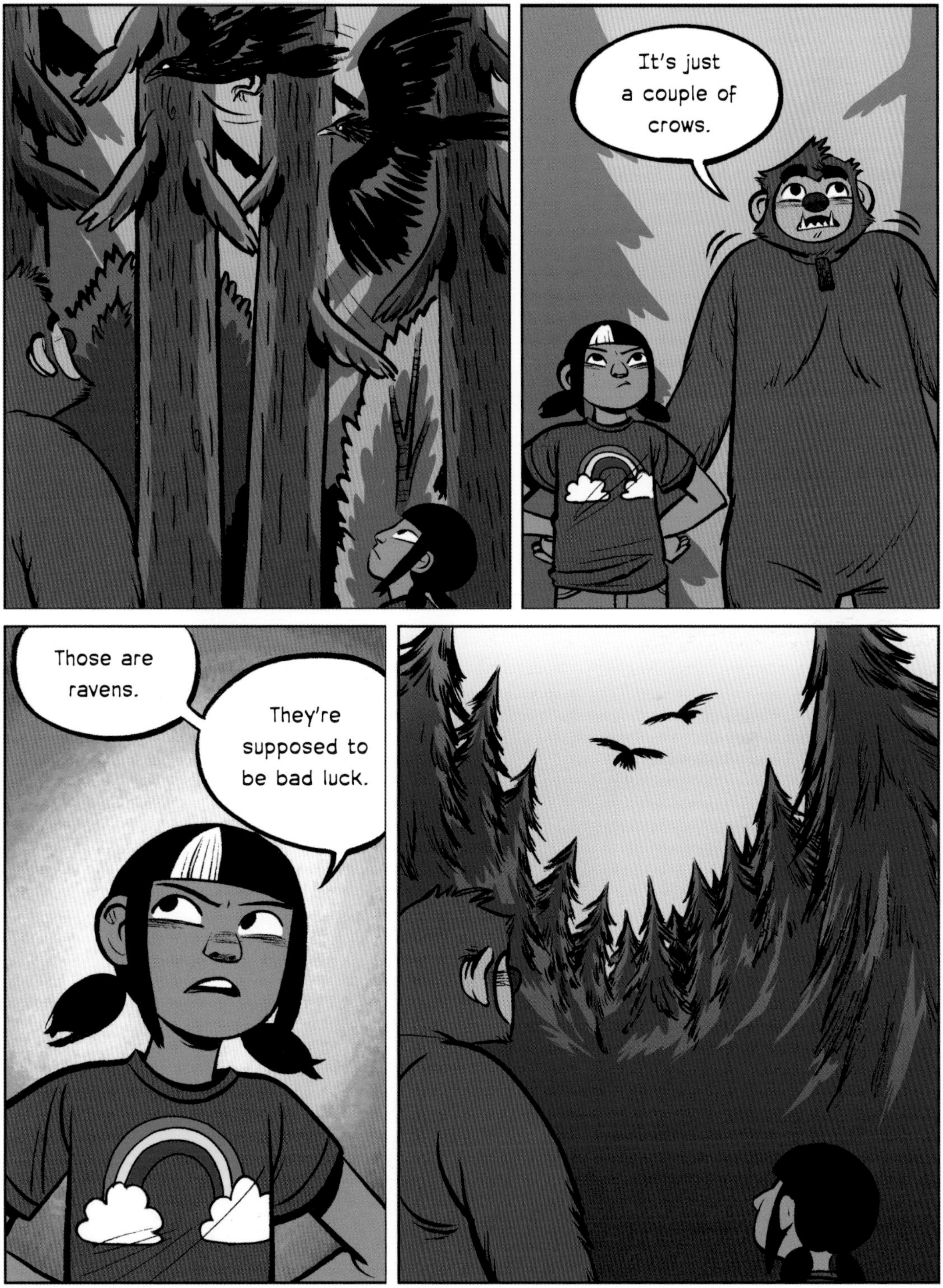
It's just a couple of crows.
Those are ravens.
They're supposed to be bad luck.

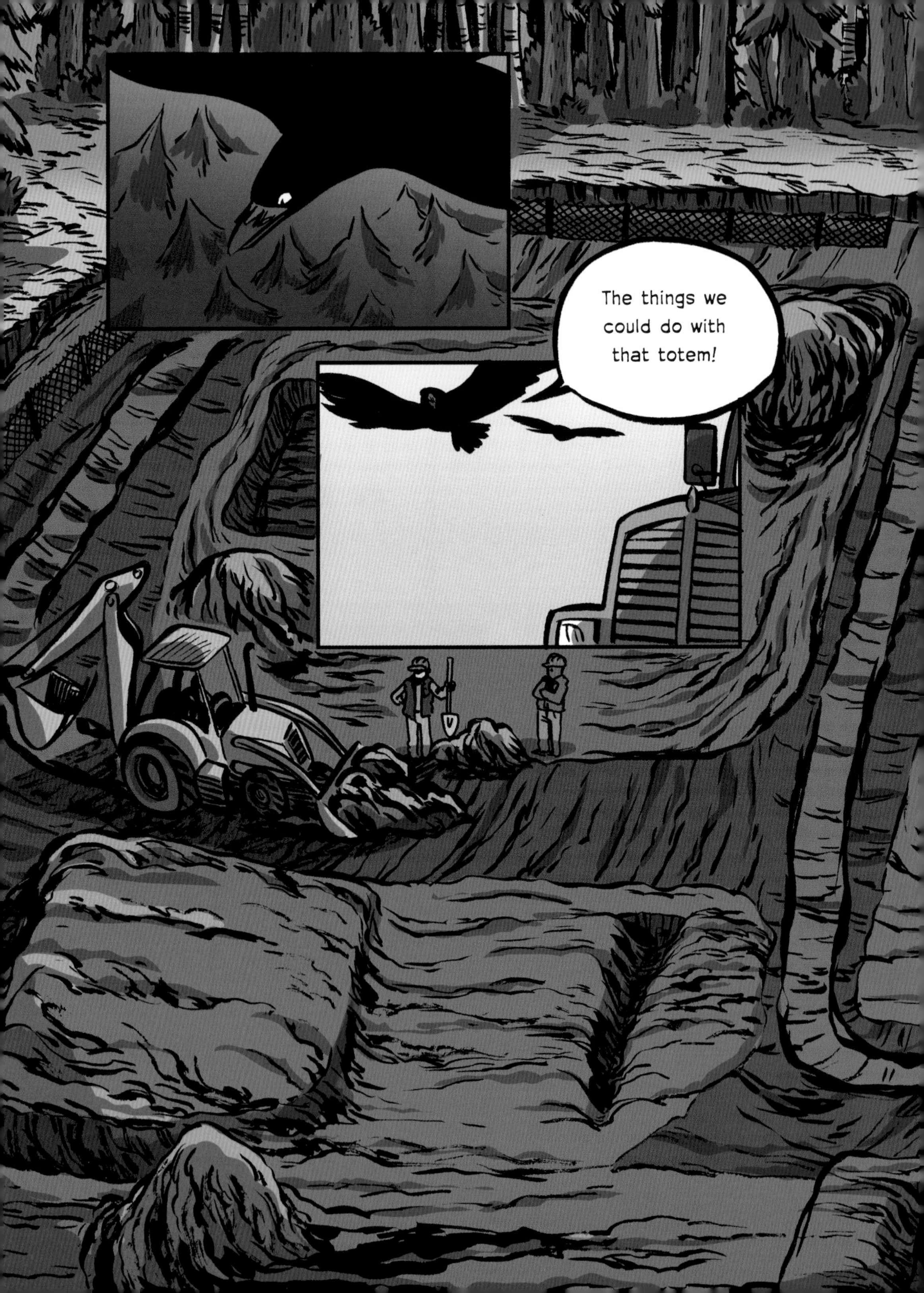
The things we could do with that totem!

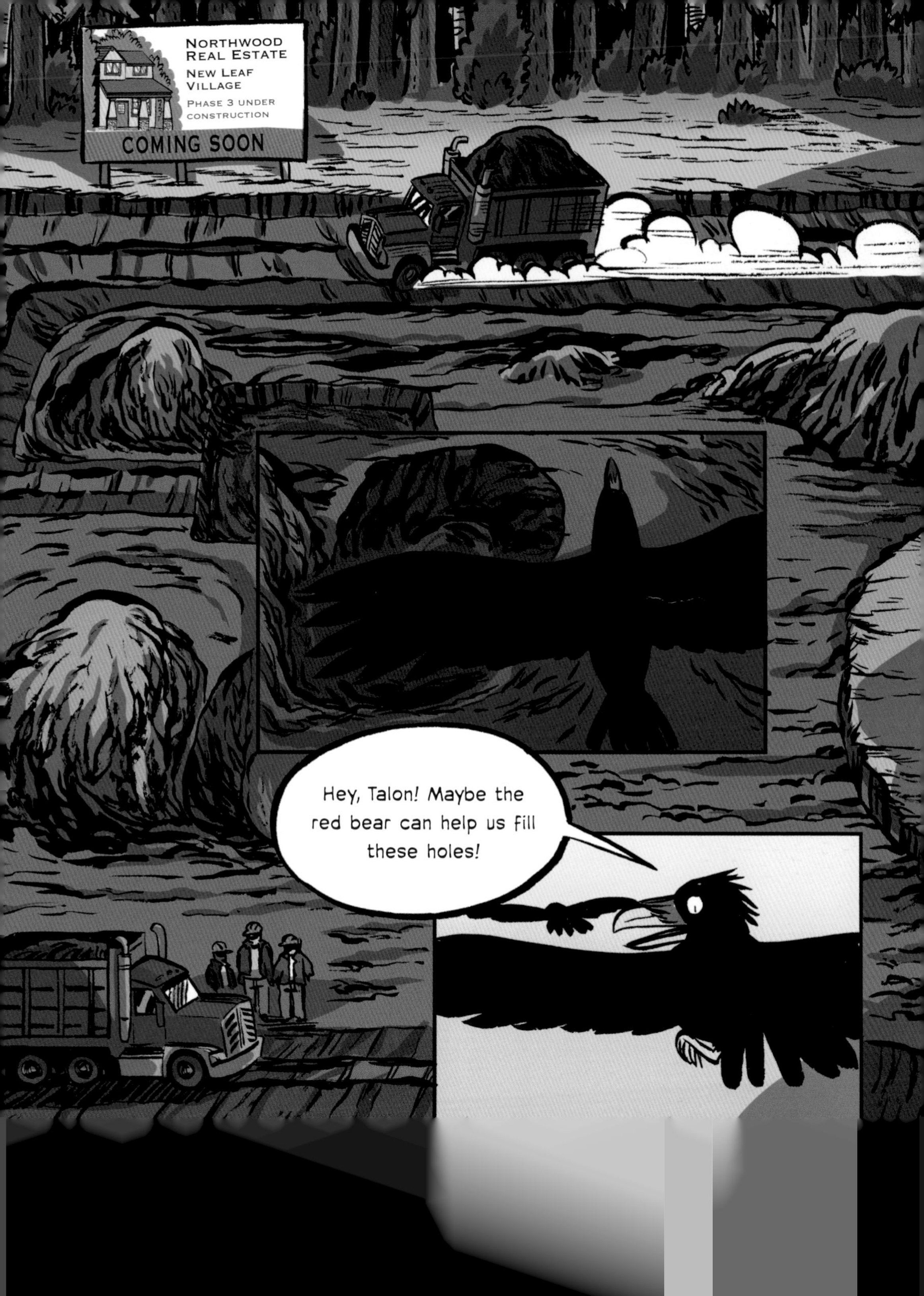
NORTHWOOD REAL ESTATE
NEW LEAF VILLAGE
PHASE 3 UNDER CONSTRUCTION
COMING SOON
Hey, Talon! Maybe the red bear can help us fill these holes!

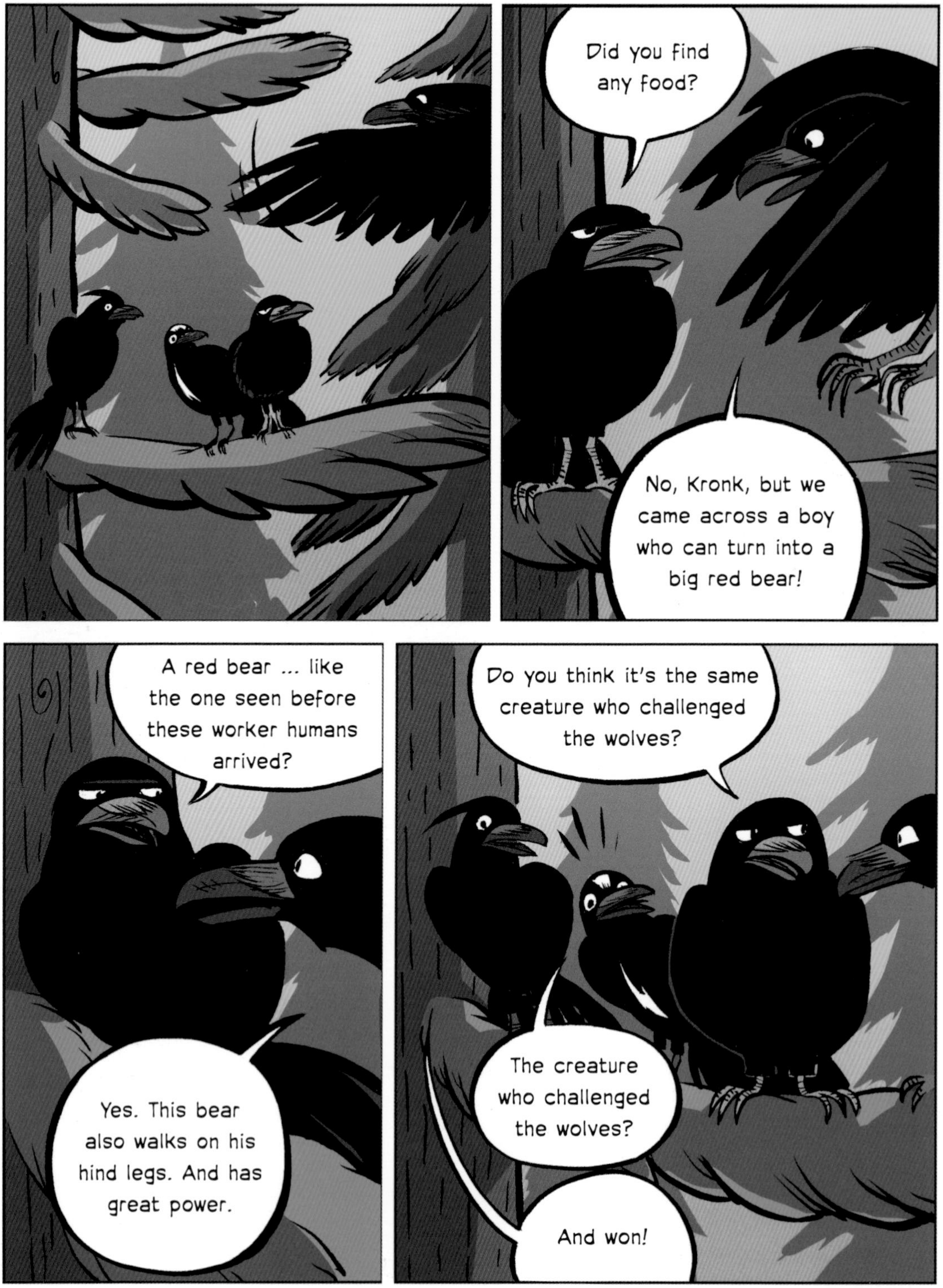
Did you find any food?
No, Kronk, but we came across a boy who can turn into a big red bear!
A red bear ... like the one seen before these worker humans arrived?
Yes. This bear also walks on his hind legs. And has great power.
Do you think it's the same creature who challenged the wolves?
The creature who challenged the wolves?
And won!

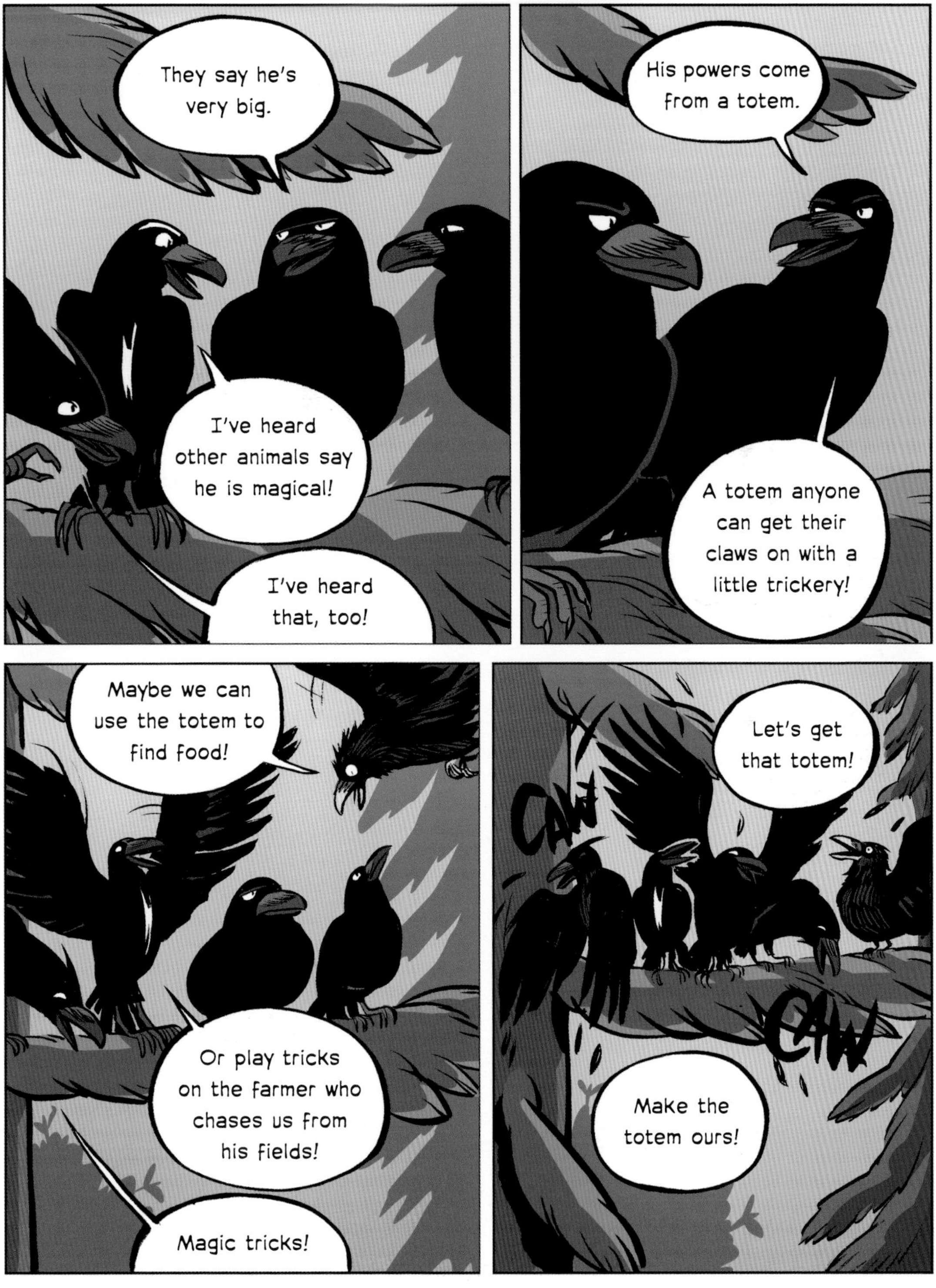

They say he's very big.
I've heard other animals say he is magical!
I've heard that, too!
His powers come from a totem.
A totem anyone can get their claws on with a little trickery!
Maybe we can use the totem to find food!
Or play tricks on the farmer who chases us from his fields!
Magic tricks!
CAW
Let's get that totem!
CAW
Make the totem ours!

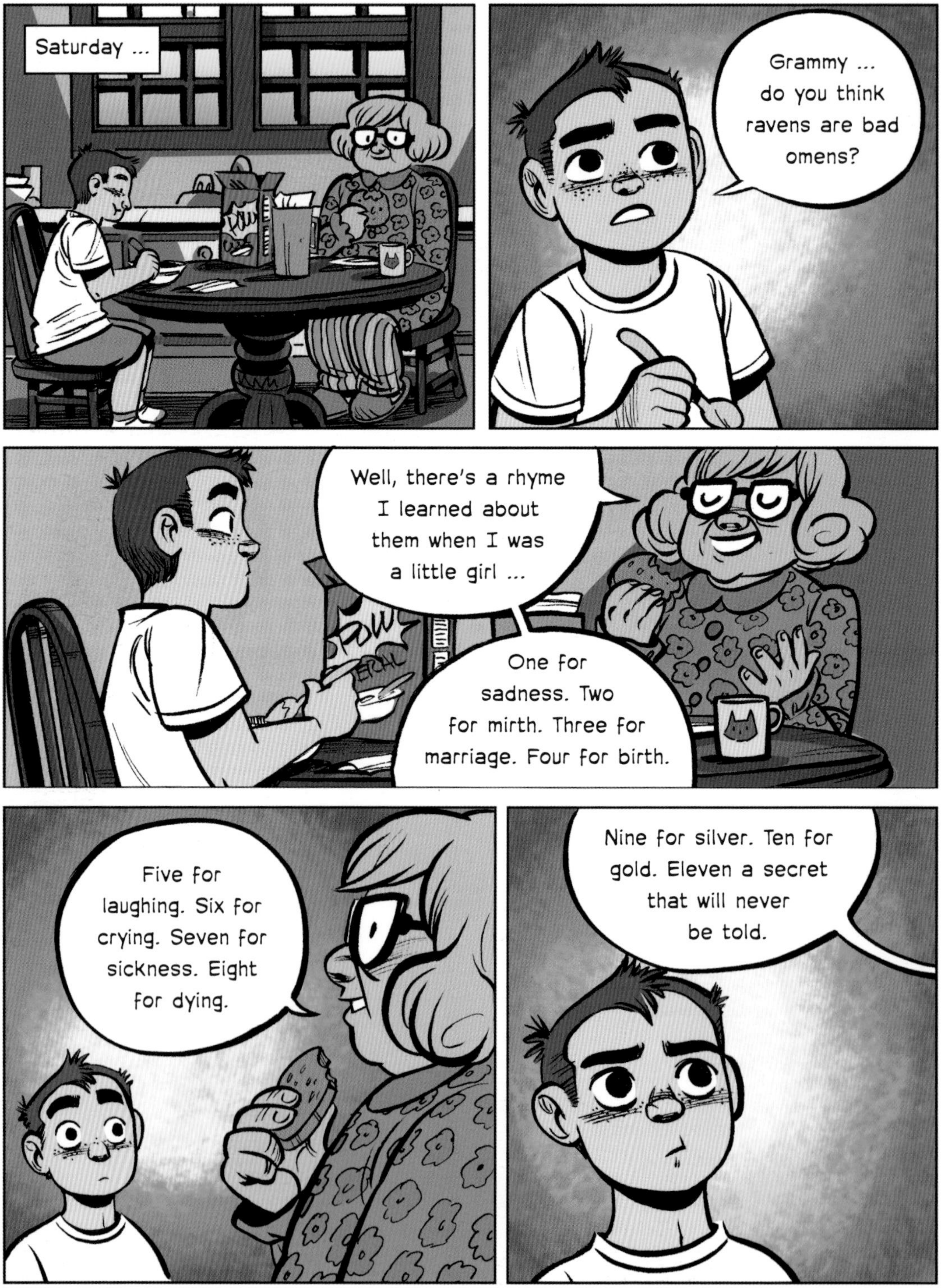
Saturday ...
Grammy ... do you think ravens are bad omens?
Well, there's a rhyme I learned about them when I was a little girl ...
One for sadness. Two for mirth. Three for marriage. Four for birth.
Five for laughing. Six for crying. Seven for sickness. Eight for dying.
Nine for silver. Ten for gold. Eleven a secret that will never be told.

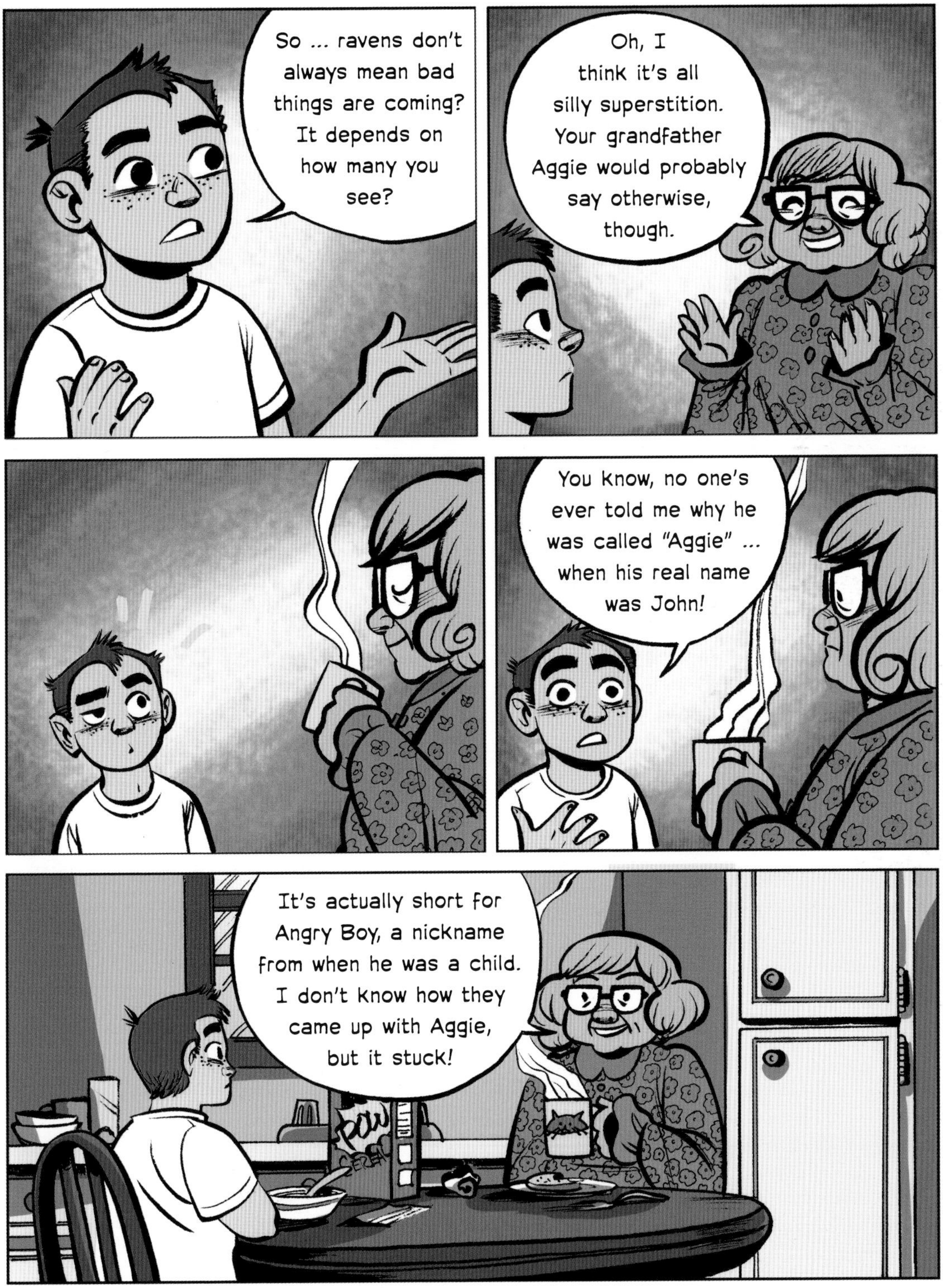
So ... ravens don't always mean bad things are coming? It depends on how many you see?
Oh, I think it's all silly superstition. Your grandfather Aggie would probably say otherwise, though.
You know, no one's ever told me why he was called "Aggie" ... when his real name was John!
It's actually short for Angry Boy, a nickname from when he was a child. I don't know how they came up with Aggie, but it stuck!
POW

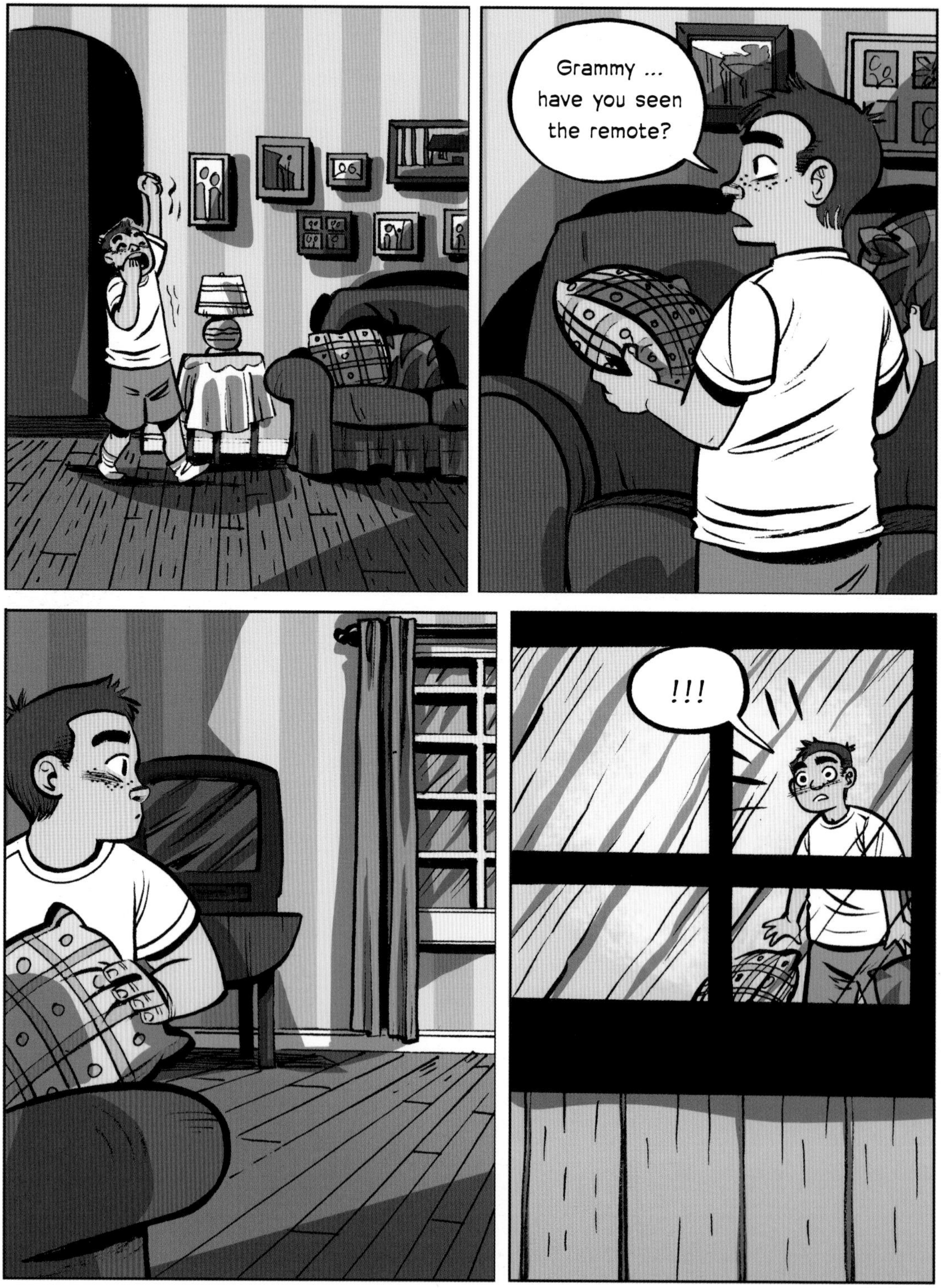
Grammy ...
have you seen
the remote?
!!!

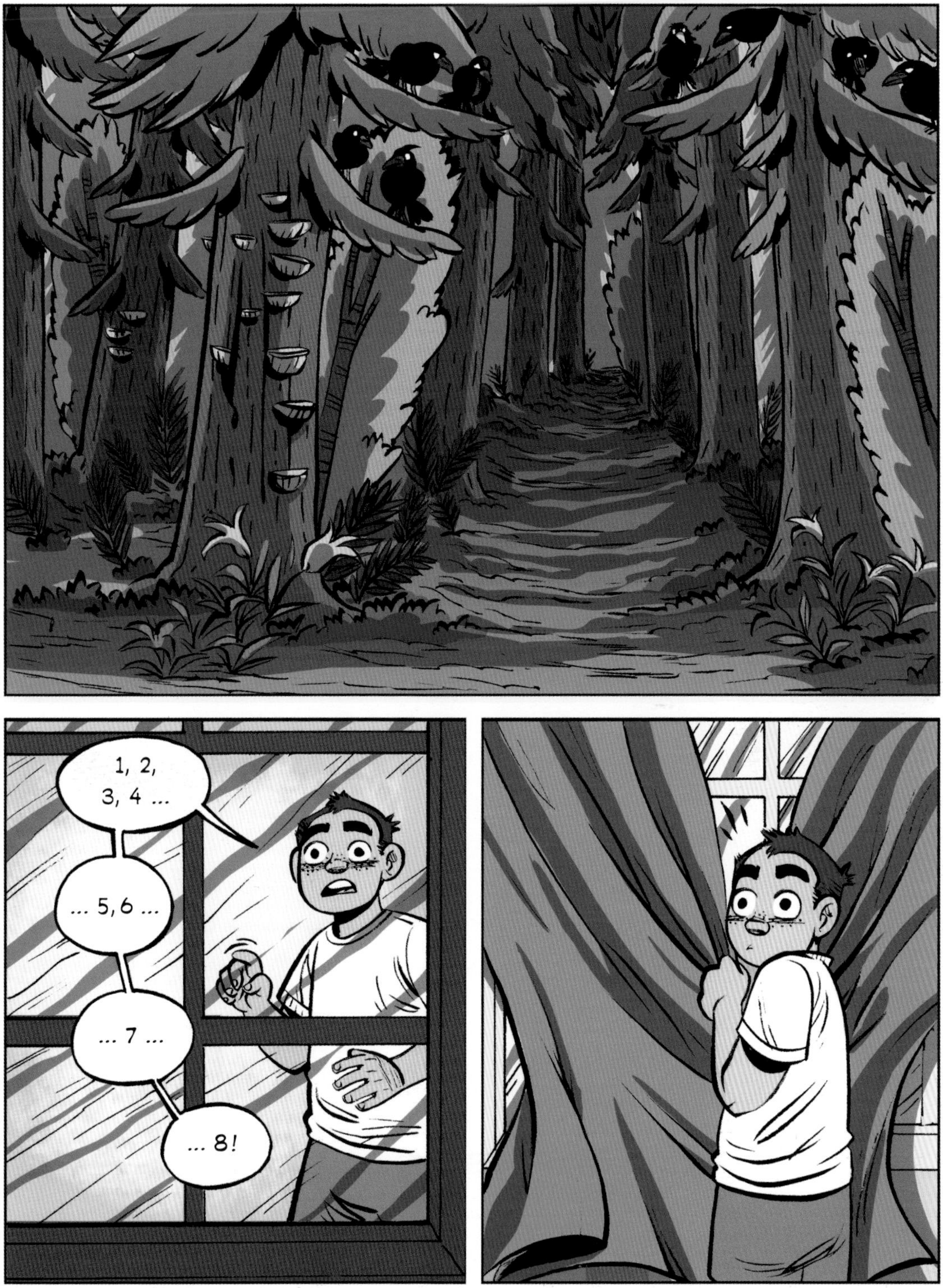
1, 2, 3, 4 ...
... 5, 6 ...
... 7 ...
... 8!

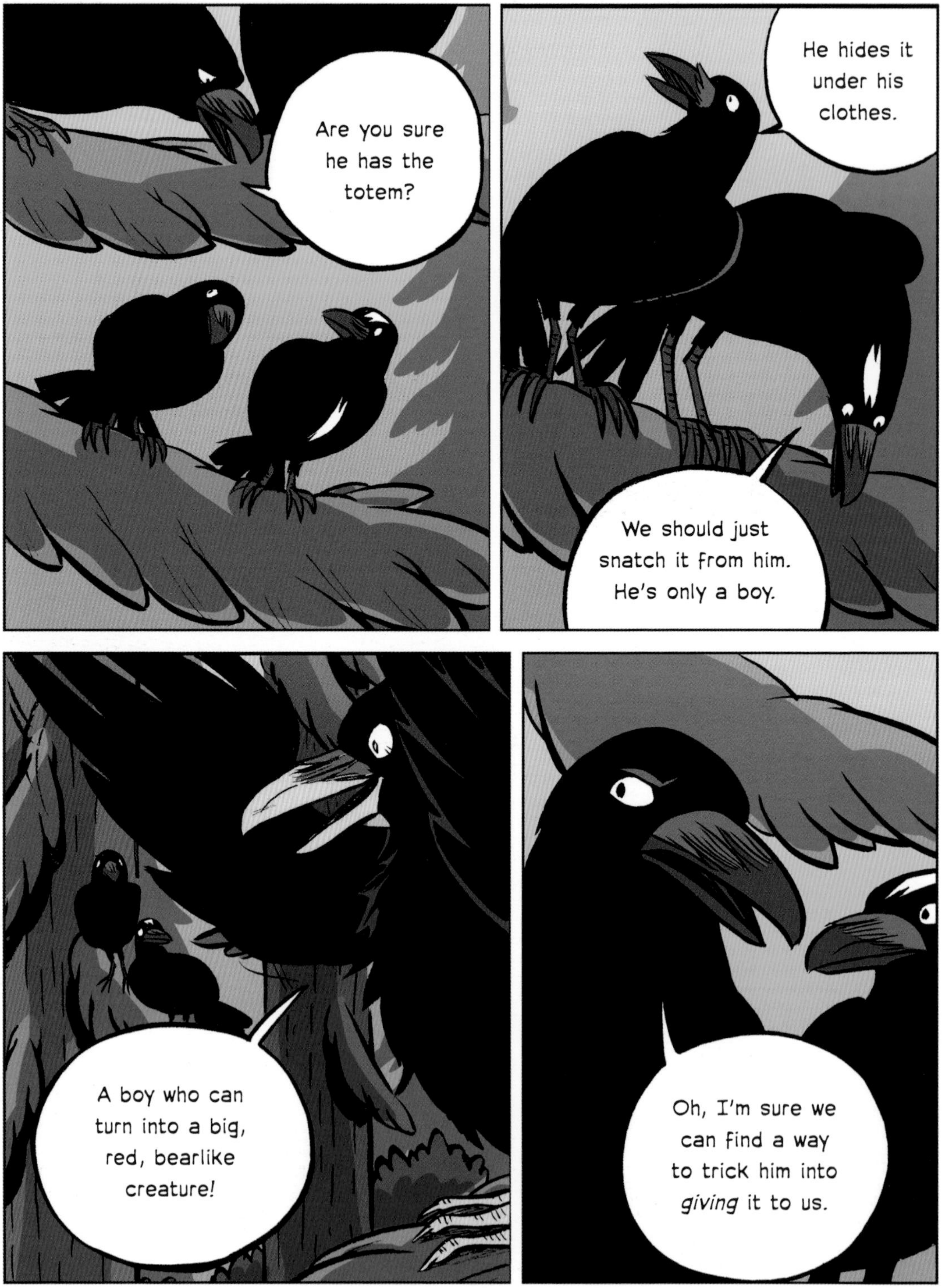
Are you sure he has the totem?
He hides it under his clothes.
We should just snatch it from him. He's only a boy.
A boy who can turn into a big, red, bearlike creature!
Oh, I'm sure we can find a way to trick him into *giving* it to us.

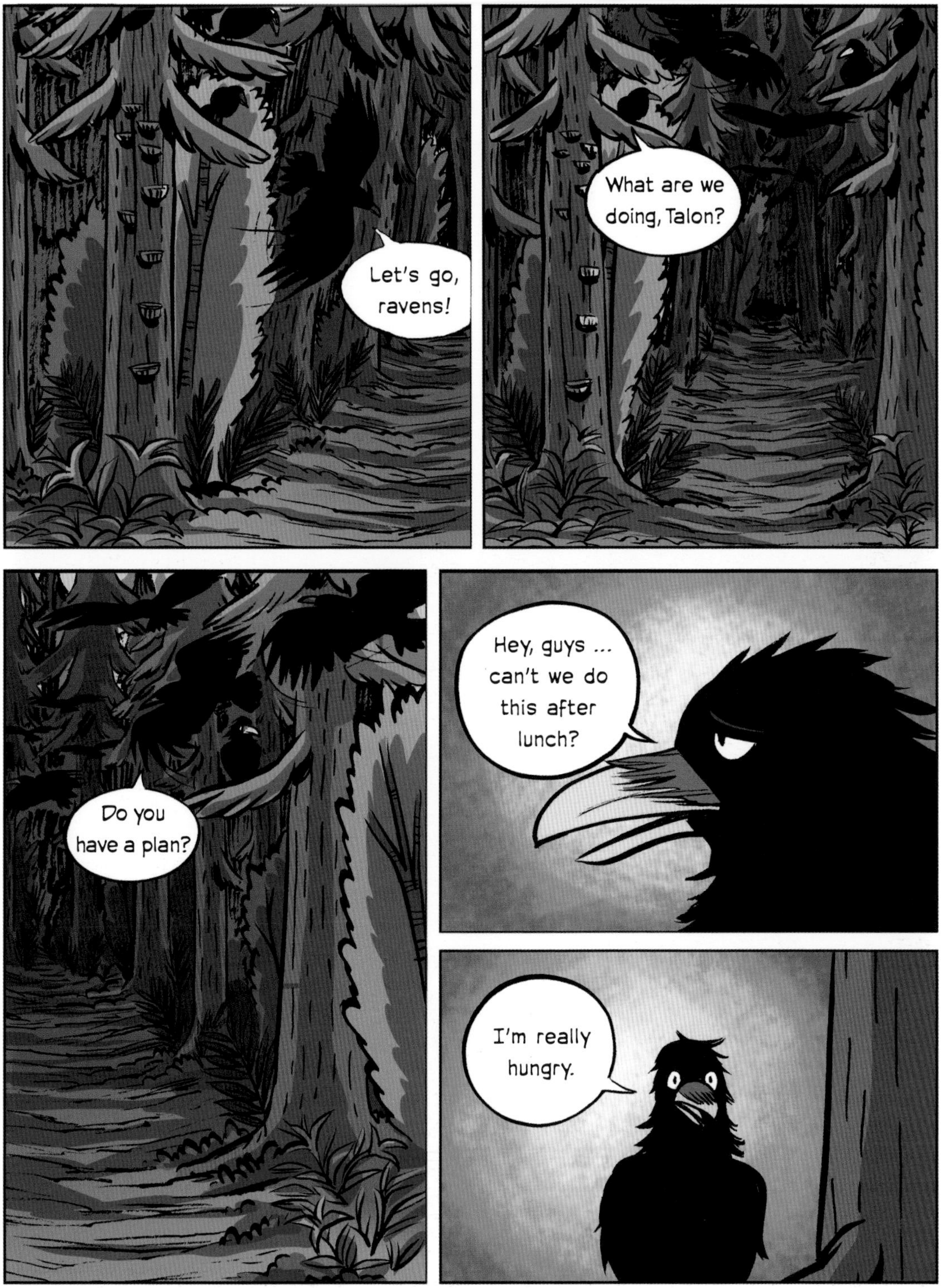
Let's go, ravens!
What are we doing, Talon?
Do you have a plan?
Hey, guys ... can't we do this after lunch?
I'm really hungry.

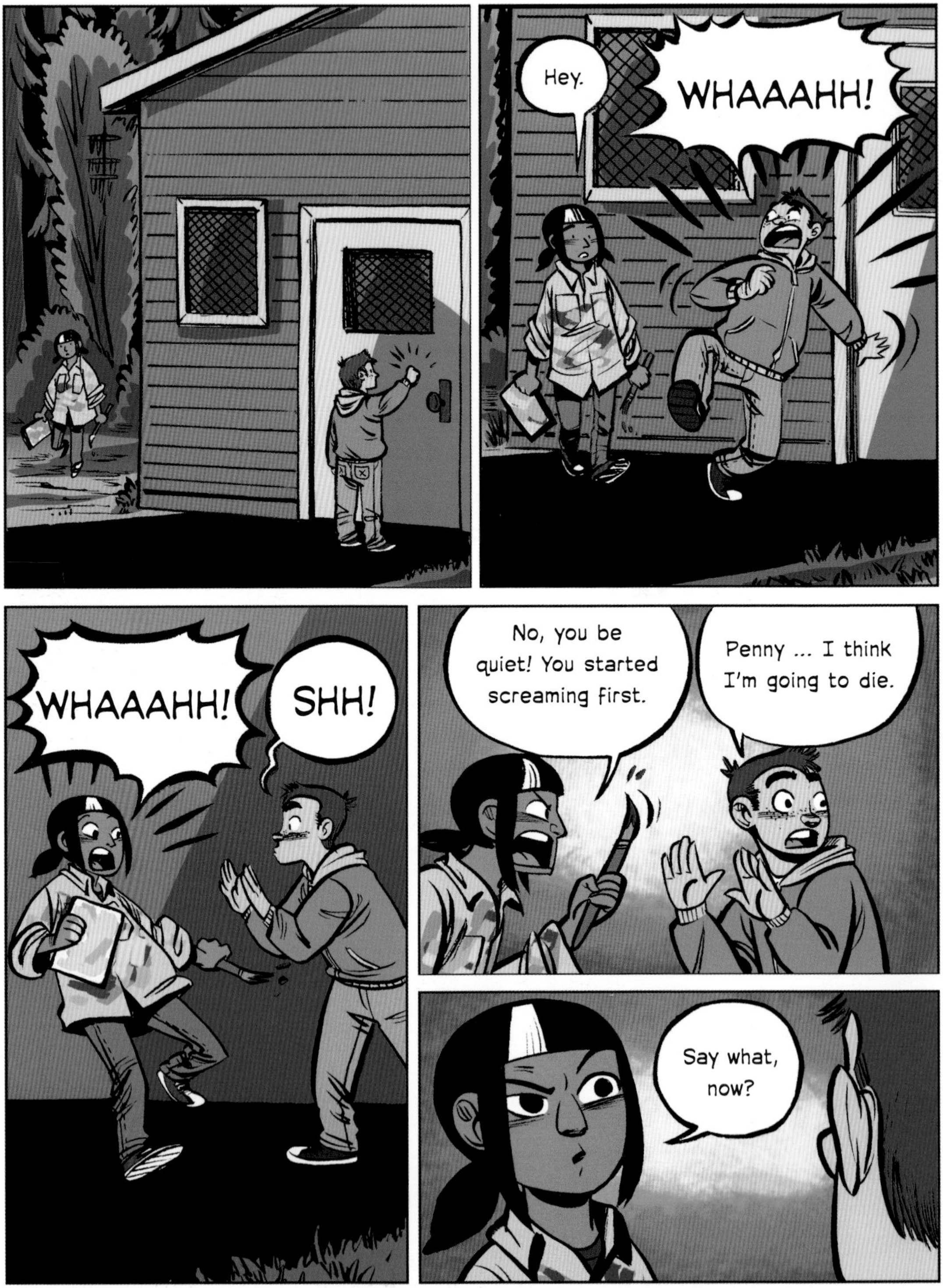
Hey.
WHAAAHH!
WHAAAHH!
SHH!
No, you be quiet! You started screaming first.
Penny ... I think I'm going to die.
Say what, now?

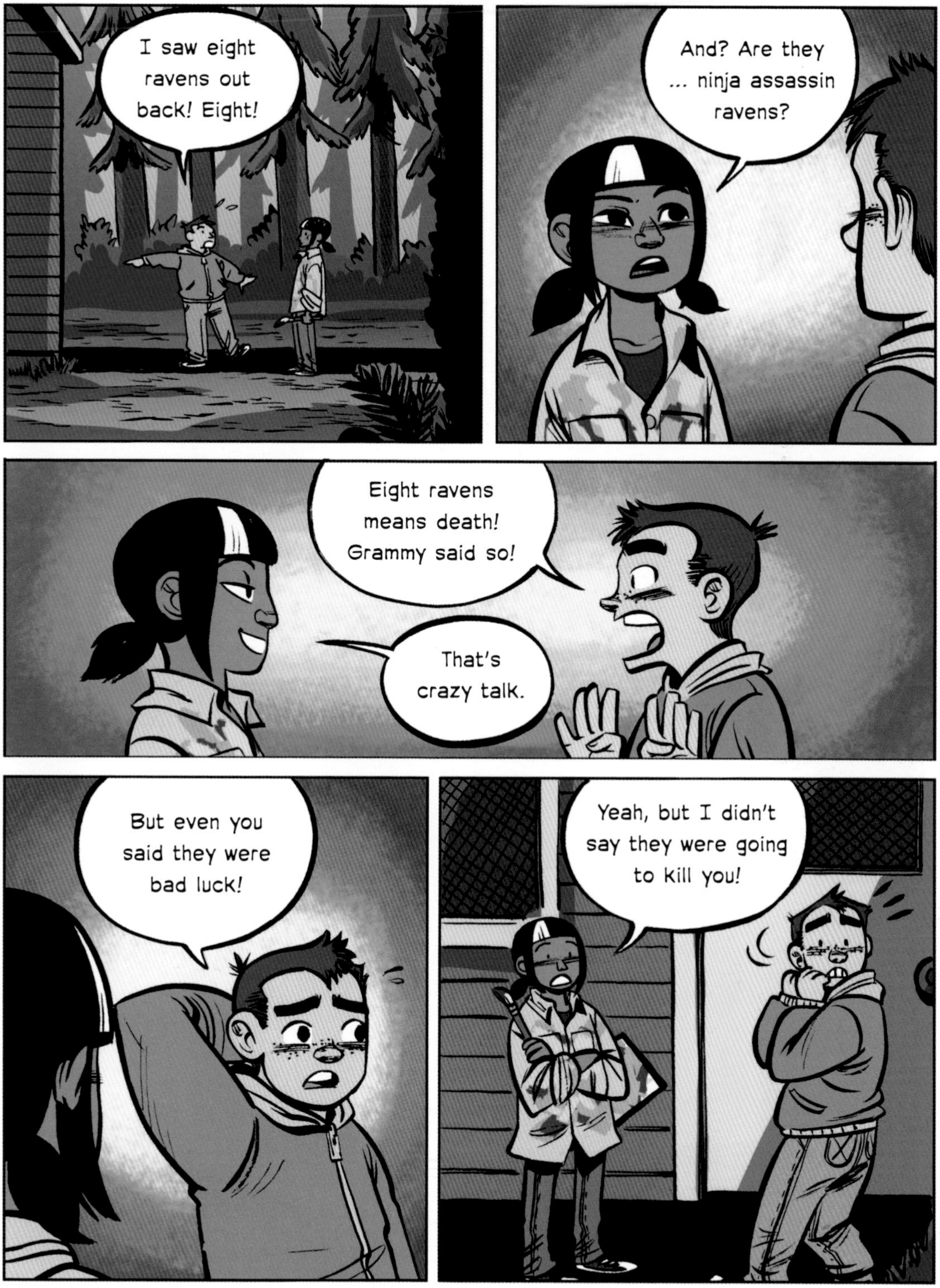
I saw eight ravens out back! Eight!
And? Are they ... ninja assassin ravens?
Eight ravens means death! Grammy said so!
That's crazy talk.
But even you said they were bad luck!
Yeah, but I didn't say they were going to kill you!

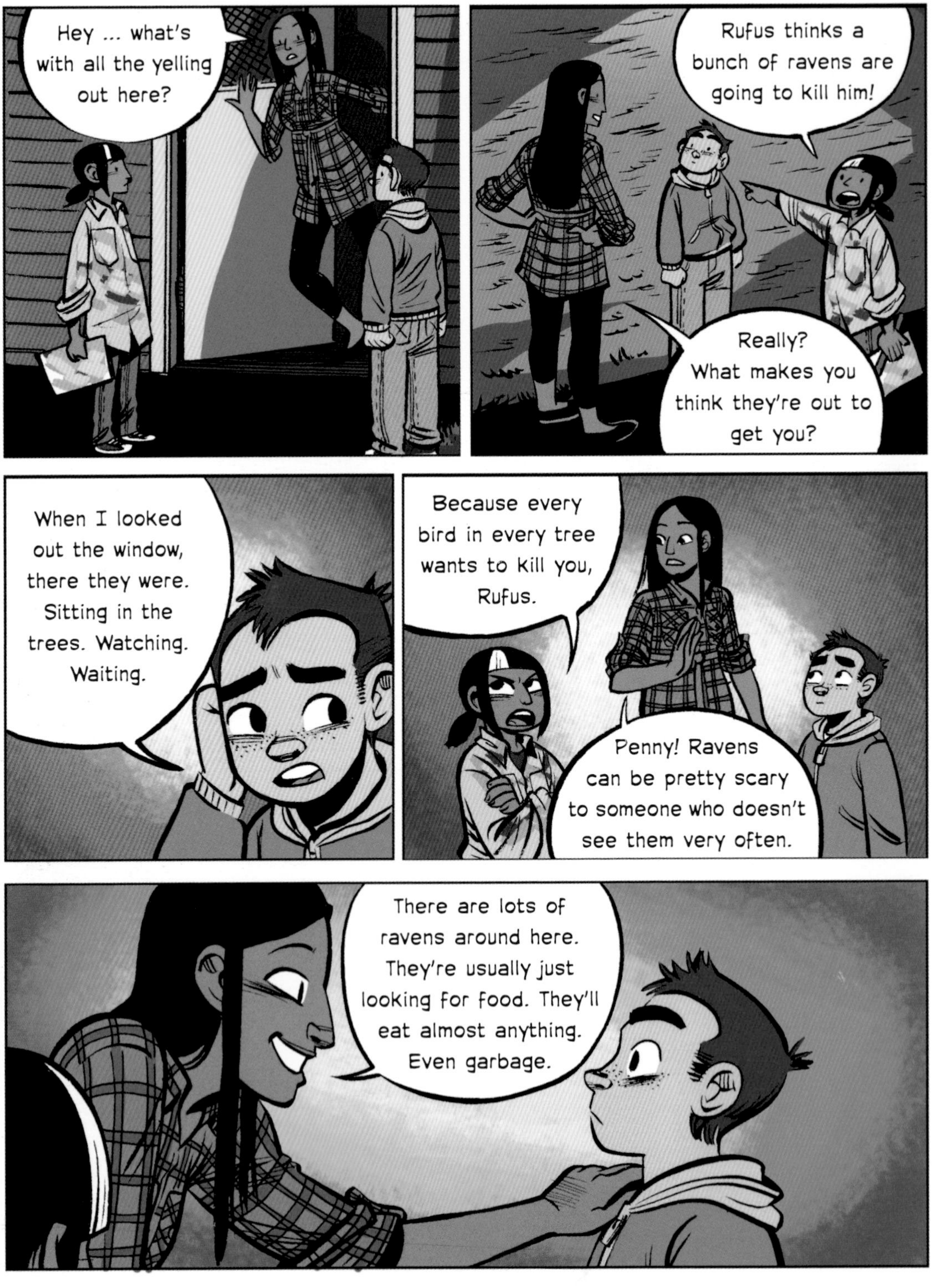

Hey ... what's with all the yelling out here?
Rufus thinks a bunch of ravens are going to kill him!
Really? What makes you think they're out to get you?
When I looked out the window, there they were. Sitting in the trees. Watching. Waiting.
Because every bird in every tree wants to kill you, Rufus.
Penny! Ravens can be pretty scary to someone who doesn't see them very often.
There are lots of ravens around here. They're usually just looking for food. They'll eat almost anything. Even garbage.

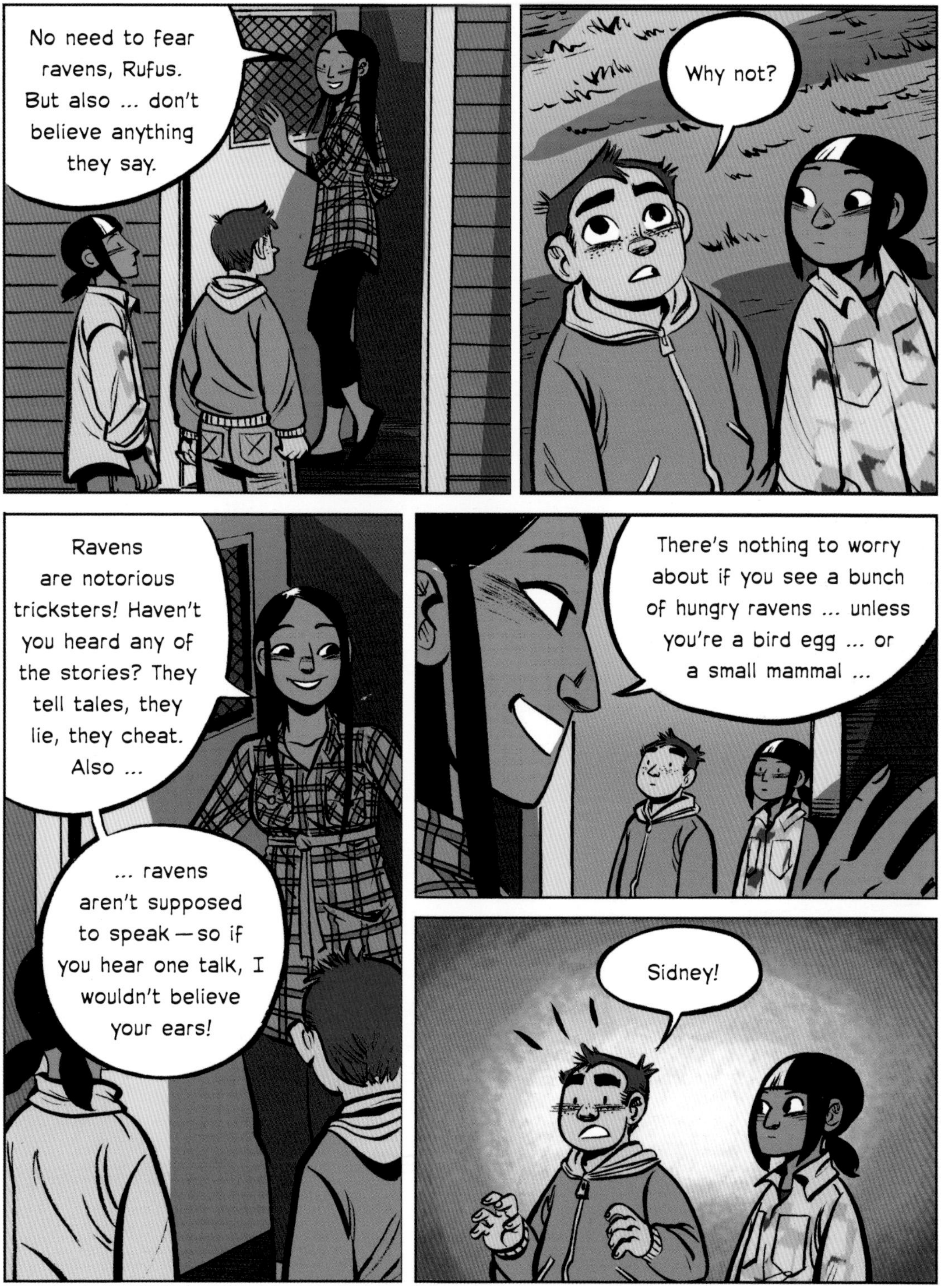
No need to fear ravens, Rufus. But also ... don't believe anything they say.
Why not?
Ravens are notorious tricksters! Haven't you heard any of the stories? They tell tales, they lie, they cheat. Also ...
... ravens aren't supposed to speak — so if you hear one talk, I wouldn't believe your ears!
There's nothing to worry about if you see a bunch of hungry ravens ... unless you're a bird egg ... or a small mammal ...
Sidney!

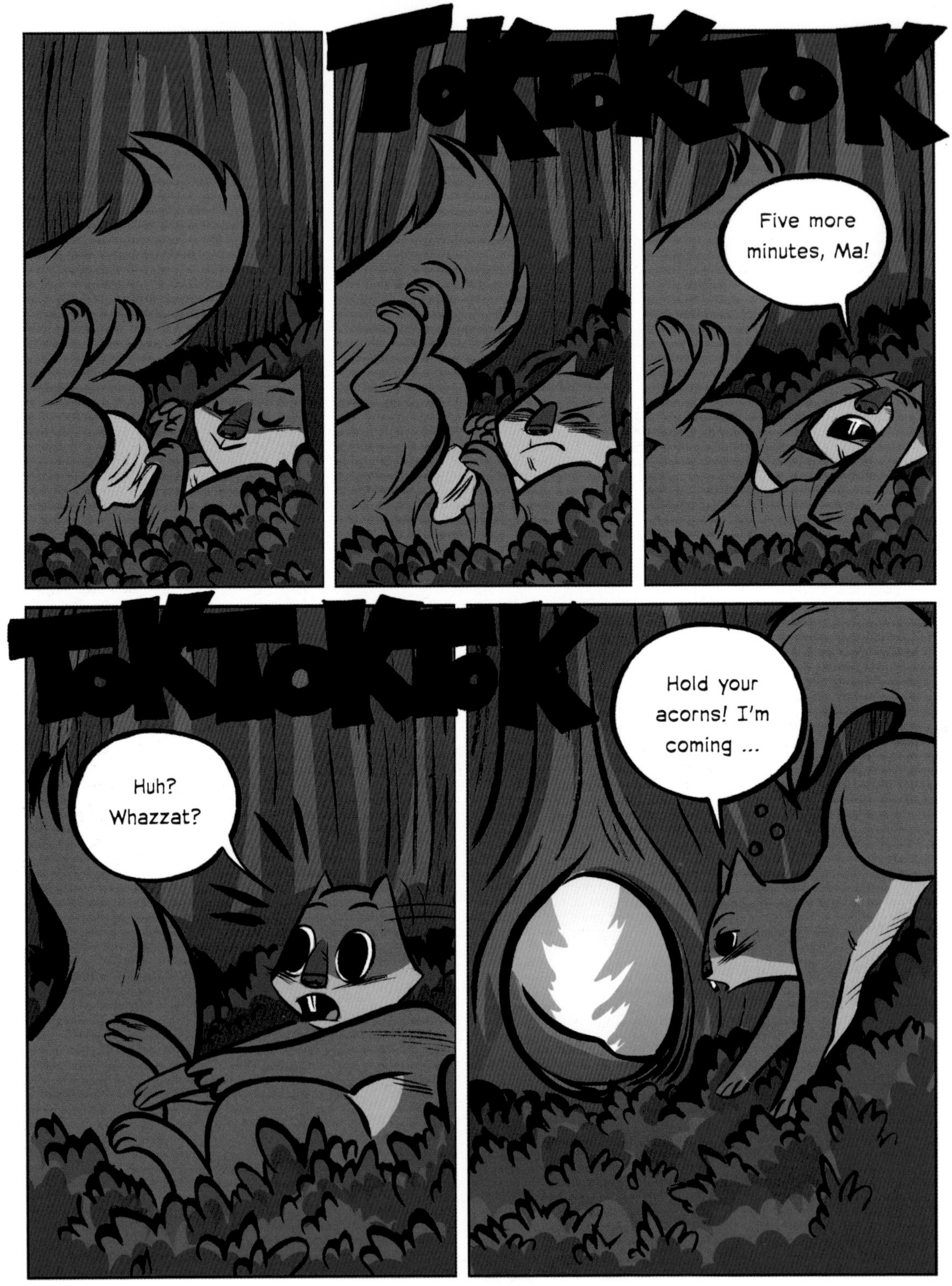
TOKTOKTOK
Five more minutes, Ma!
TOKTOKTOK
Huh? Whazzat?
Hold your acorns! I'm coming ...

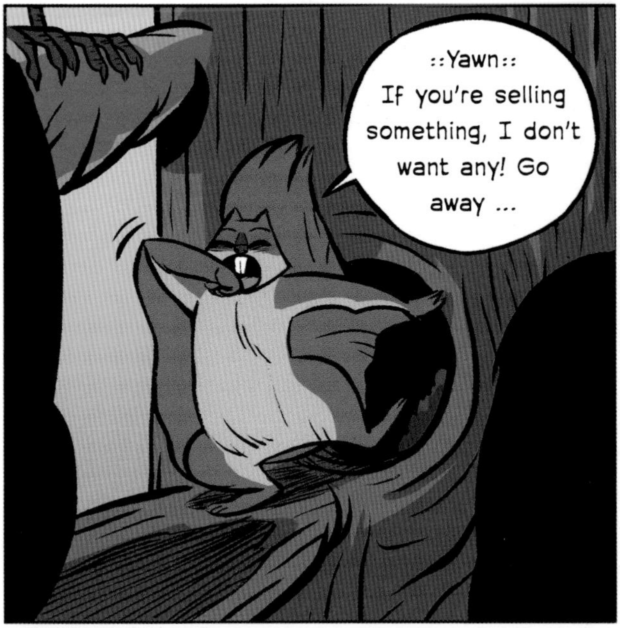
::Yawn:: If you're selling something, I don't want any! Go away ...

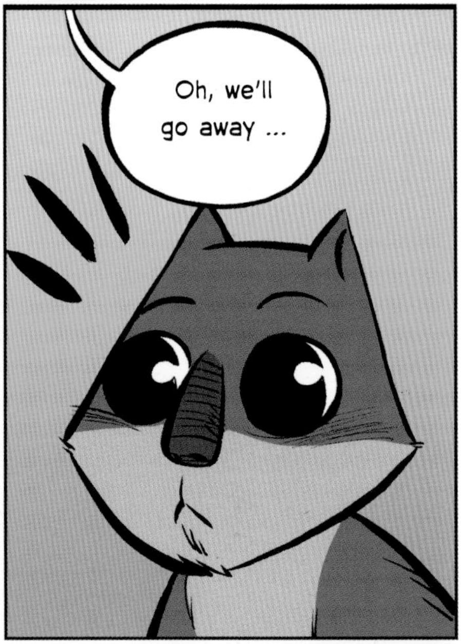
Oh, we'll go away ...

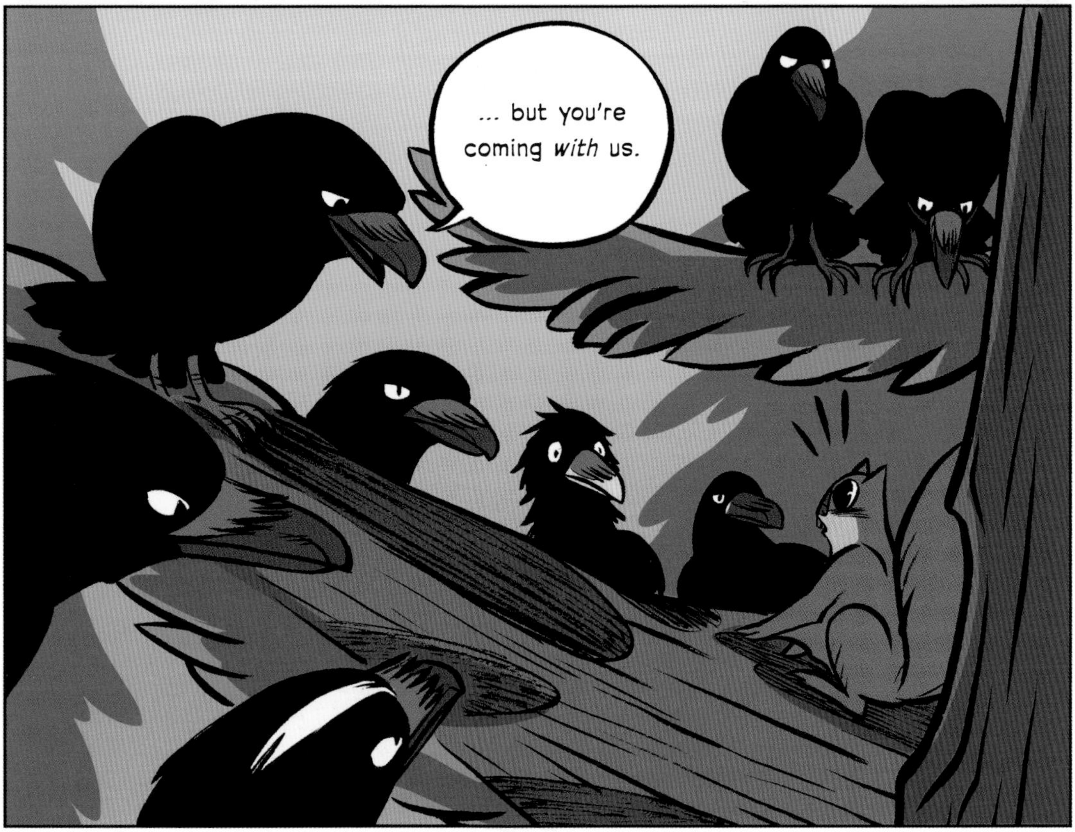
... but you're coming *with* us.

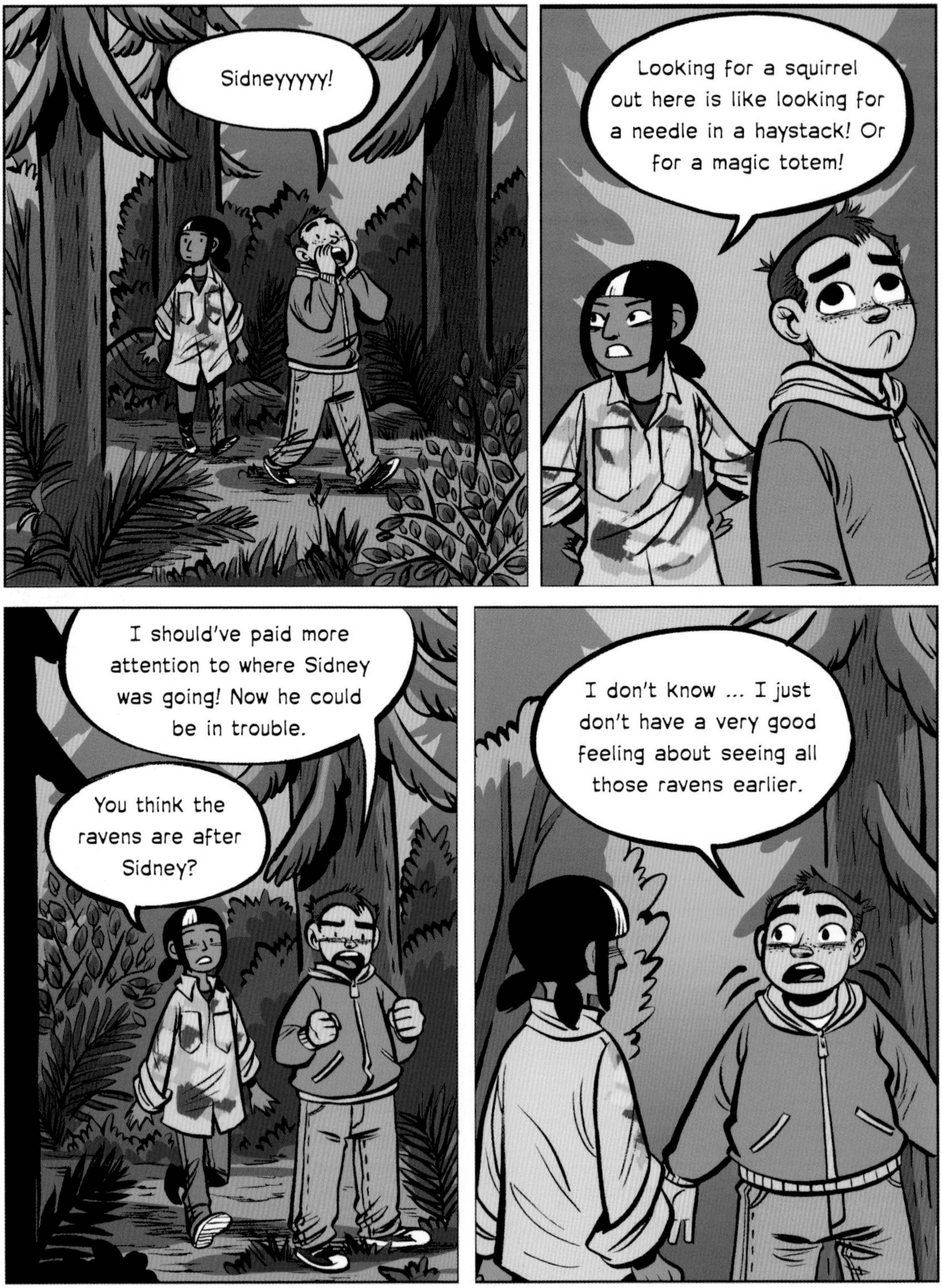
Sidneyyyyy!
Looking for a squirrel out here is like looking for a needle in a haystack! Or for a magic totem!
I should've paid more attention to where Sidney was going! Now he could be in trouble.
You think the ravens are after Sidney?
I don't know ... I just don't have a very good feeling about seeing all those ravens earlier.

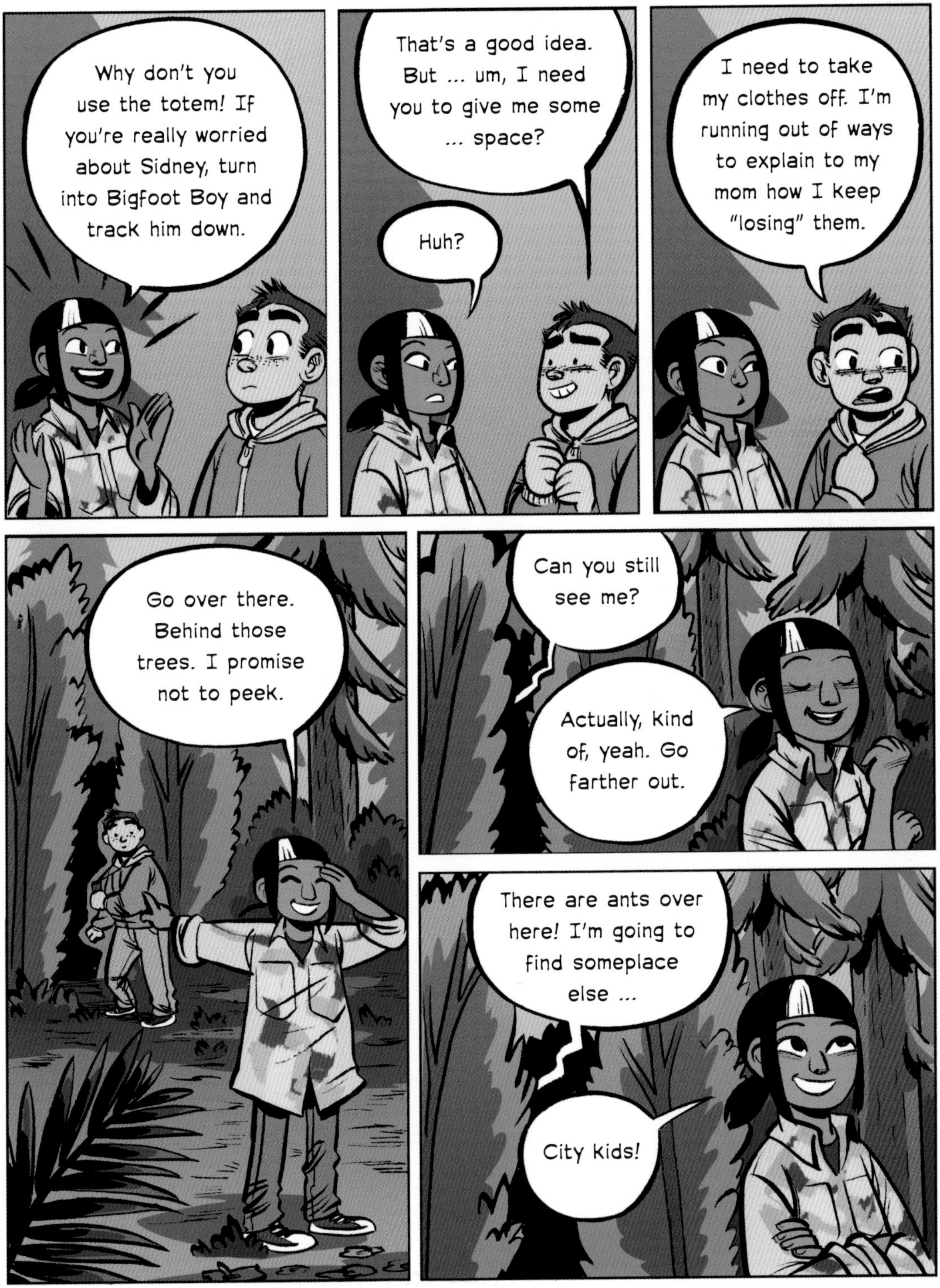
Why don't you use the totem! If you're really worried about Sidney, turn into Bigfoot Boy and track him down.
That's a good idea. But ... um, I need you to give me some ... space?
Huh?
I need to take my clothes off. I'm running out of ways to explain to my mom how I keep "losing" them.
Go over there. Behind those trees. I promise not to peek.
Can you still see me?
Actually, kind of, yeah. Go farther out.
There are ants over here! I'm going to find someplace else ...
City kids!

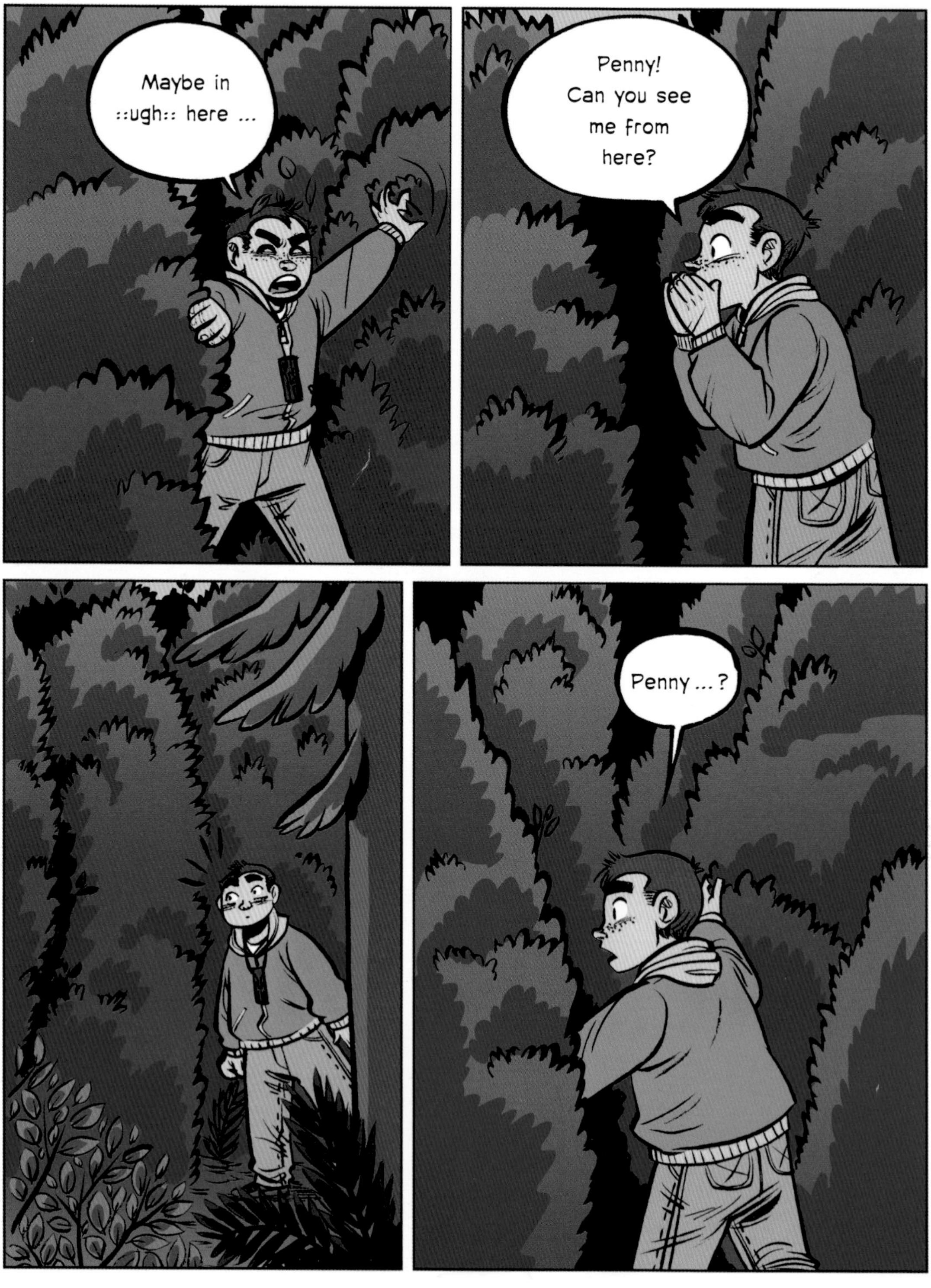
Maybe in ::ugh:: here ...
Penny! Can you see me from here?
Penny ... ?

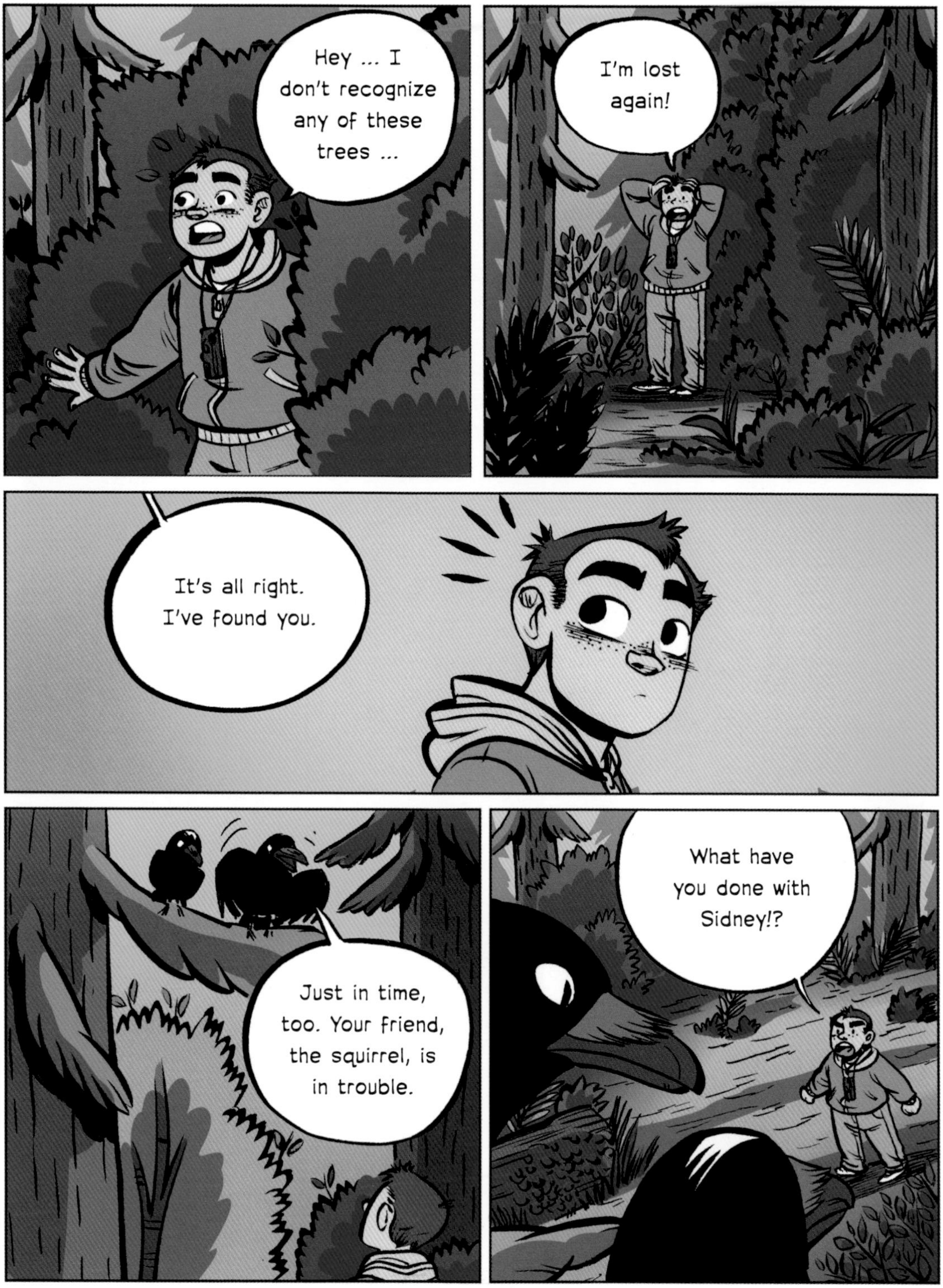
Hey ... I don't recognize any of these trees ...
I'm lost again!
It's all right. I've found you.
Just in time, too. Your friend, the squirrel, is in trouble.
What have you done with Sidney!?

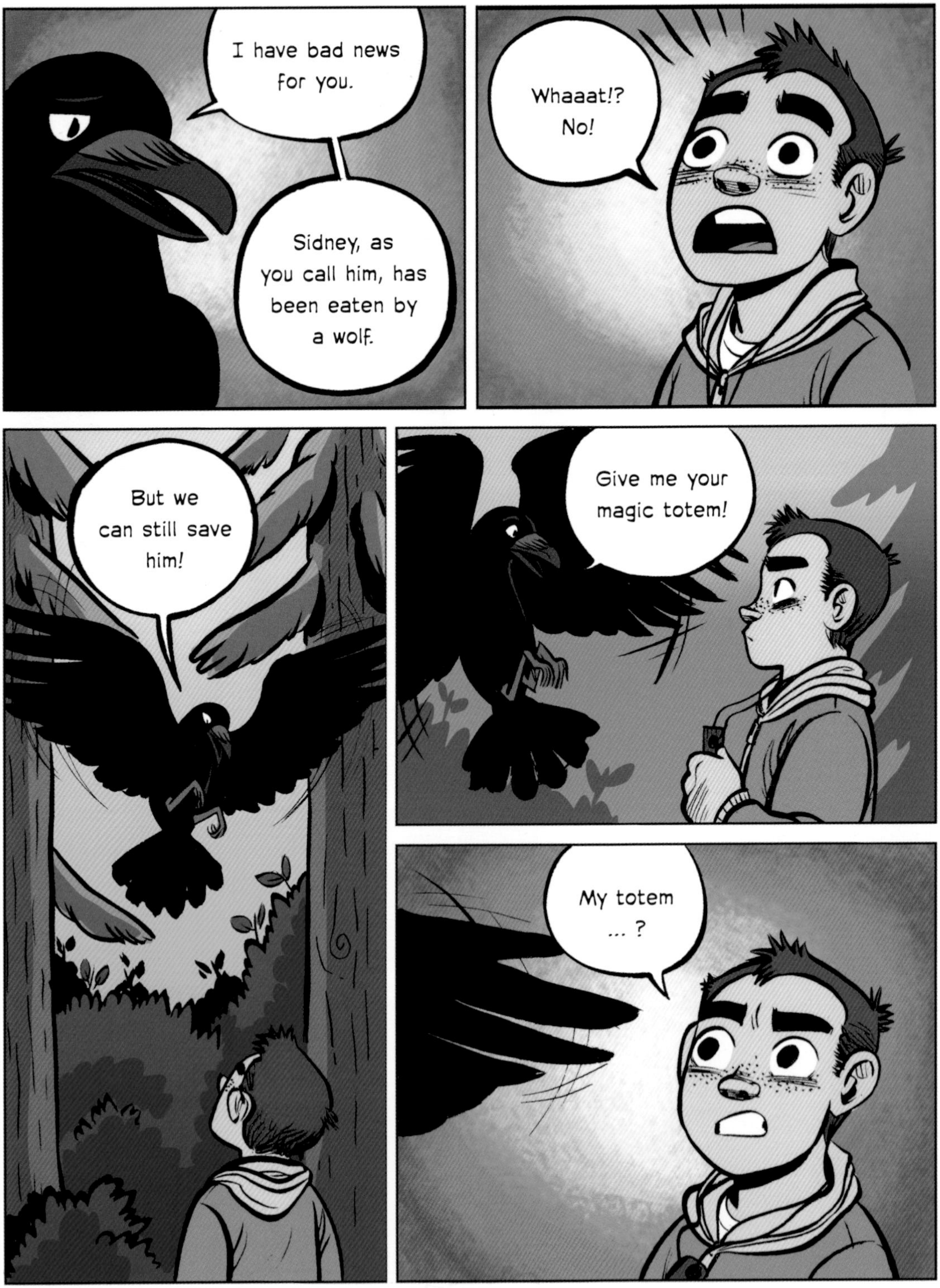
I have bad news for you.
Sidney, as you call him, has been eaten by a wolf.
Whaaat!? No!
But we can still save him!
Give me your magic totem!
My totem ... ?

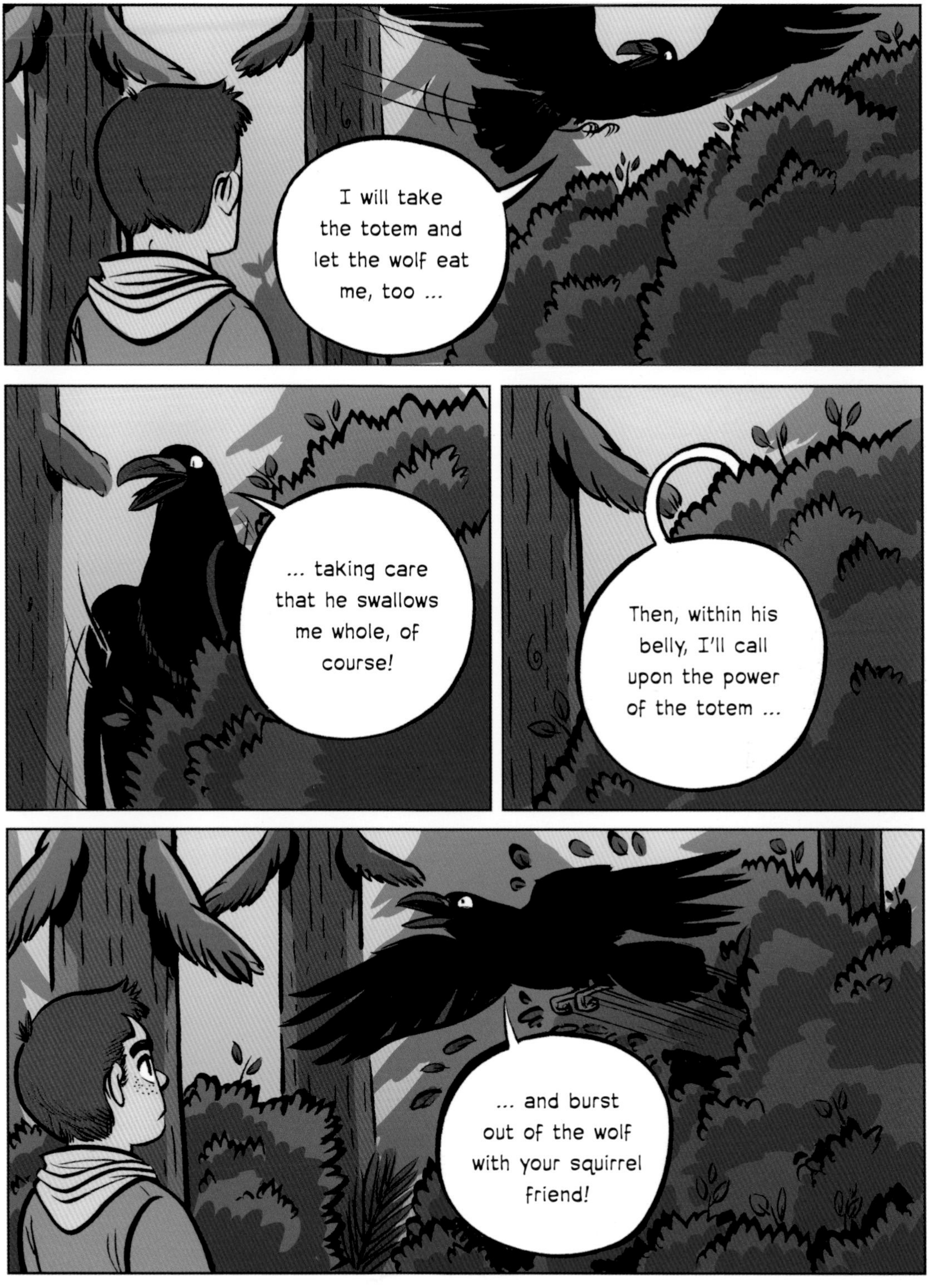
I will take the totem and let the wolf eat me, too ...
... taking care that he swallows me whole, of course!
Then, within his belly, I'll call upon the power of the totem ...
... and burst out of the wolf with your squirrel friend!

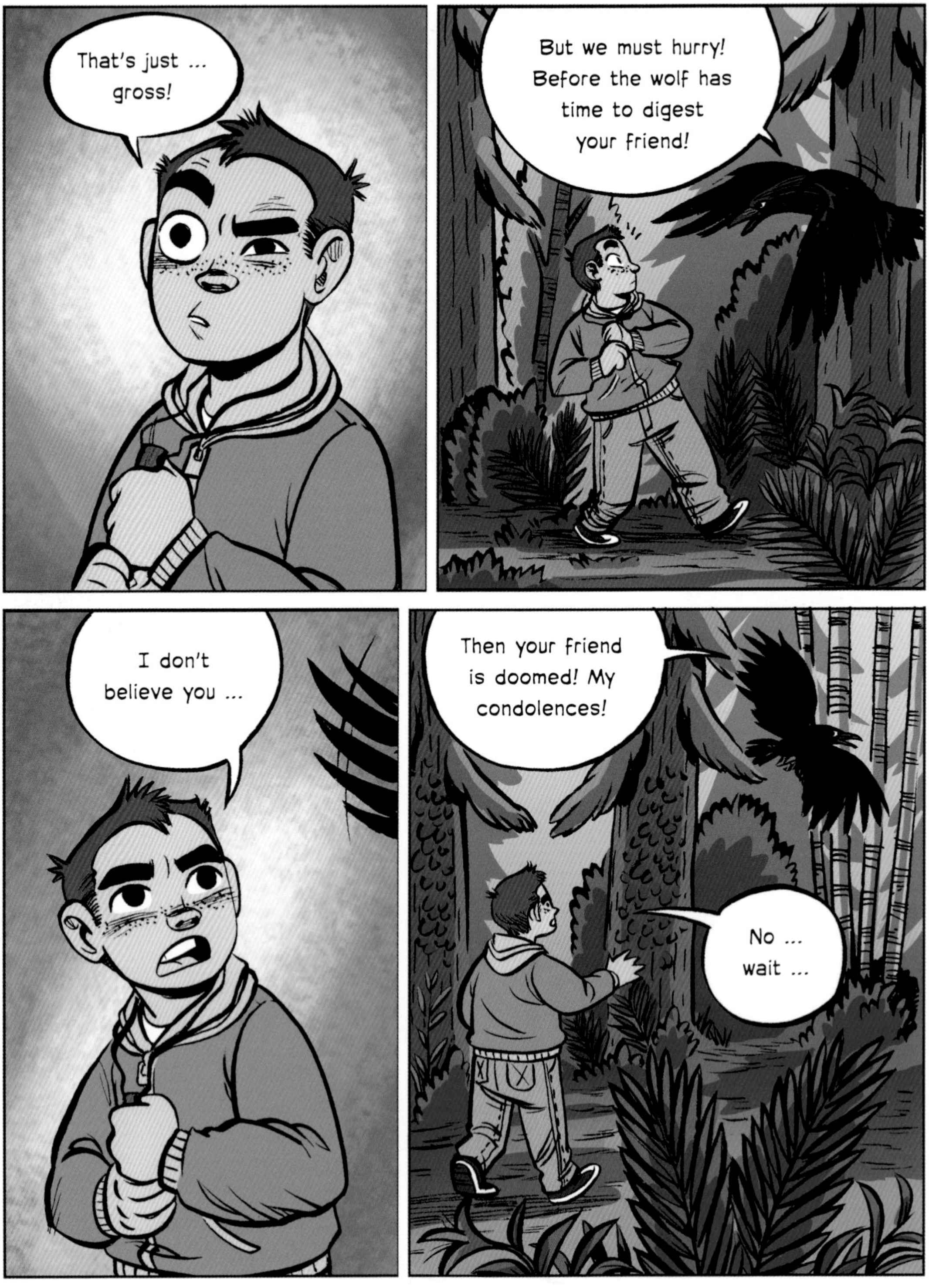

That's just ... gross!
But we must hurry! Before the wolf has time to digest your friend!
I don't believe you ...
Then your friend is doomed! My condolences!
No ... wait ...

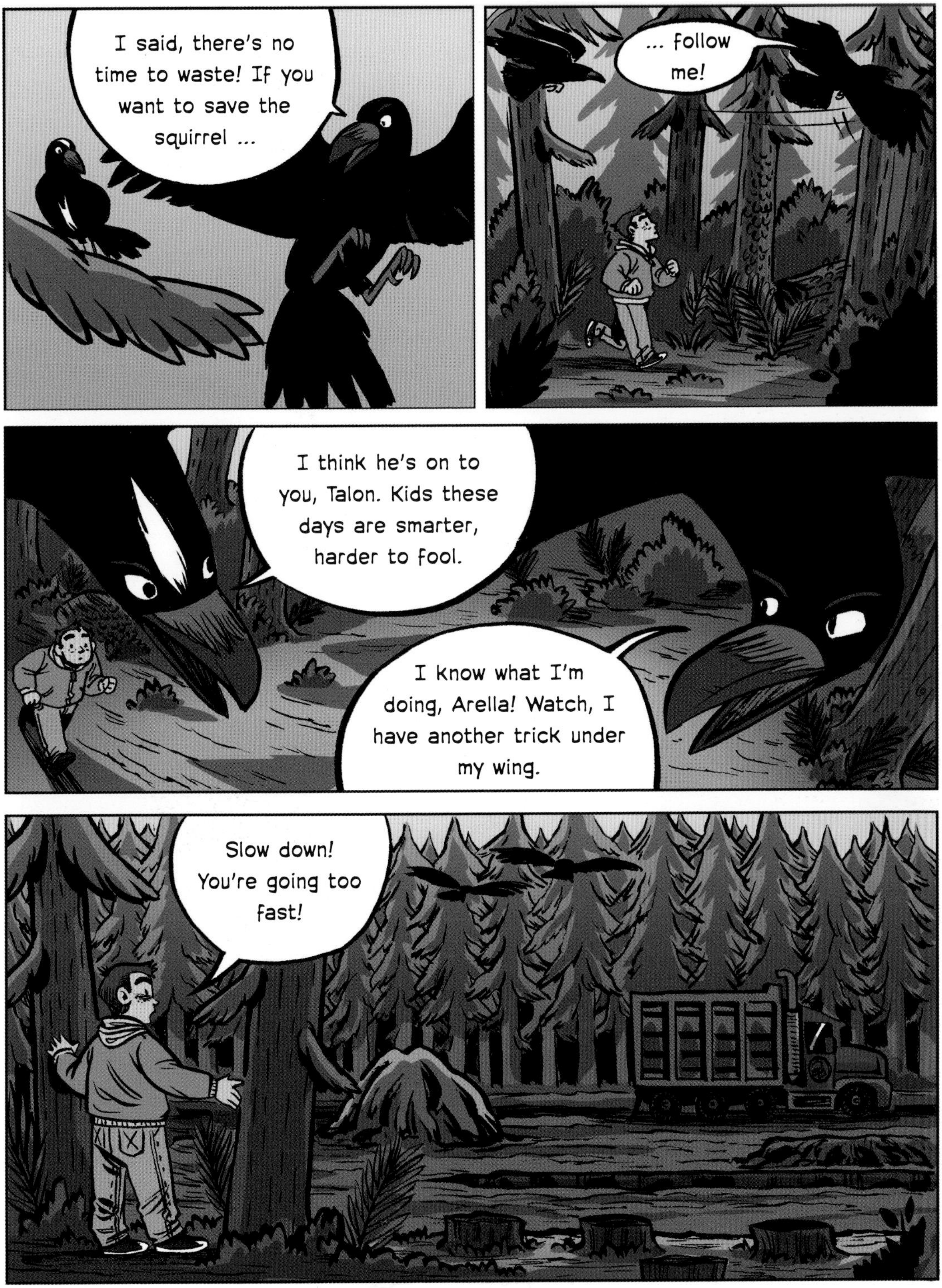
I said, there's no time to waste! If you want to save the squirrel ...
... follow me!
I think he's on to you, Talon. Kids these days are smarter, harder to fool.
I know what I'm doing, Arella! Watch, I have another trick under my wing.
Slow down! You're going too fast!

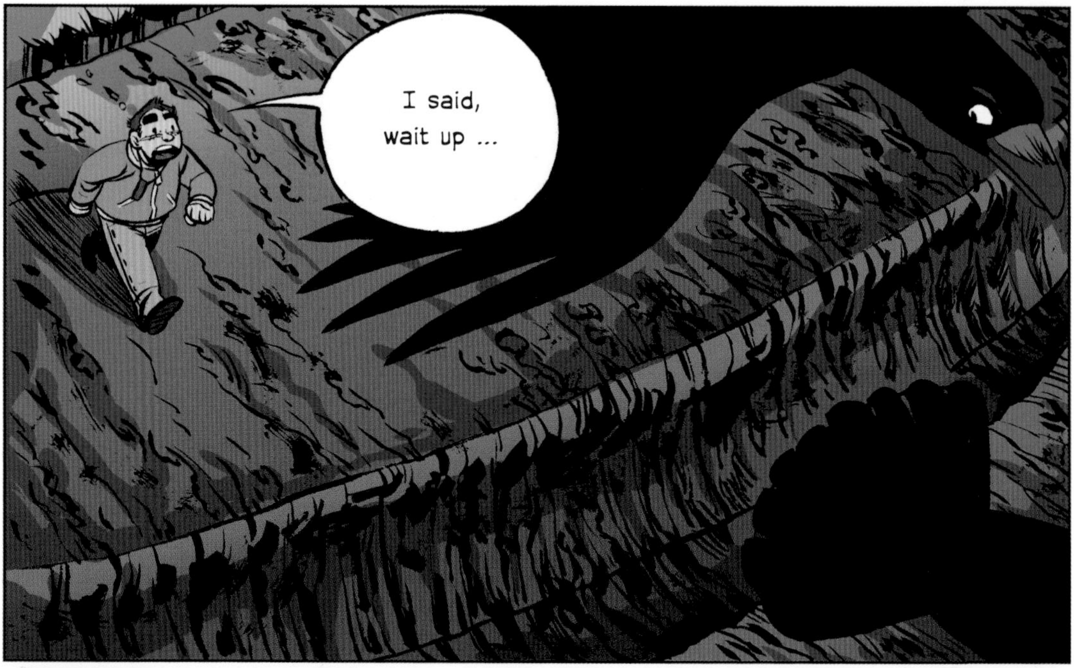
I said,
wait up ...

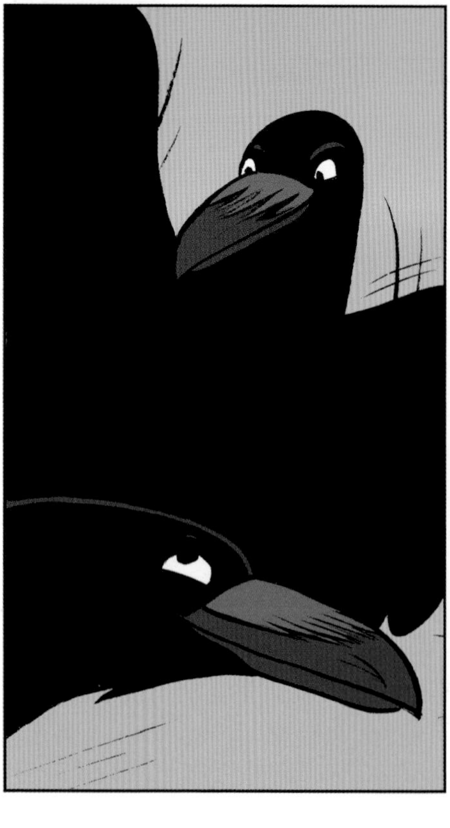

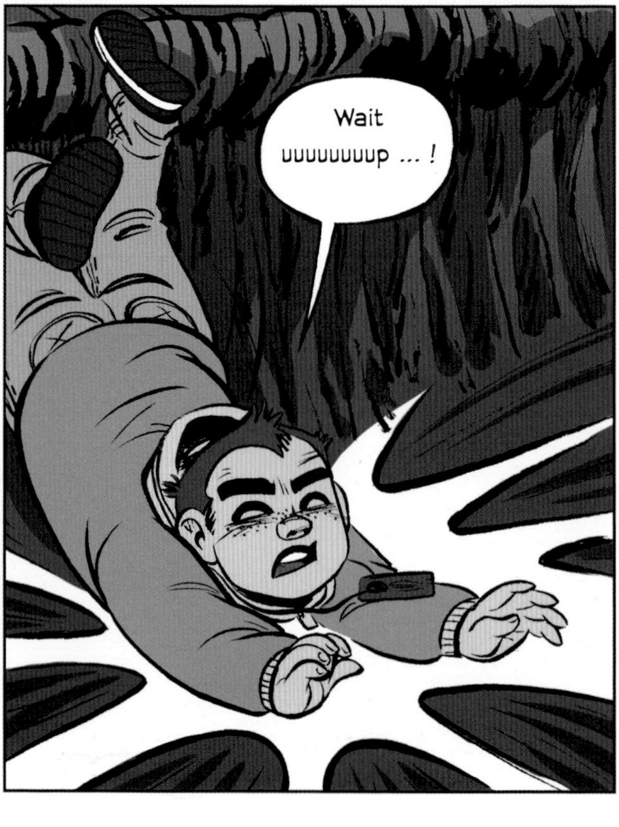
Wait
uuuuuuuup ... !

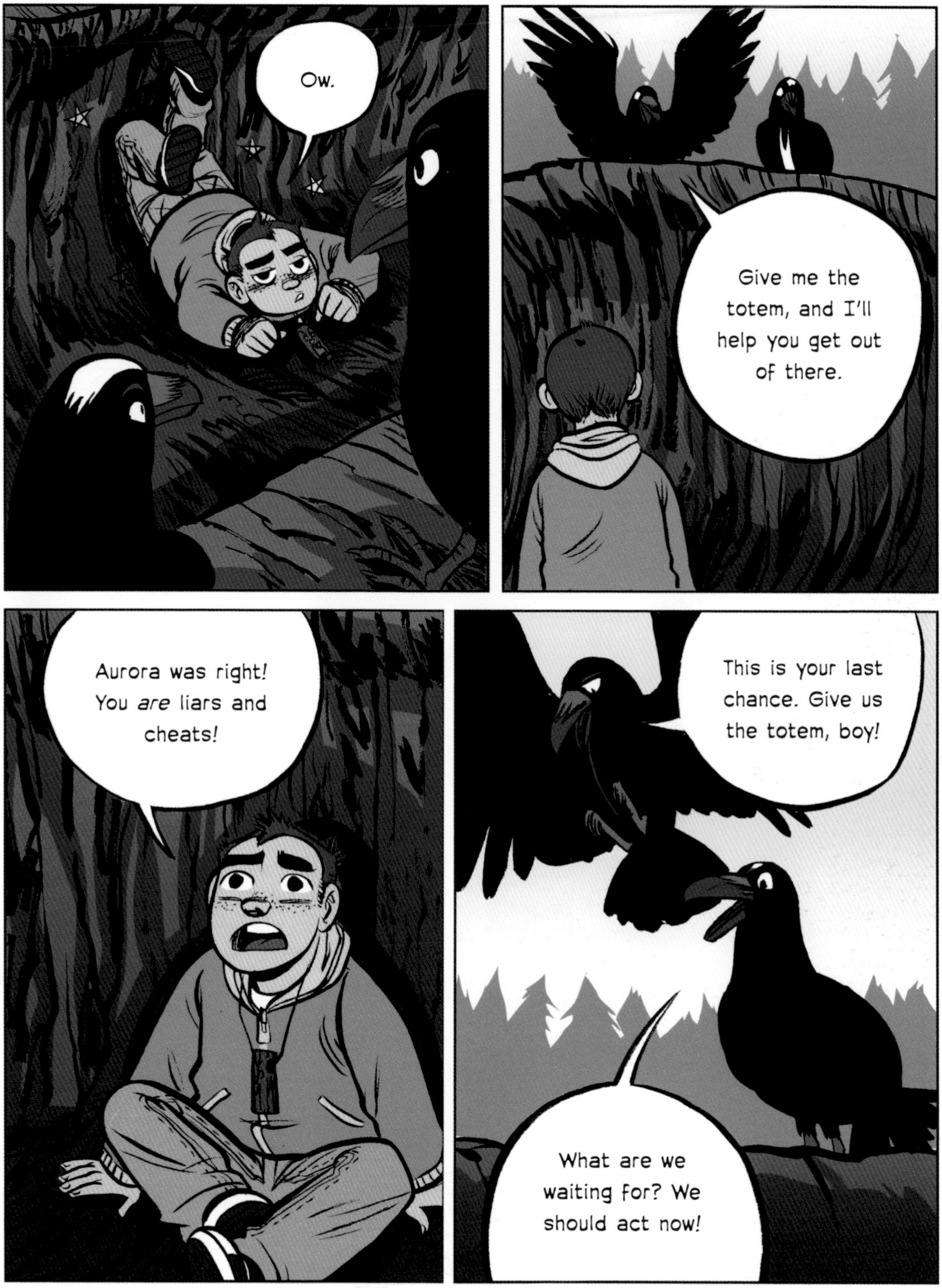
Ow.
Give me the totem, and I'll help you get out of there.
Aurora was right! You *are* liars and cheats!
This is your last chance. Give us the totem, boy!
What are we waiting for? We should act now!

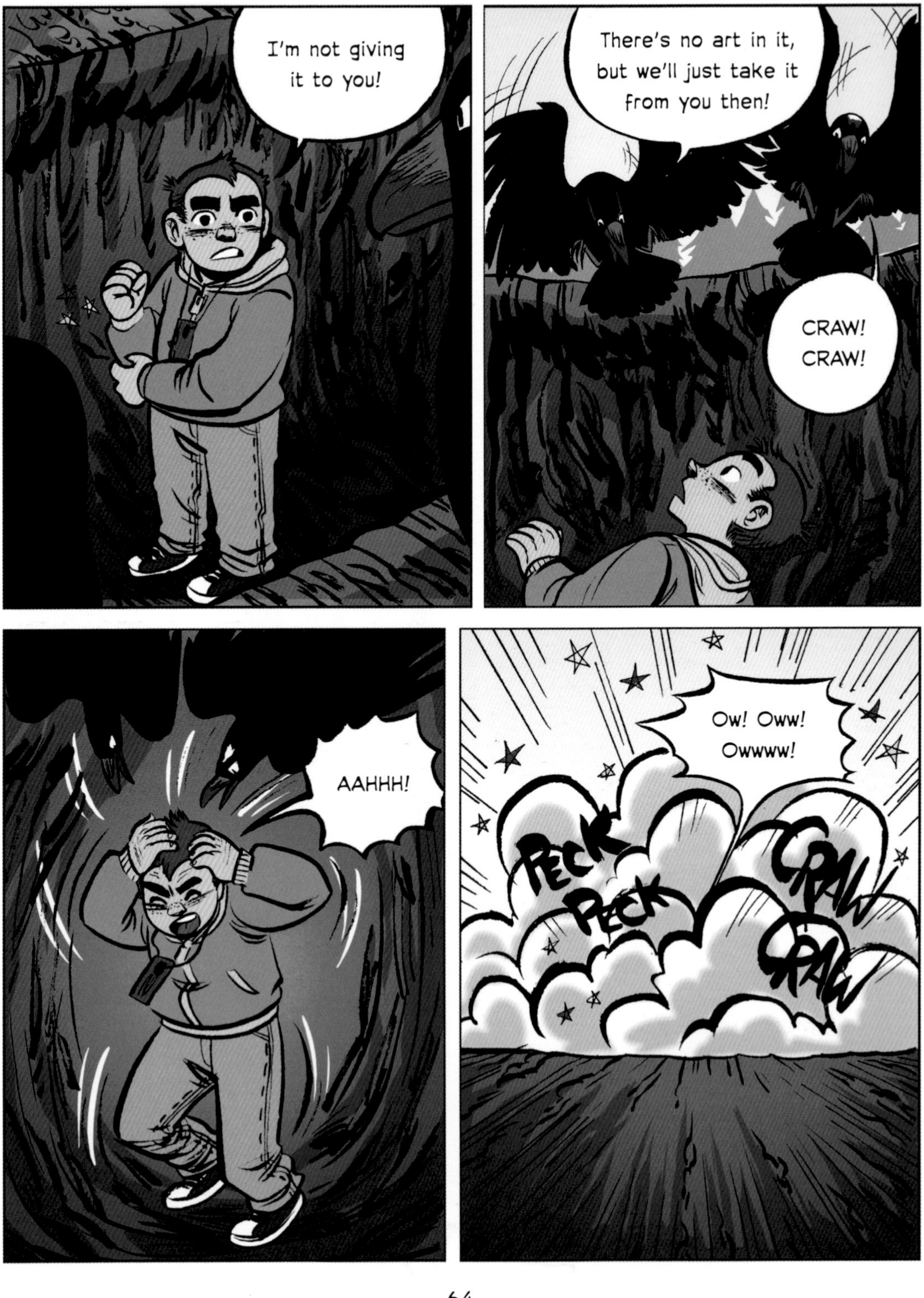
I'm not giving it to you!
There's no art in it, but we'll just take it from you then!
CRAW! CRAW!
AAHHH!
Ow! Oww! Owwww!
PECK PECK
CRAW CRAW

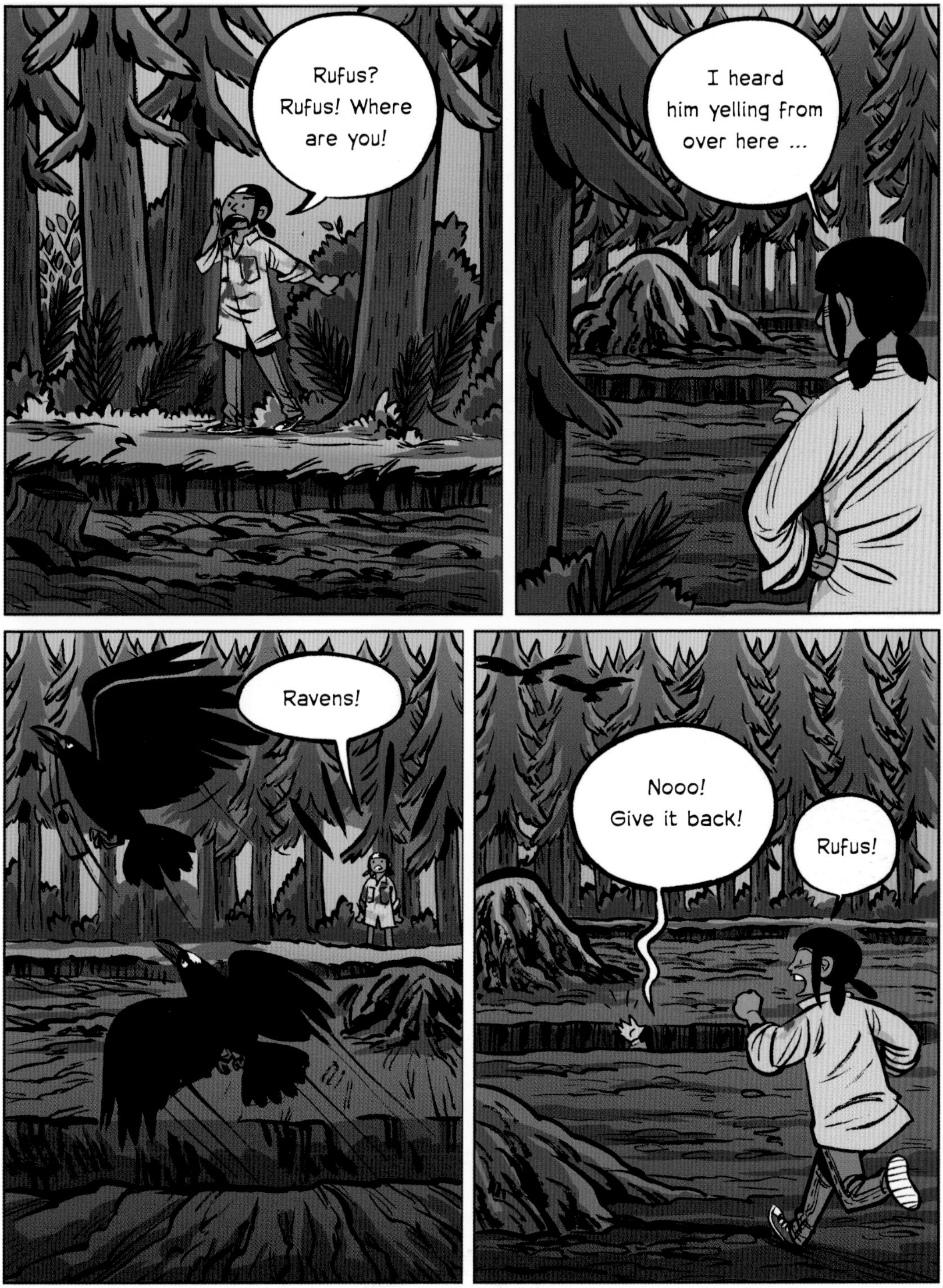
Rufus? Rufus! Where are you!
I heard him yelling from over here ...
Ravens!
Nooo! Give it back!
Rufus!

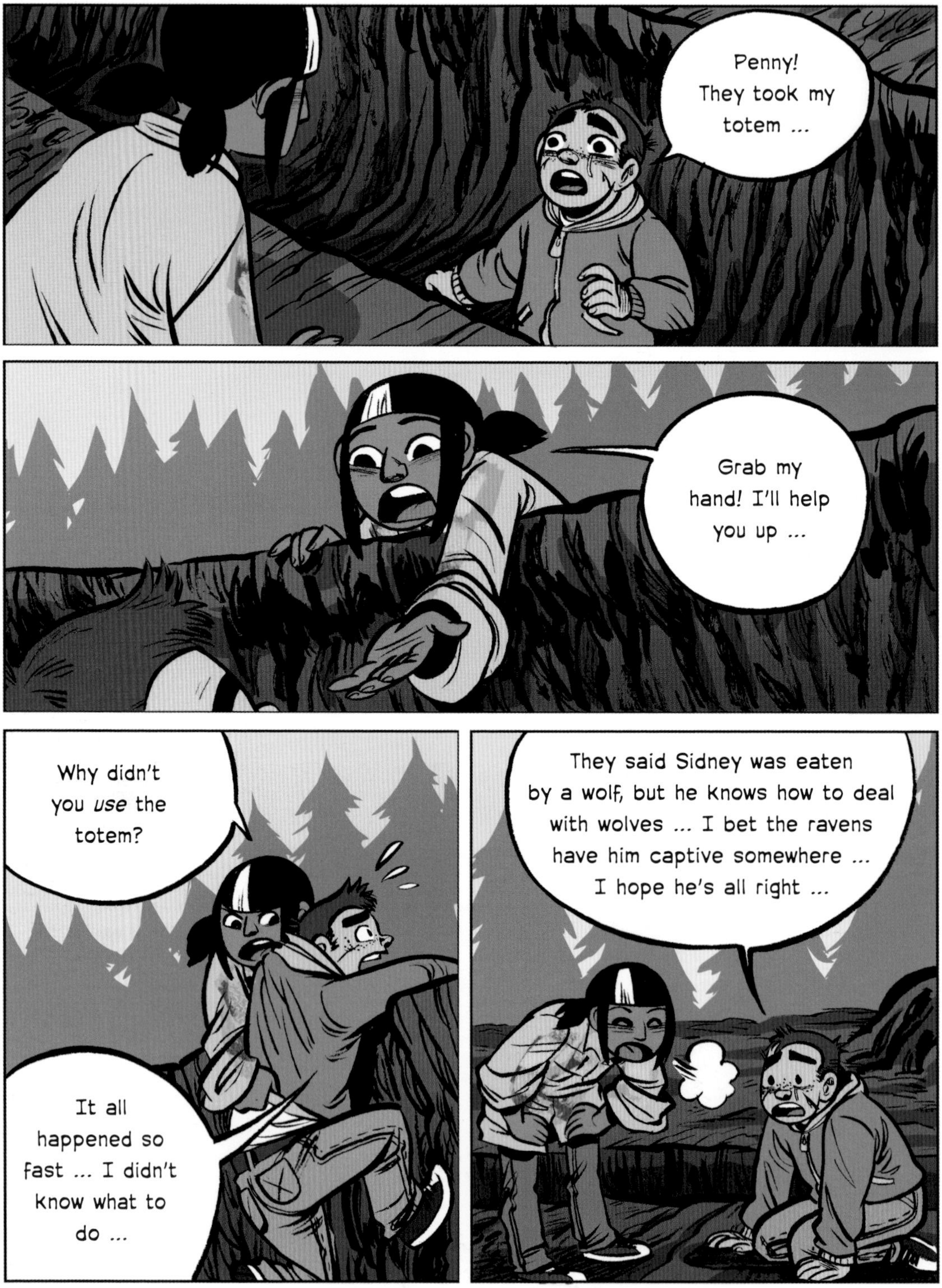

Penny! They took my totem ...
Grab my hand! I'll help you up ...
Why didn't you *use* the totem?
It all happened so fast ... I didn't know what to do ...
They said Sidney was eaten by a wolf, but he knows how to deal with wolves ... I bet the ravens have him captive somewhere ... I hope he's all right ...

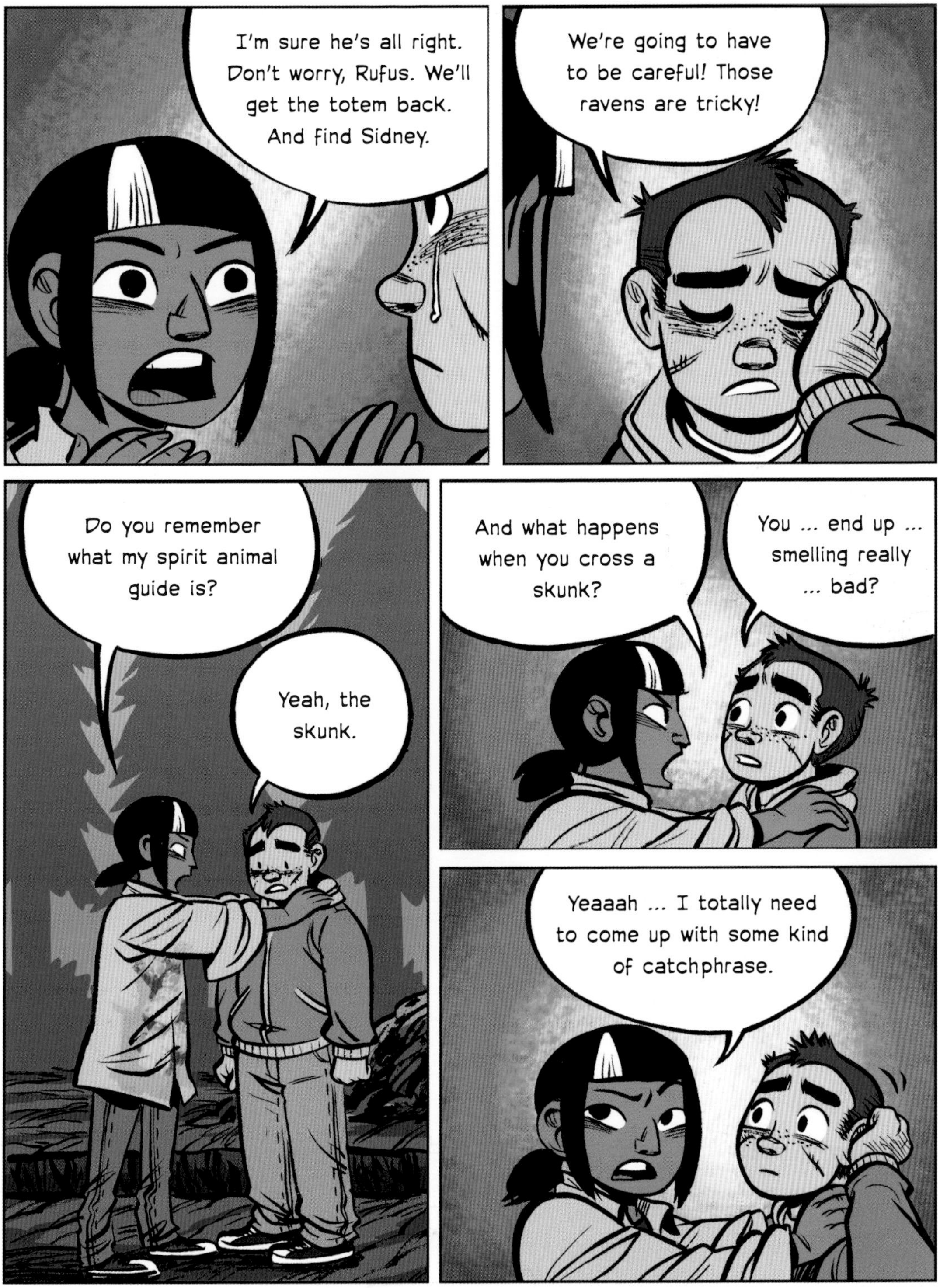
I'm sure he's all right. Don't worry, Rufus. We'll get the totem back. And find Sidney.
We're going to have to be careful! Those ravens are tricky!
Do you remember what my spirit animal guide is?
Yeah, the skunk.
And what happens when you cross a skunk?
You ... end up ... smelling really ... bad?
Yeaaah ... I totally need to come up with some kind of catchphrase.

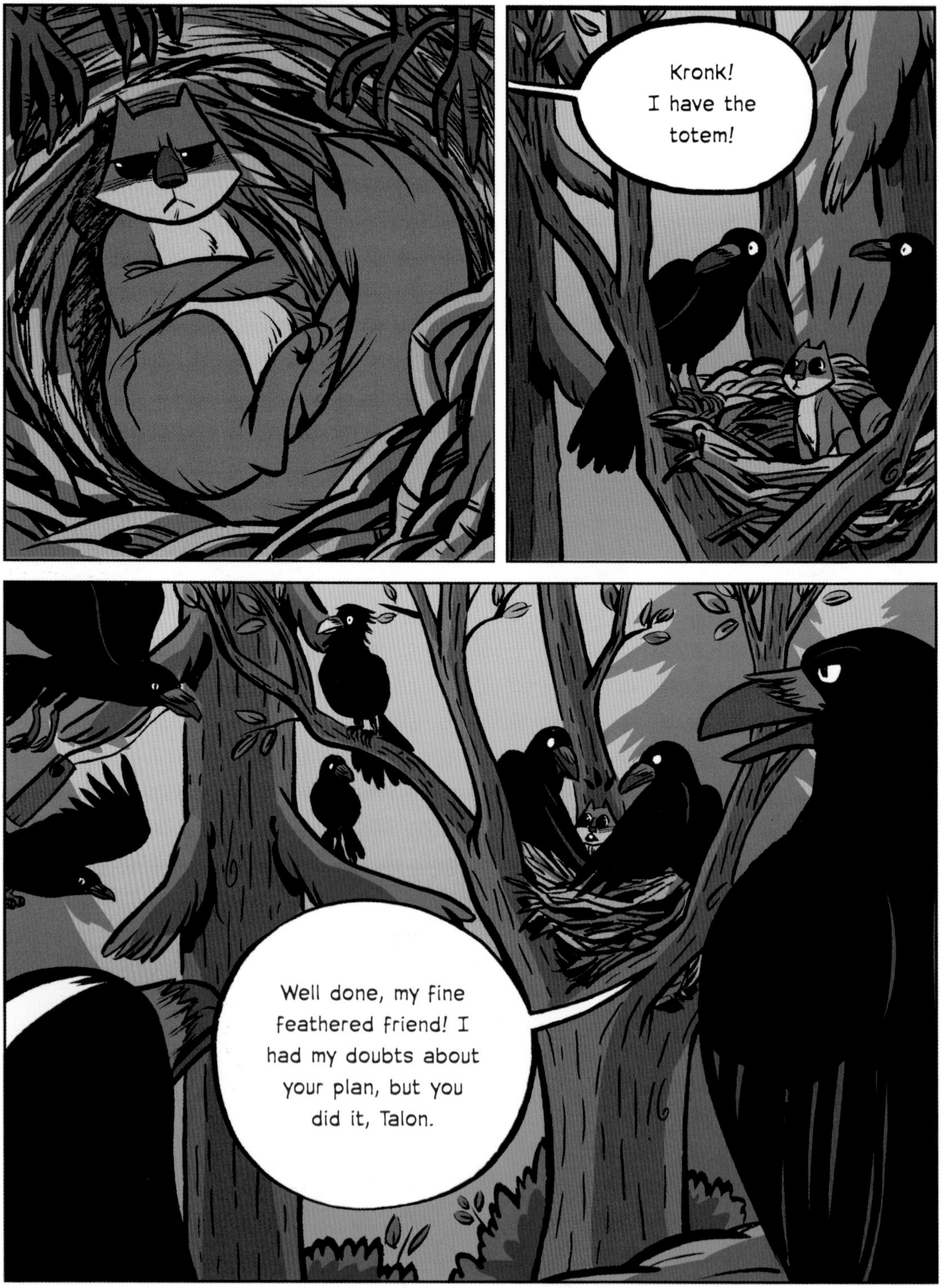
Kronk! I have the totem!
Well done, my fine feathered friend! I had my doubts about your plan, but you did it, Talon.

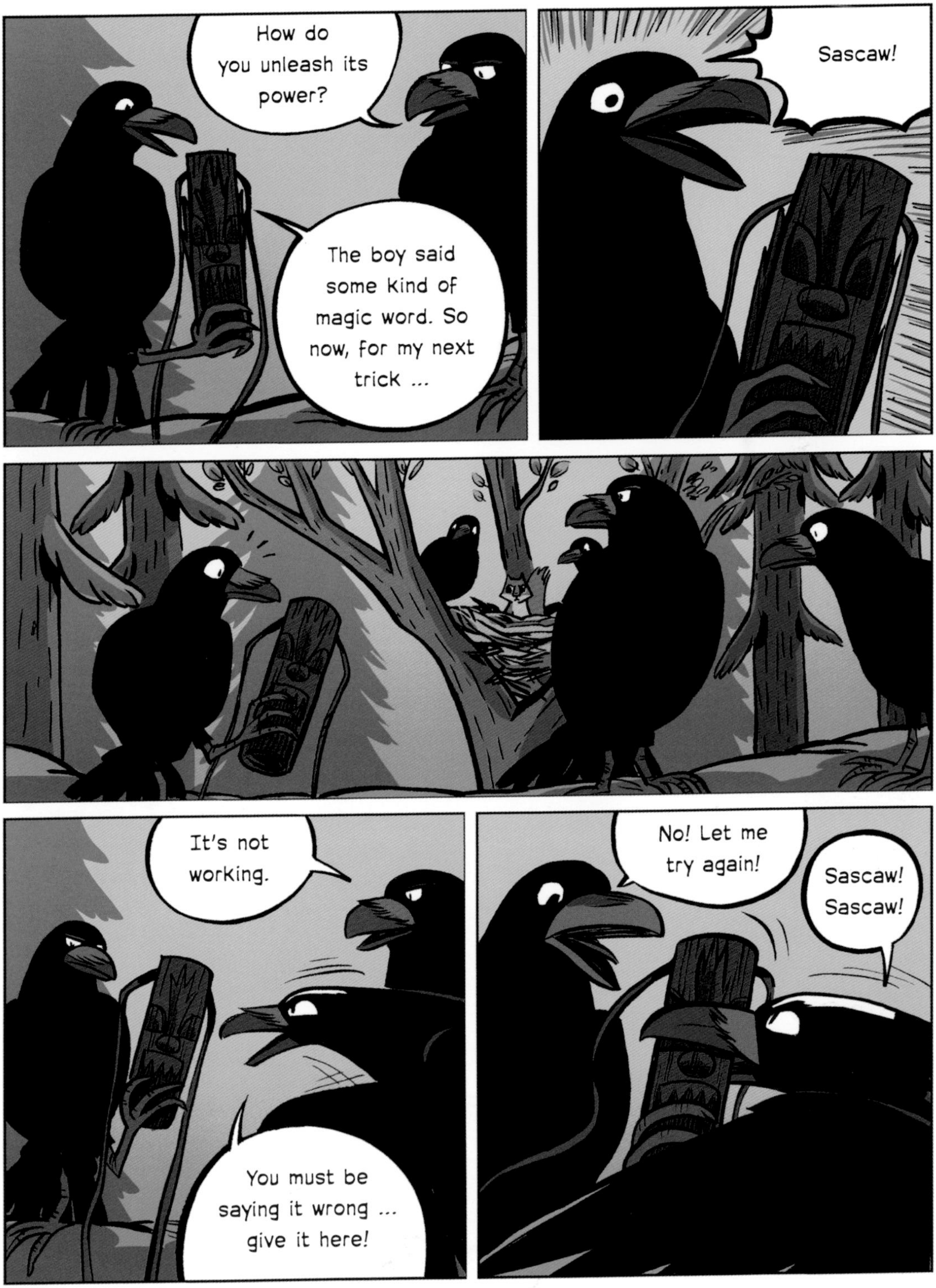
How do you unleash its power?
The boy said some kind of magic word. So now, for my next trick ...
Sascaw!
It's not working.
You must be saying it wrong ... give it here!
No! Let me try again!
Sascaw! Sascaw!

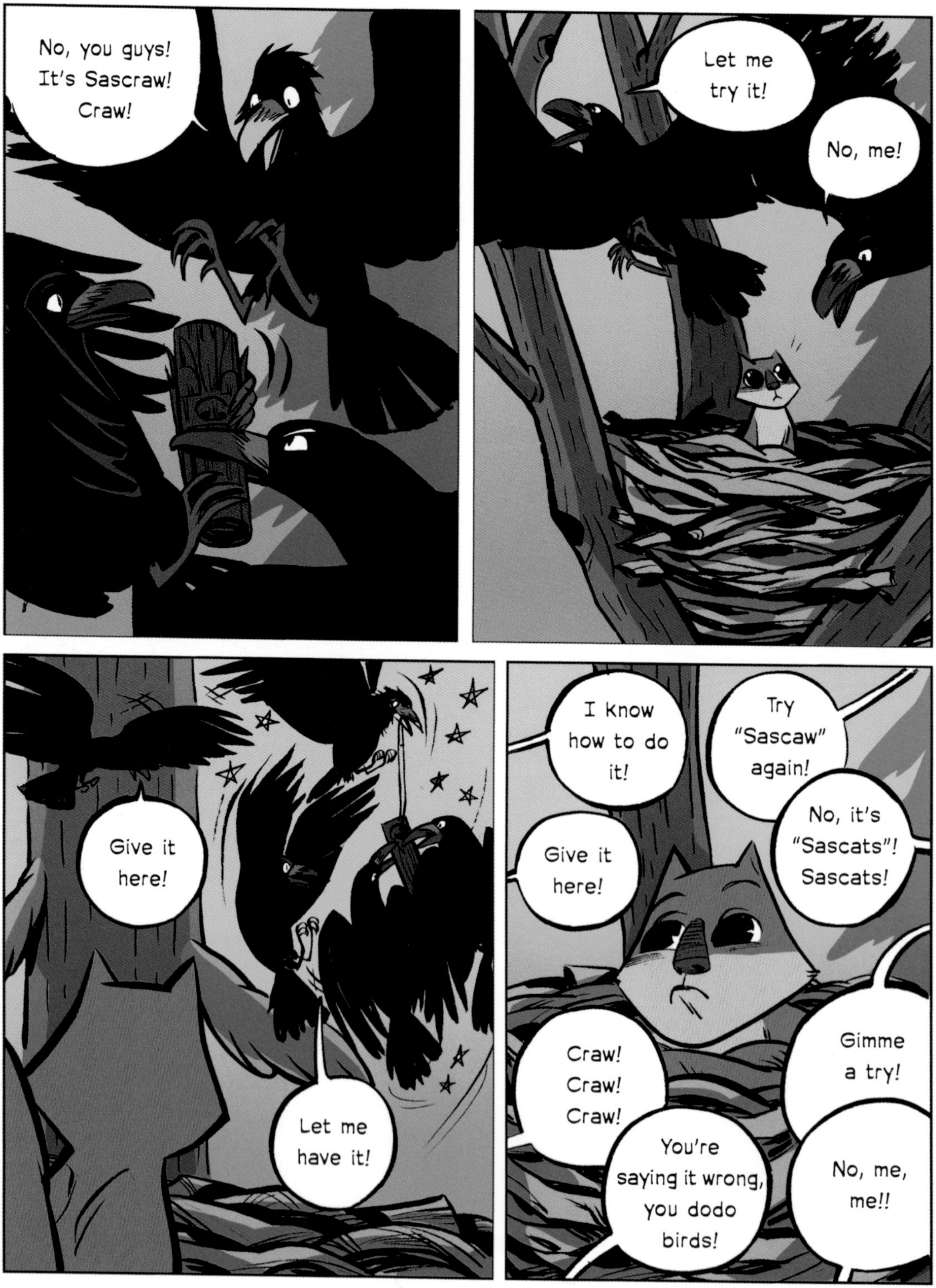

No, you guys! It's Sascraw! Craw!
Let me try it!
No, me!
Give it here!
Let me have it!
I know how to do it!
Try "Sascaw" again!
Give it here!
No, it's "Sascats"! Sascats!
Craw! Craw! Craw!
Gimme a try!
You're saying it wrong, you dodo birds!
No, me, me!!

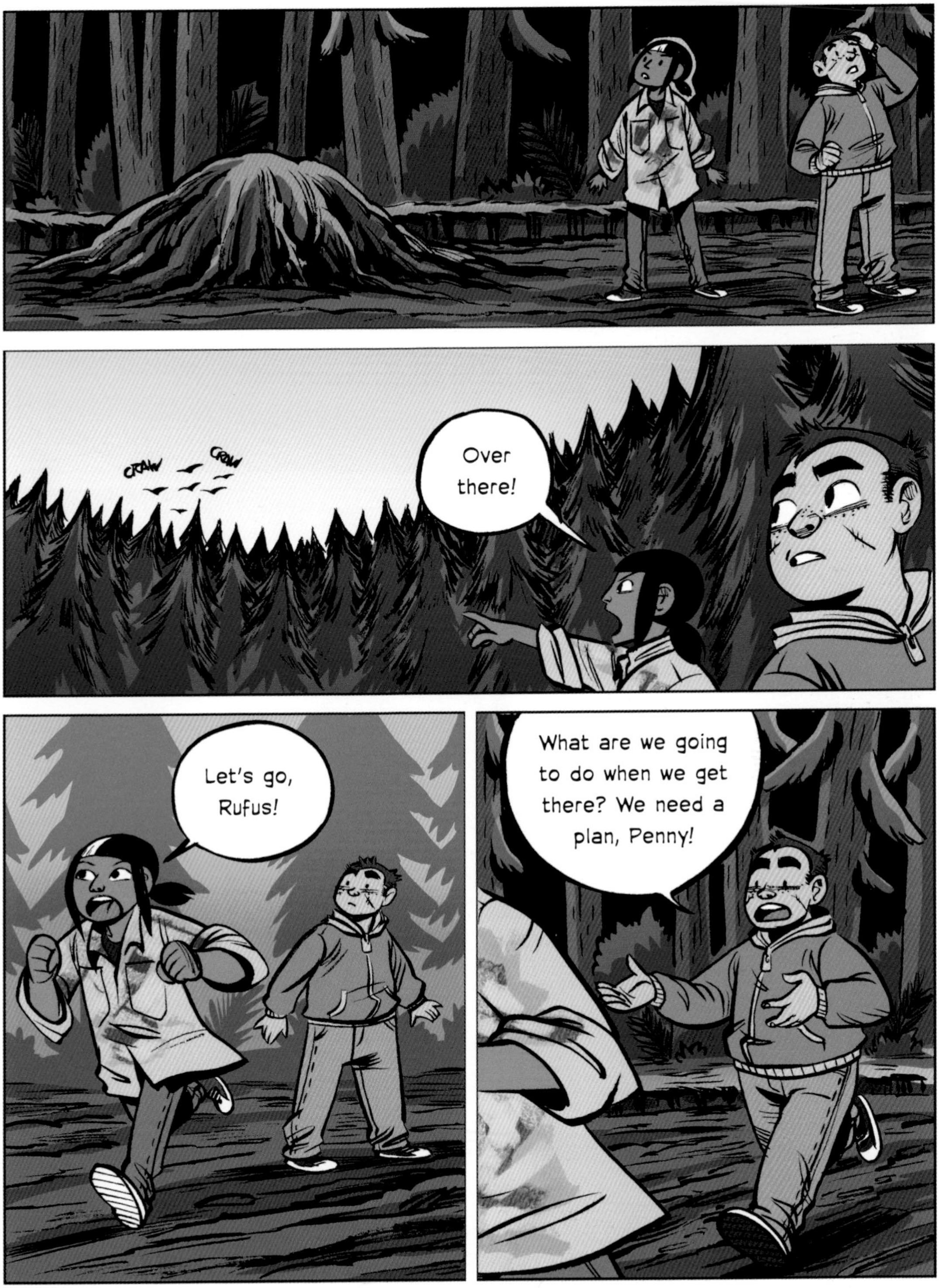
CRAW
CRAW
Over there!
Let's go, Rufus!
What are we going to do when we get there? We need a plan, Penny!

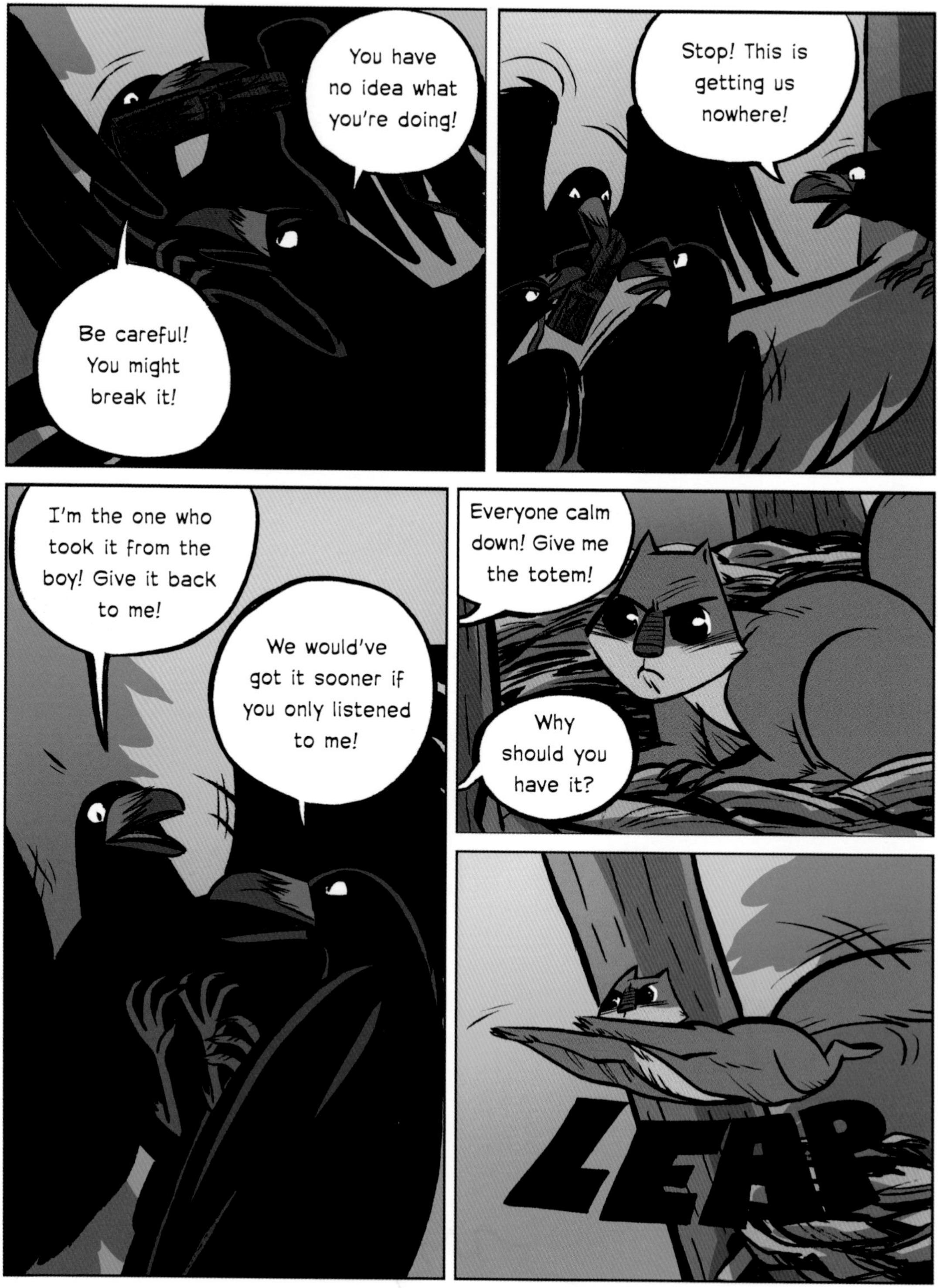
You have no idea what you're doing!
Be careful! You might break it!
Stop! This is getting us nowhere!
I'm the one who took it from the boy! Give it back to me!
We would've got it sooner if you only listened to me!
Everyone calm down! Give me the totem!
Why should you have it?
LEAP

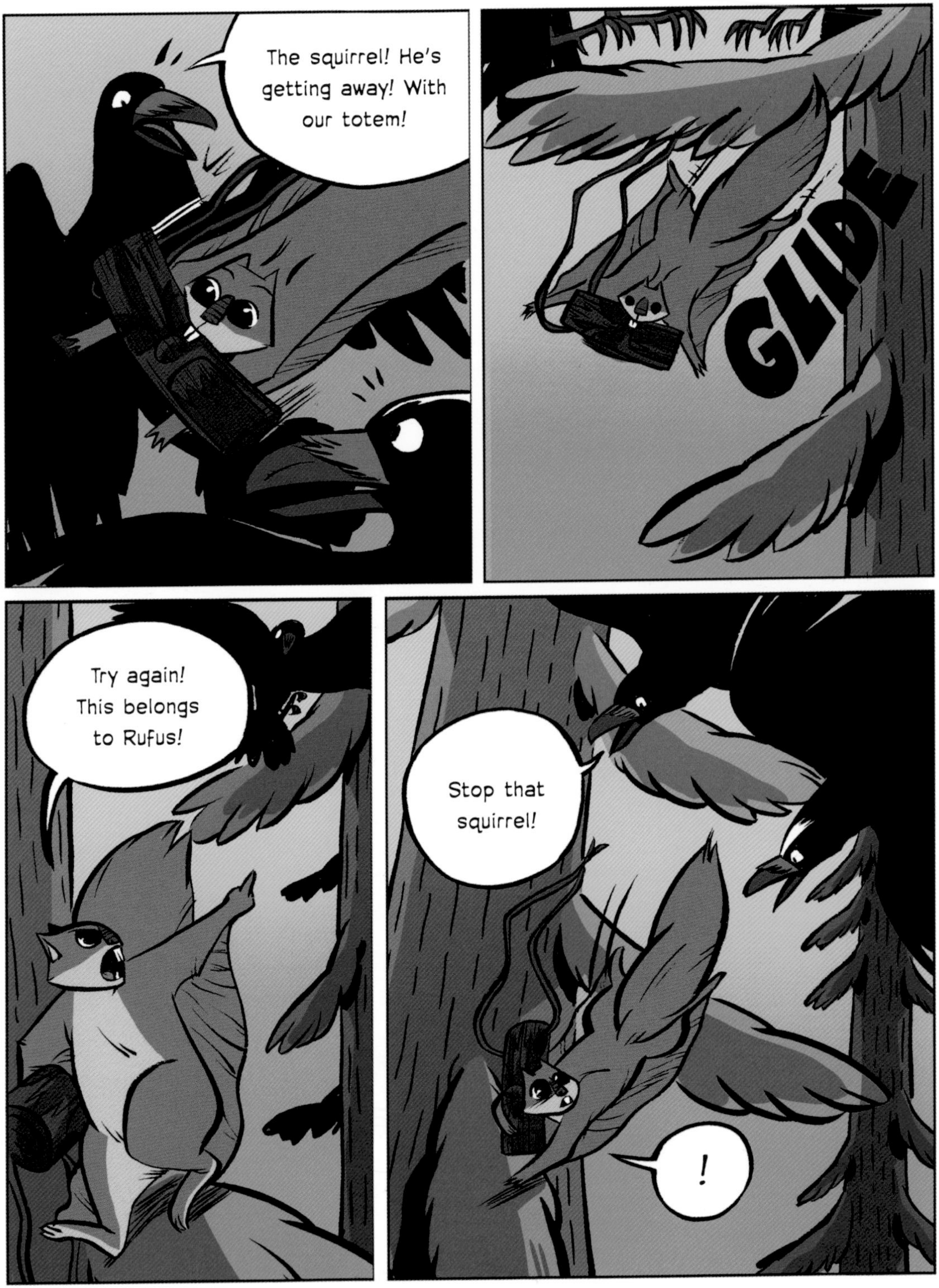
The squirrel! He's getting away! With our totem!
GLIDE
Try again! This belongs to Rufus!
Stop that squirrel!
!

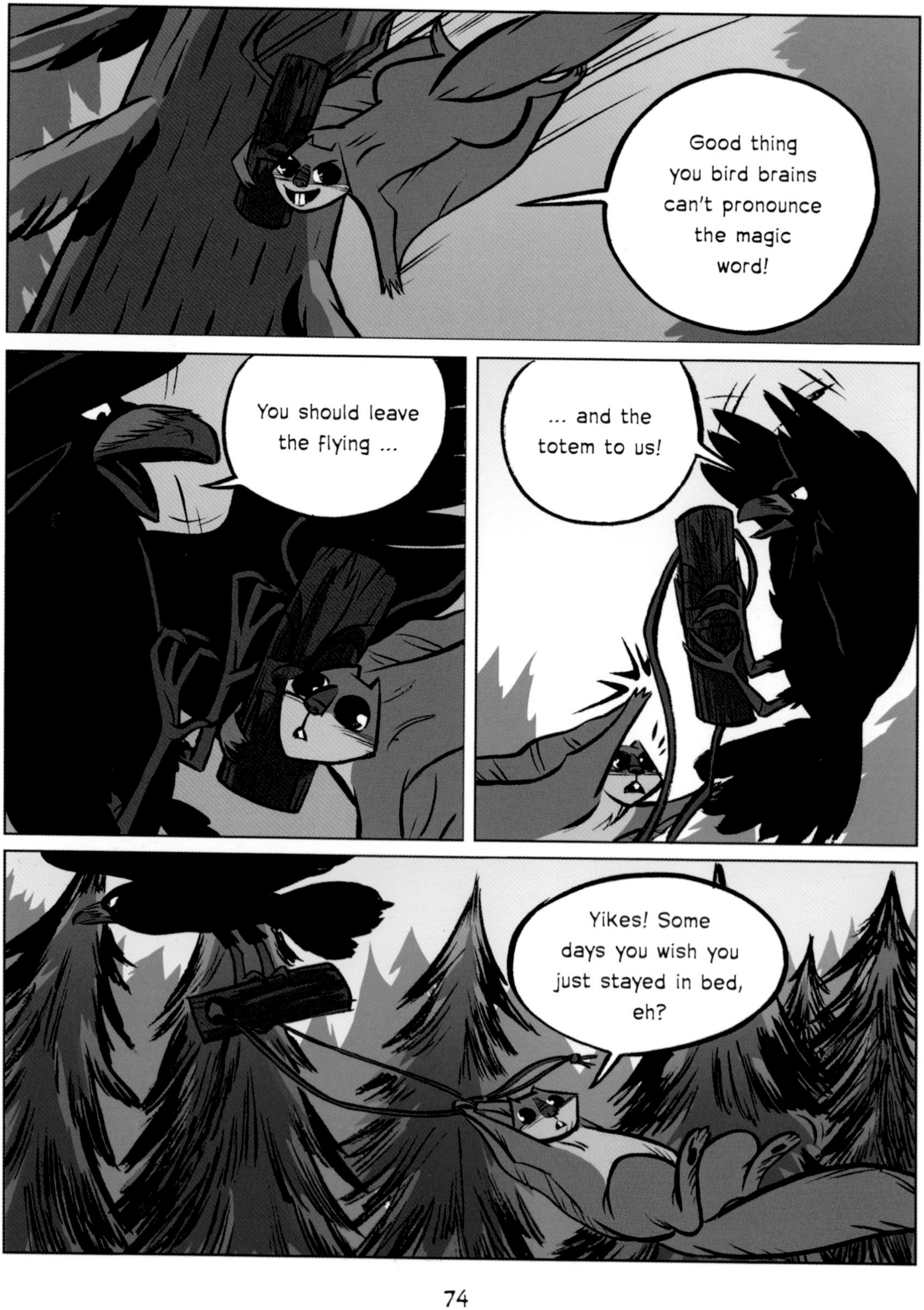
Good thing you bird brains can't pronounce the magic word!
You should leave the flying ...
... and the totem to us!
Yikes! Some days you wish you just stayed in bed, eh?

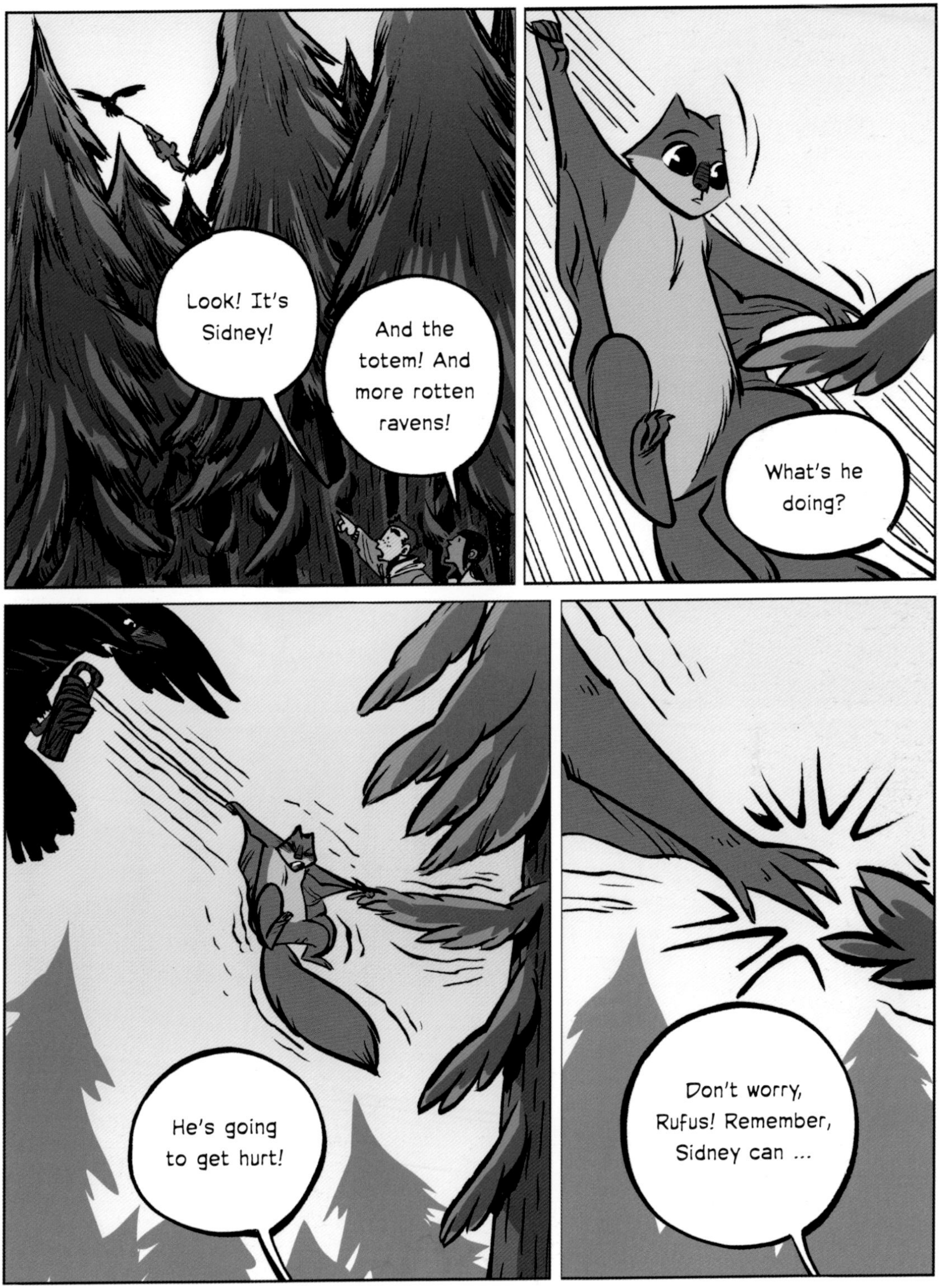
Look! It's Sidney!
And the totem! And more rotten ravens!
What's he doing?
He's going to get hurt!
Don't worry, Rufus! Remember, Sidney can ...

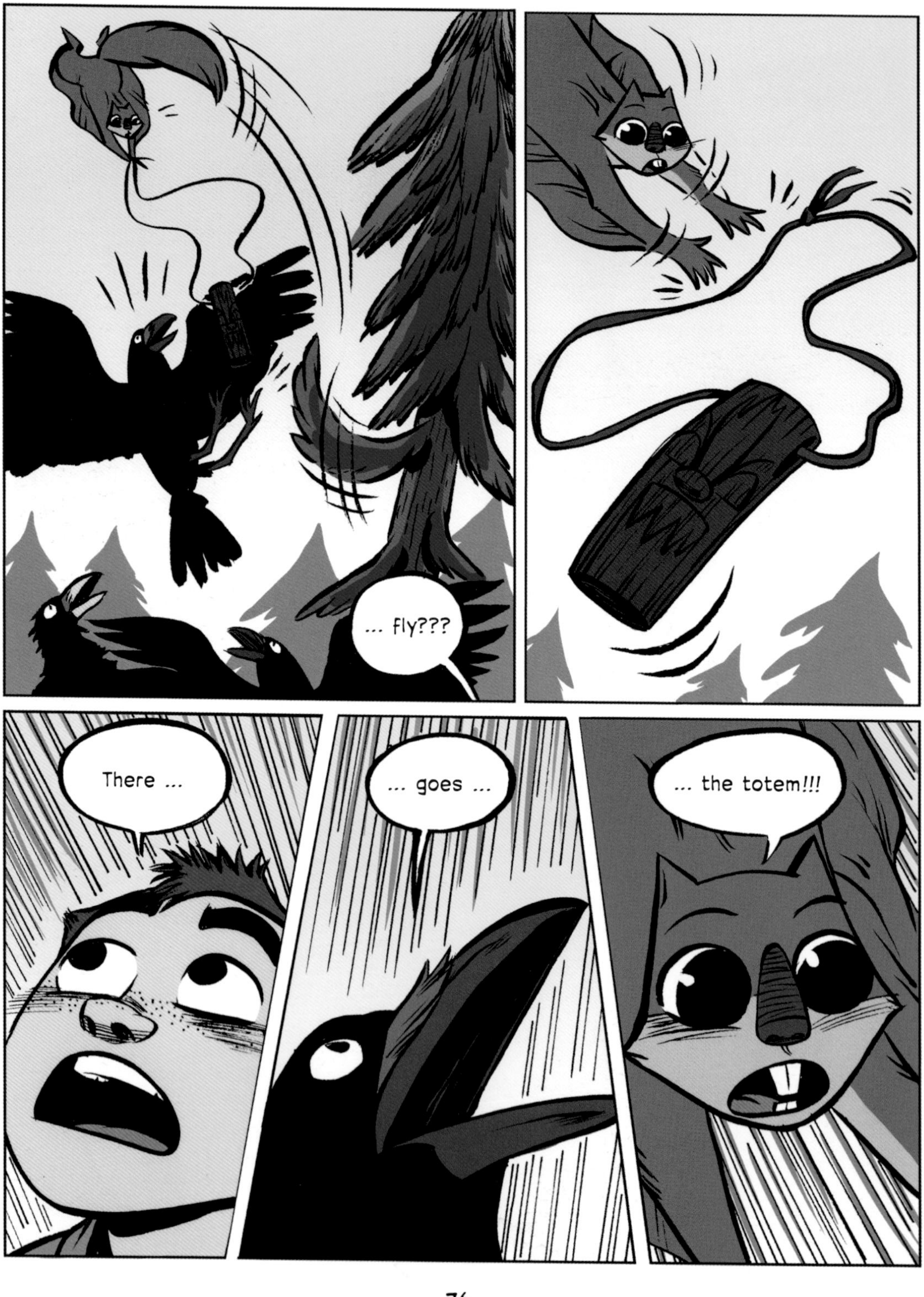
... fly???
There ...
... goes ...
... the totem!!!

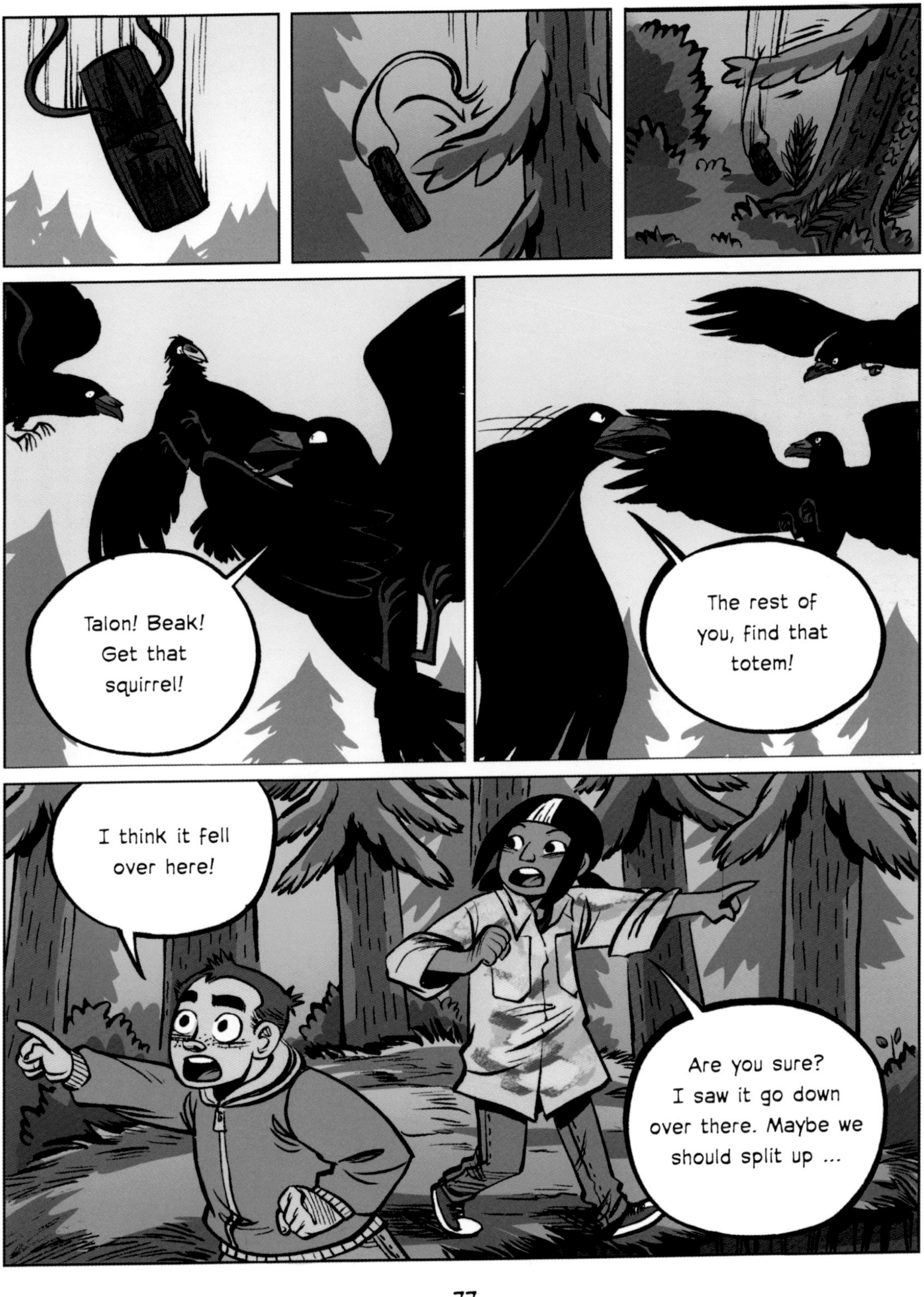
Talon! Beak!
Get that
squirrel!
The rest of
you, find that
totem!
I think it fell
over here!
Are you sure?
I saw it go down
over there. Maybe we
should split up ...

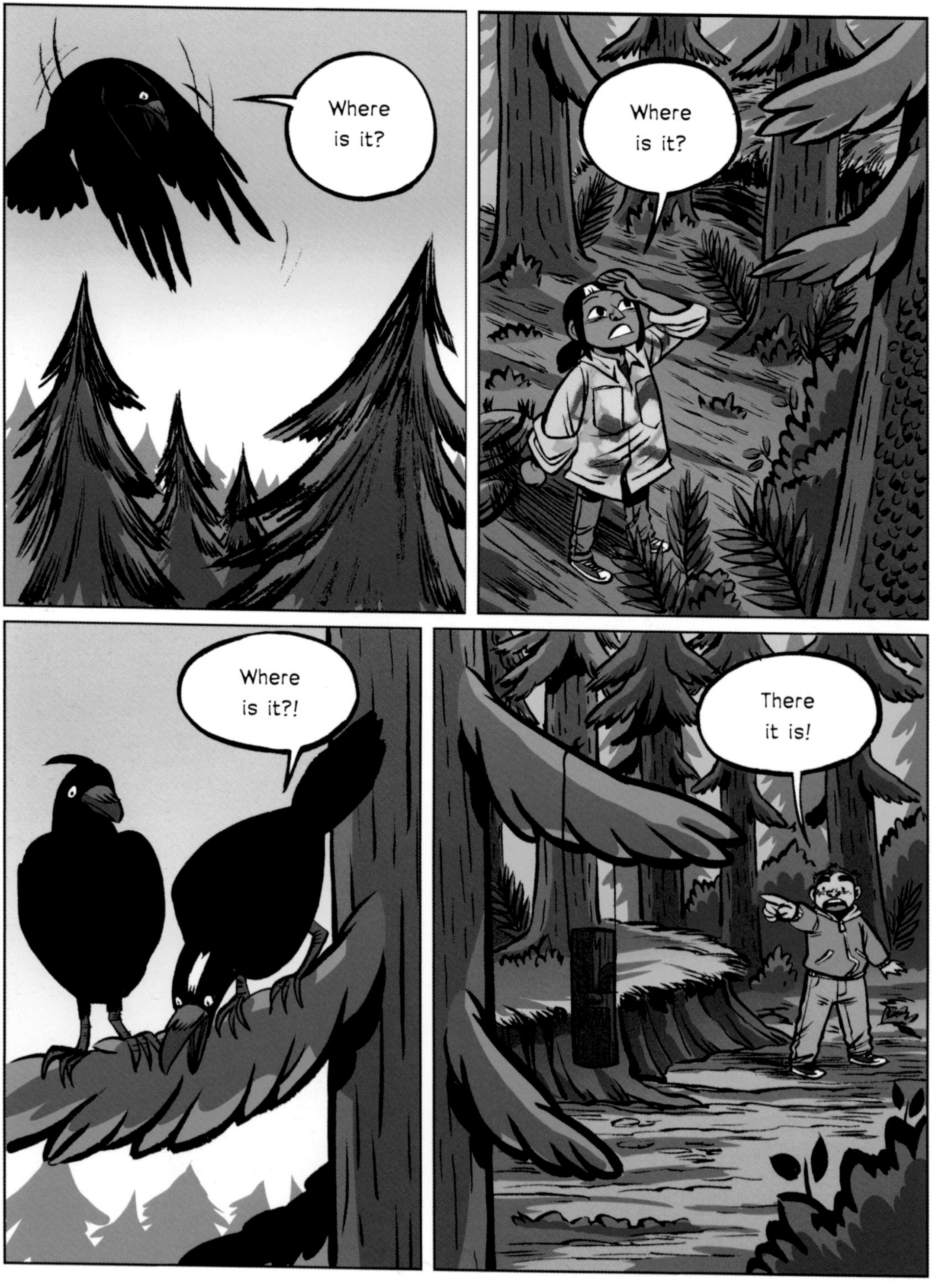
Where is it?
Where is it?
Where is it?!
There it is!

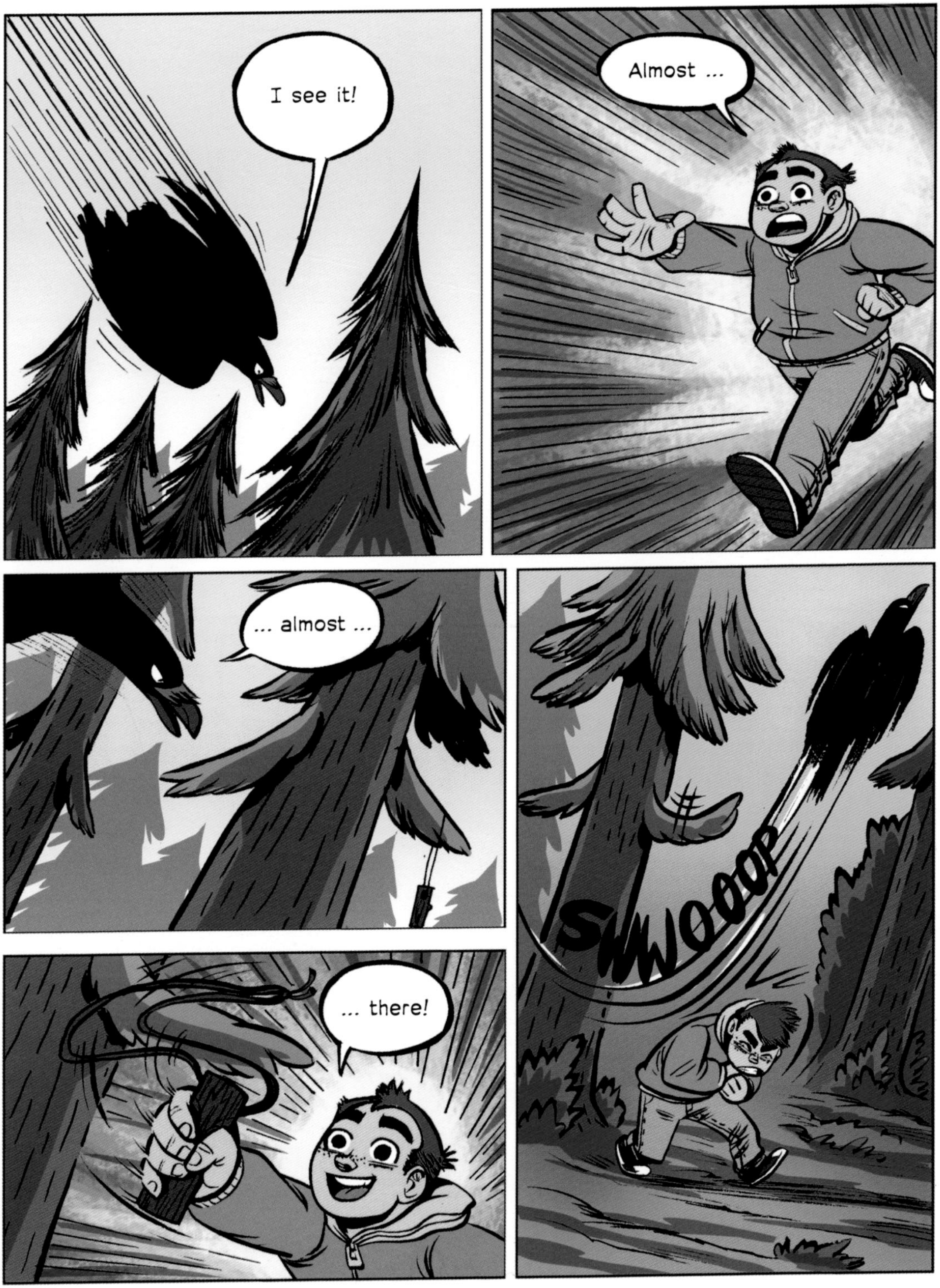
I see it!
Almost ...
... almost ...
... there!
SWOOOP

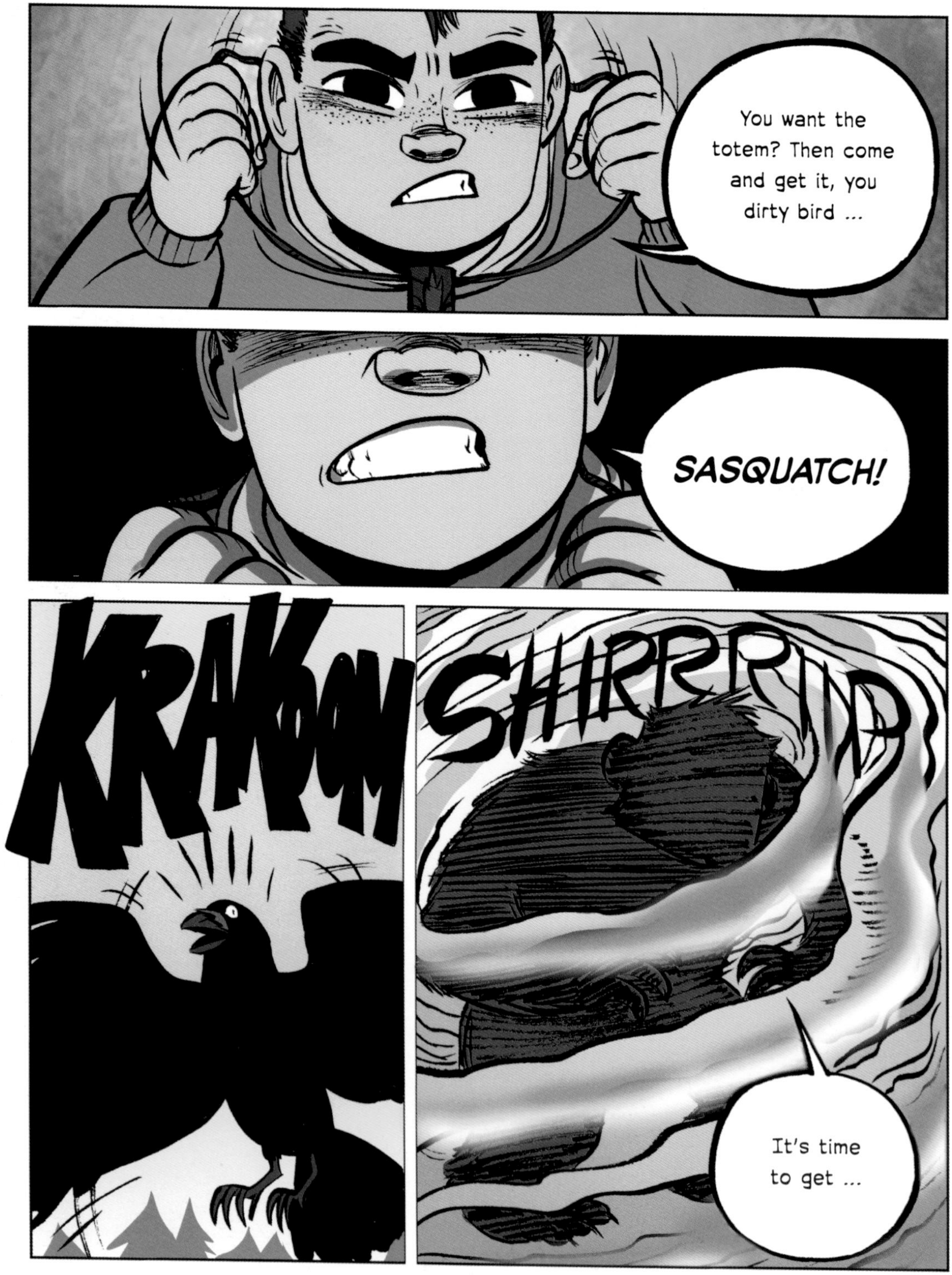
You want the totem? Then come and get it, you dirty bird ...
SASQUATCH!
KRAKOOM
SHIRRRIIP
It's time to get ...

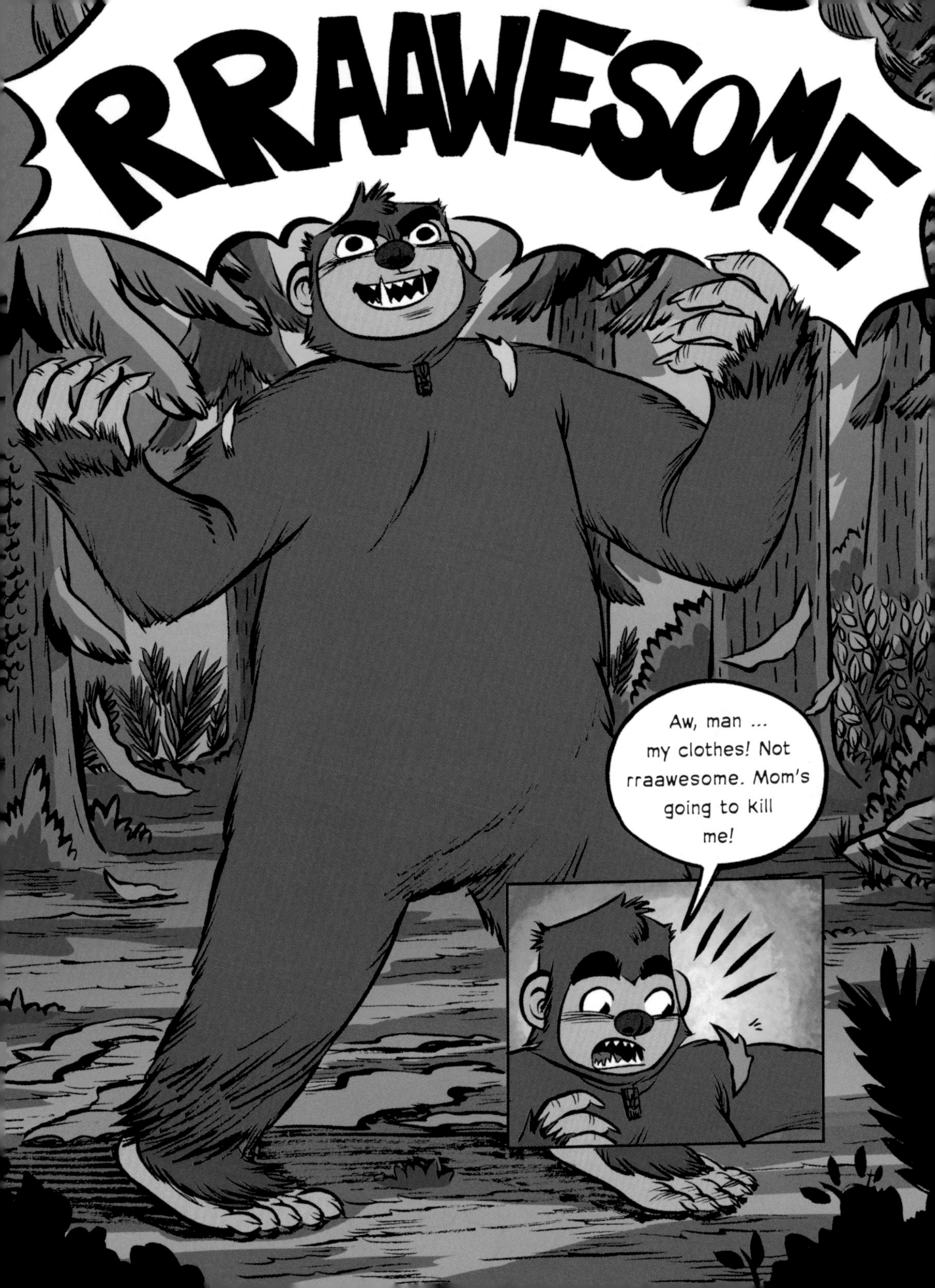
RRAAWESOME
Aw, man ... my clothes! Not rraawesome. Mom's going to kill me!

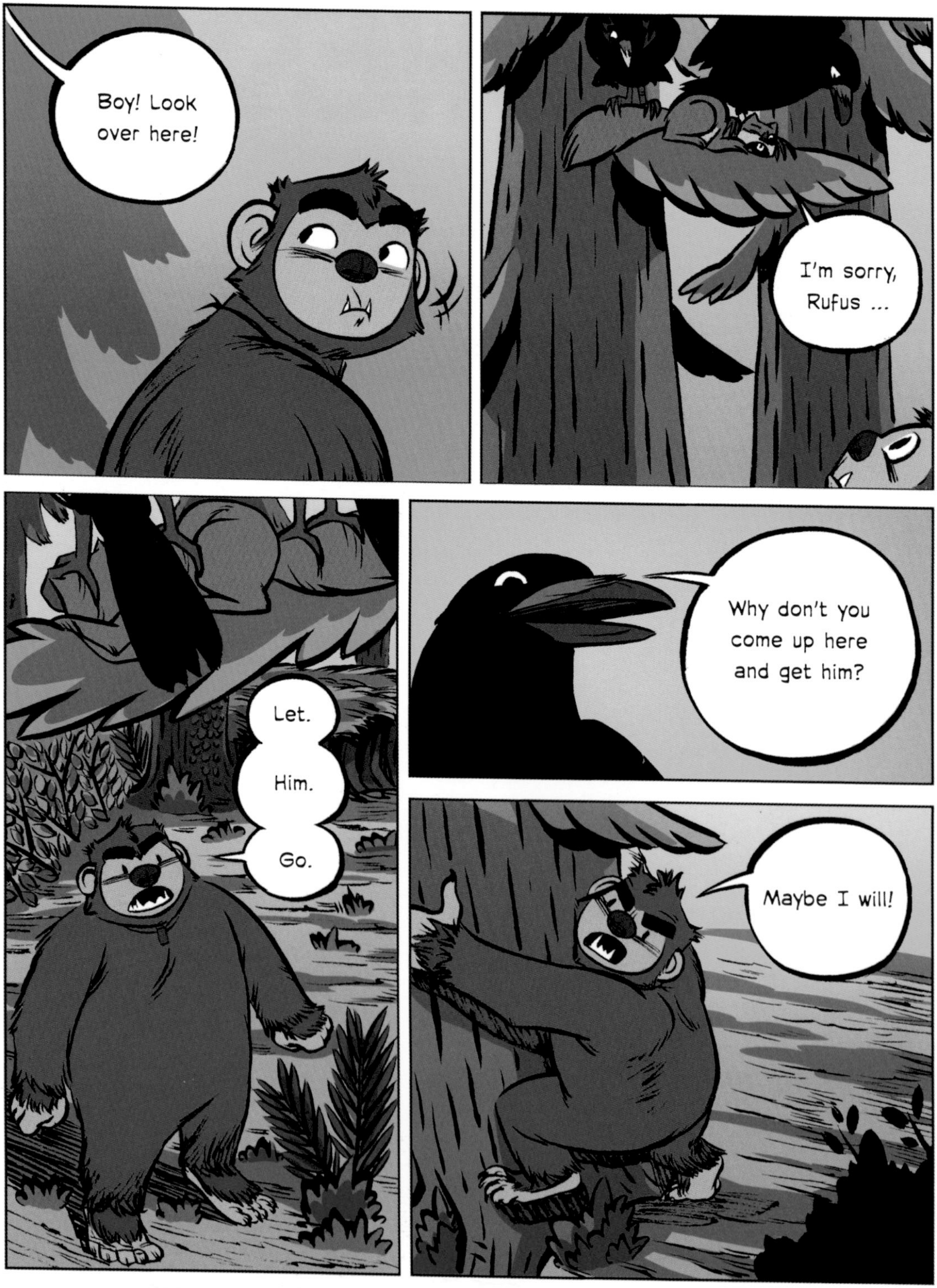
Boy! Look over here!
I'm sorry, Rufus ...
Let.
Him.
Go.
Why don't you come up here and get him?
Maybe I will!

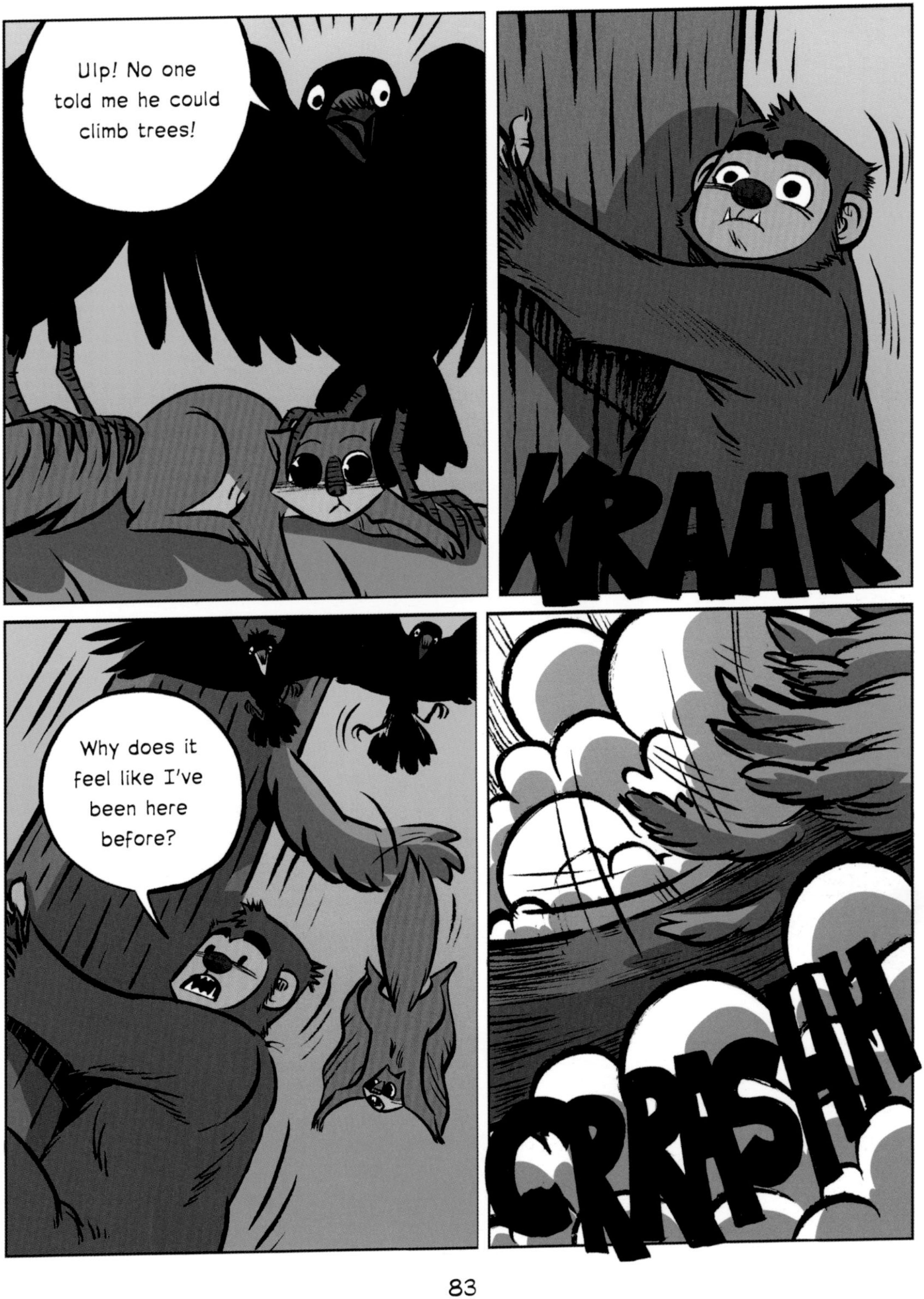
Ulp! No one told me he could climb trees!
KRAAK
Why does it feel like I've been here before?
CRRASHH

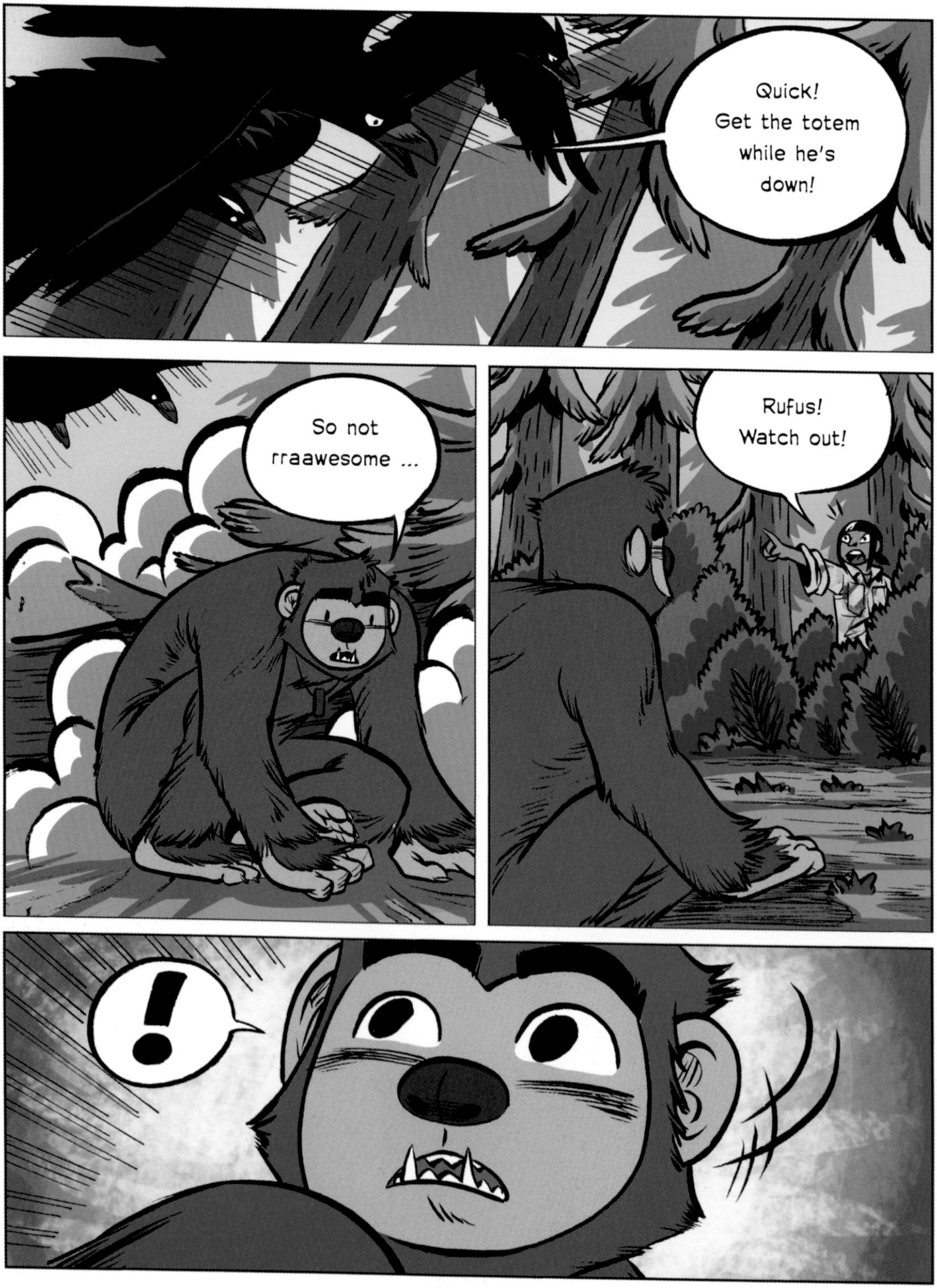
Quick! Get the totem while he's down!
So not rraawesome ...
Rufus! Watch out!
!

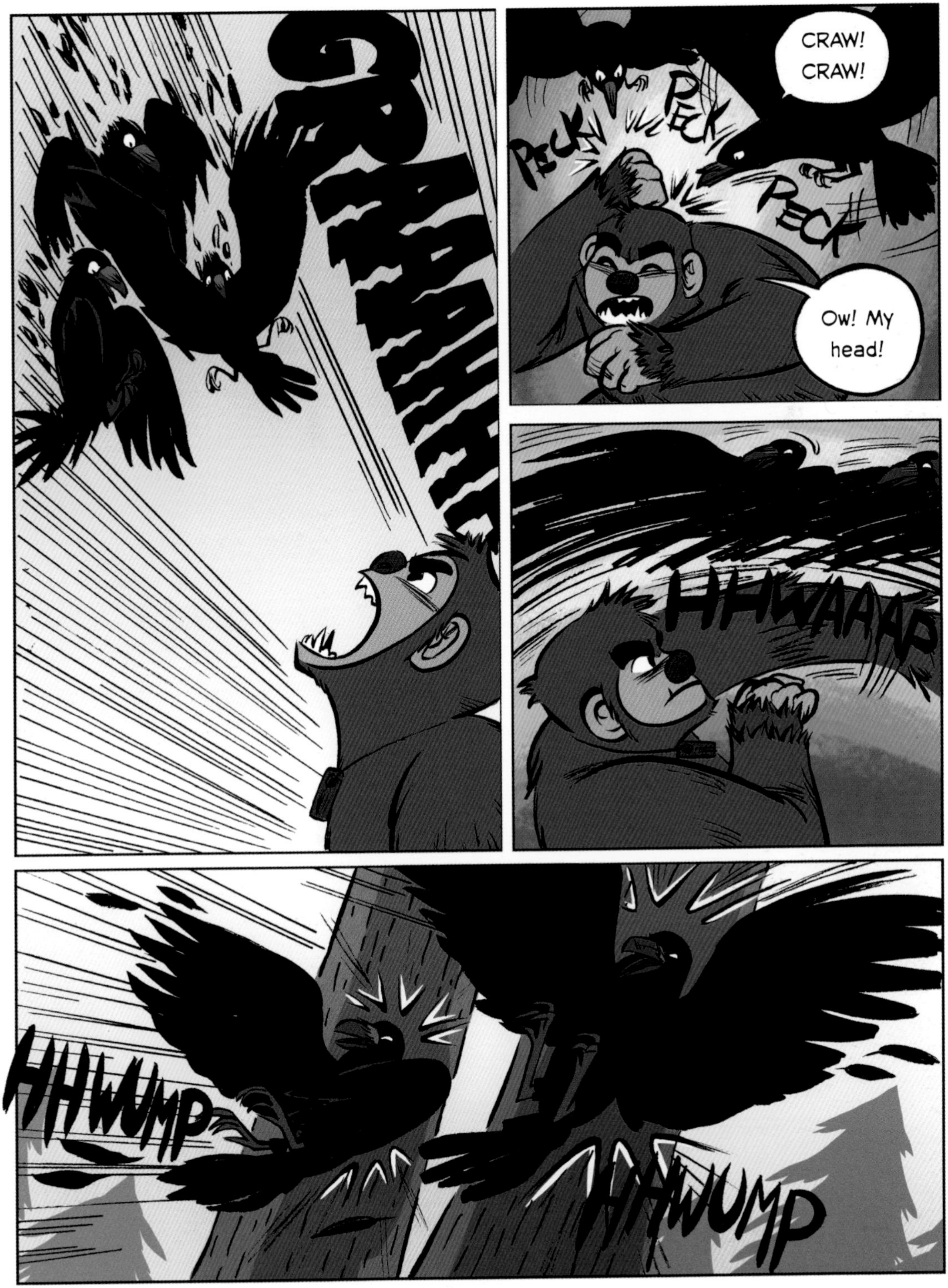
GRAAHHHH
CRAW! CRAW!
PECK PECK PECK
Ow! My head!
HHWAAAP
HHWUMP
HHWUMP

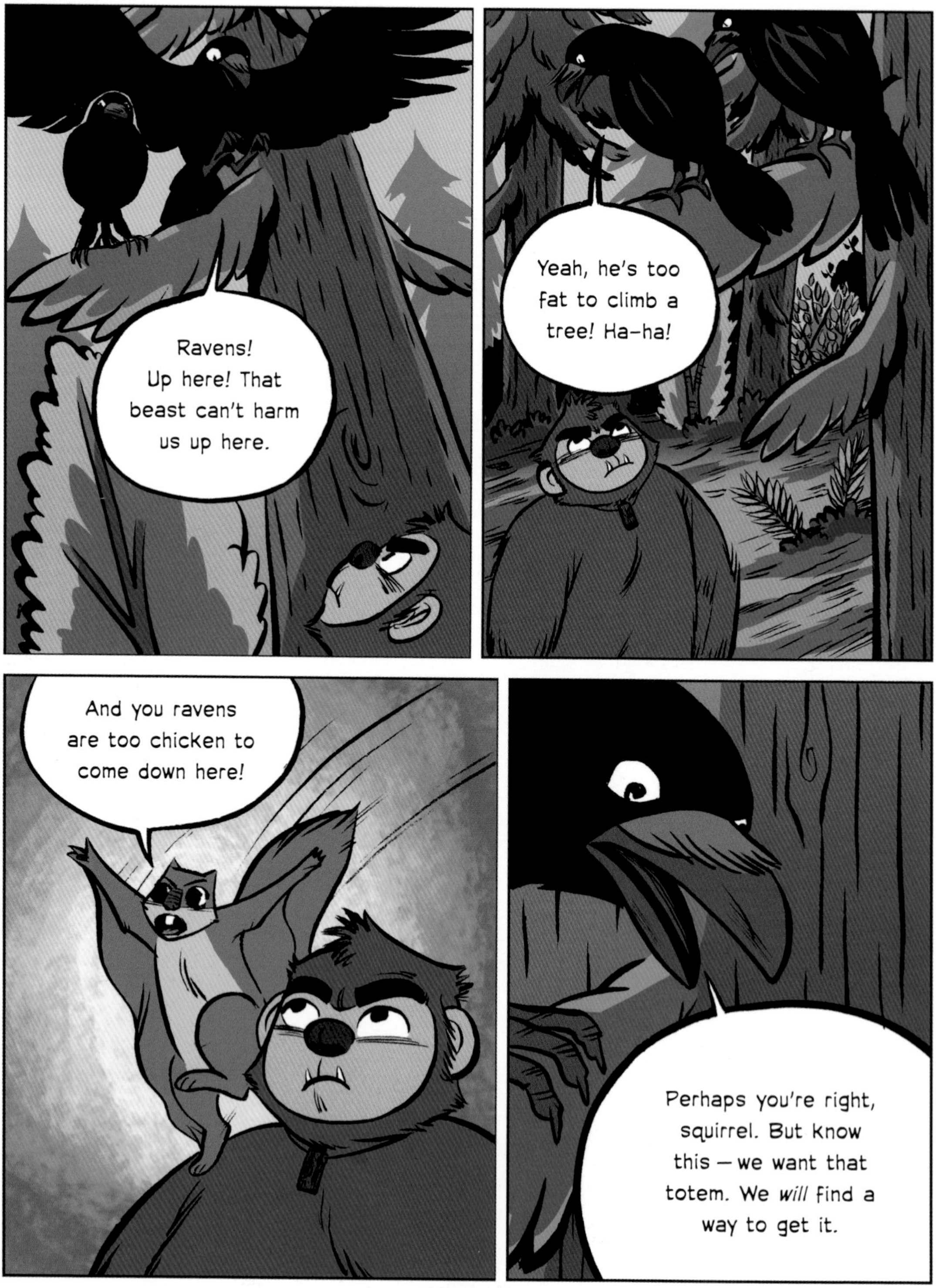
Ravens! Up here! That beast can't harm us up here.
Yeah, he's too fat to climb a tree! Ha-ha!
And you ravens are too chicken to come down here!
Perhaps you're right, squirrel. But know this — we want that totem. We *will* find a way to get it.

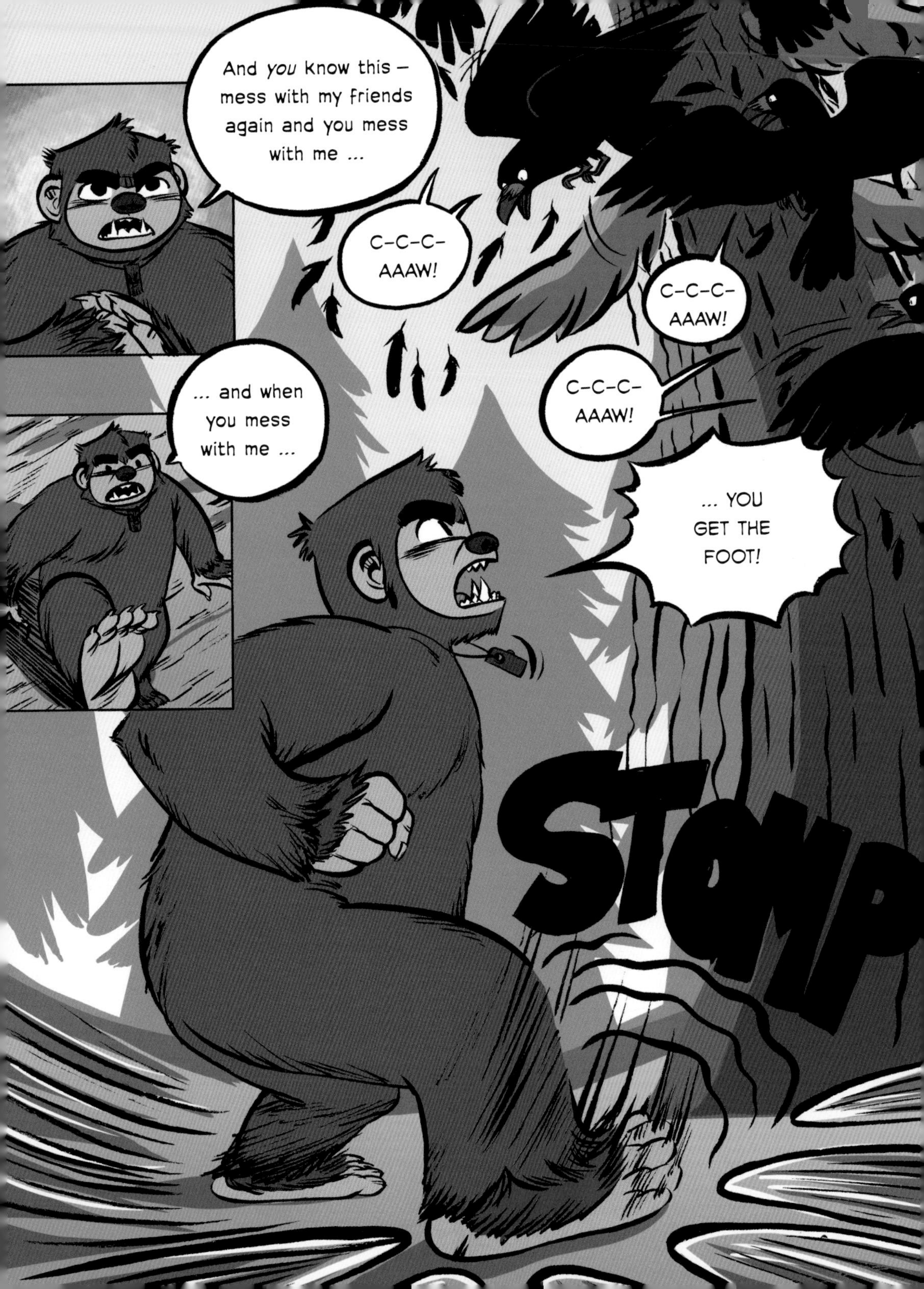
And *you* know this – mess with my friends again and you mess with me ...
C-C-C-AAAW!
C-C-C-AAAW!
... and when you mess with me ...
C-C-C-AAAW!
... YOU GET THE FOOT!
STOMP

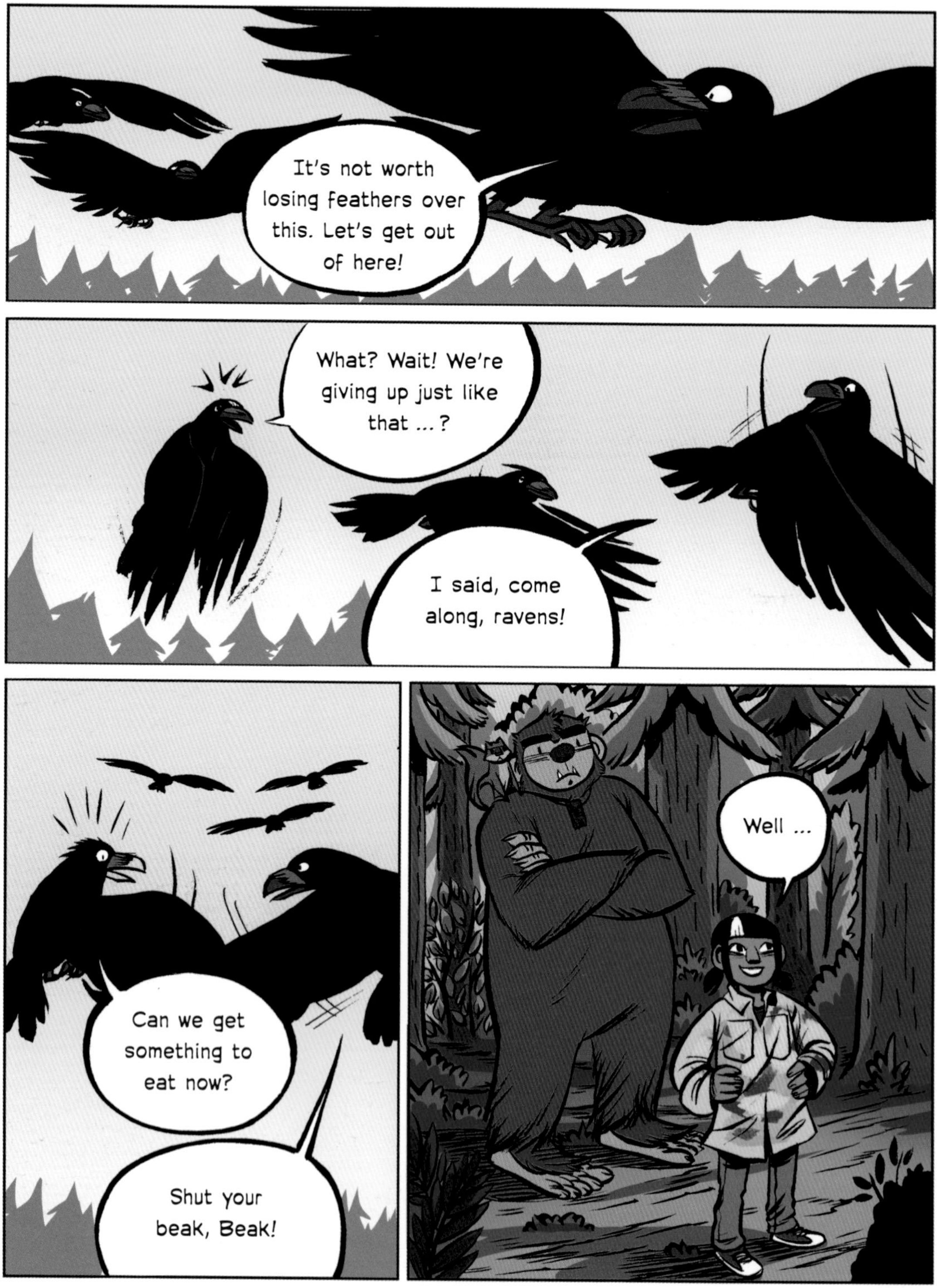
It's not worth losing feathers over this. Let's get out of here!
What? Wait! We're giving up just like that ... ?
I said, come along, ravens!
Can we get something to eat now?
Shut your beak, Beak!
Well ...

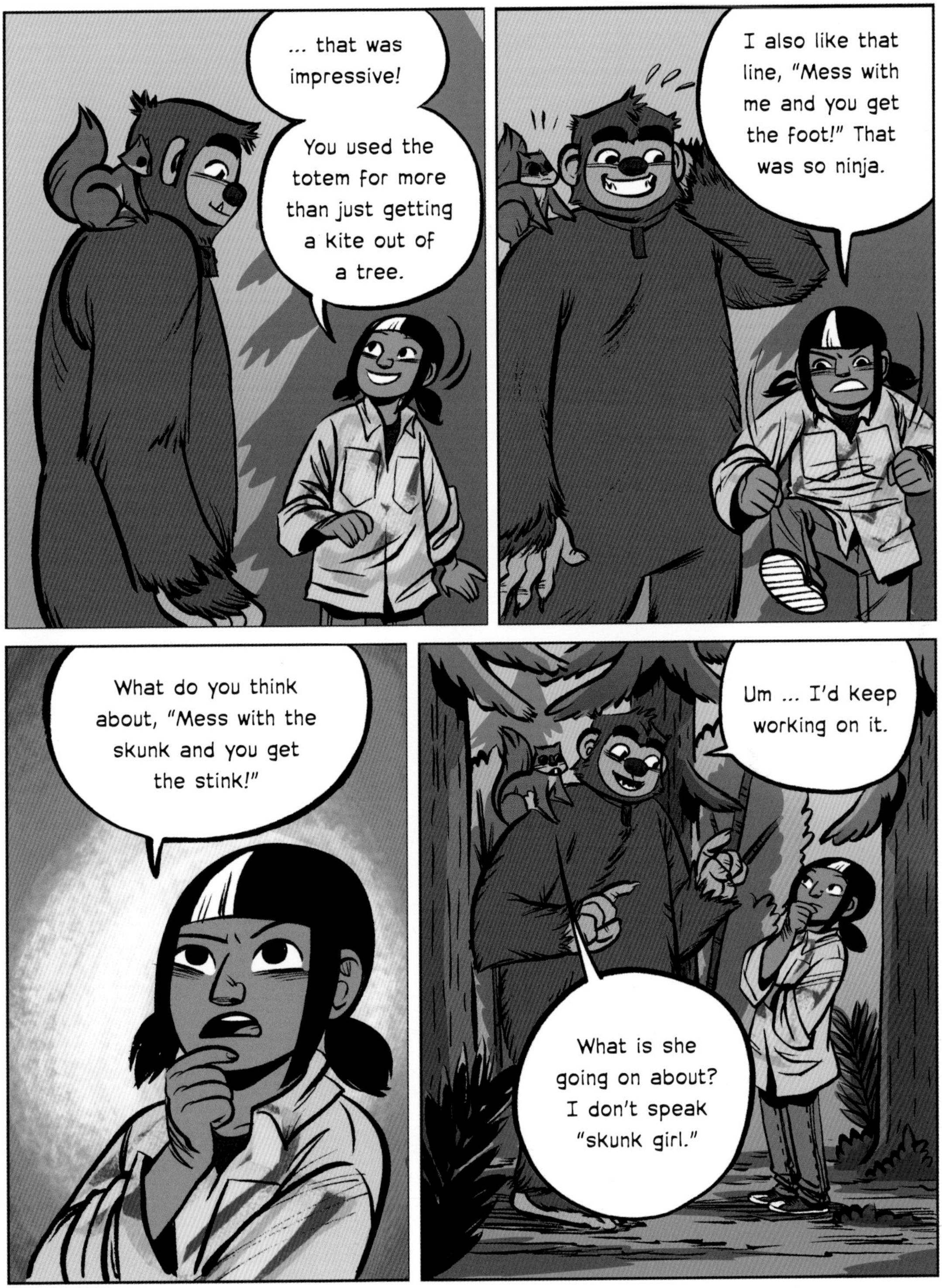
... that was impressive!
You used the totem for more than just getting a kite out of a tree.
I also like that line, "Mess with me and you get the foot!" That was so ninja.
What do you think about, "Mess with the skunk and you get the stink!"
Um ... I'd keep working on it.
What is she going on about? I don't speak "skunk girl."

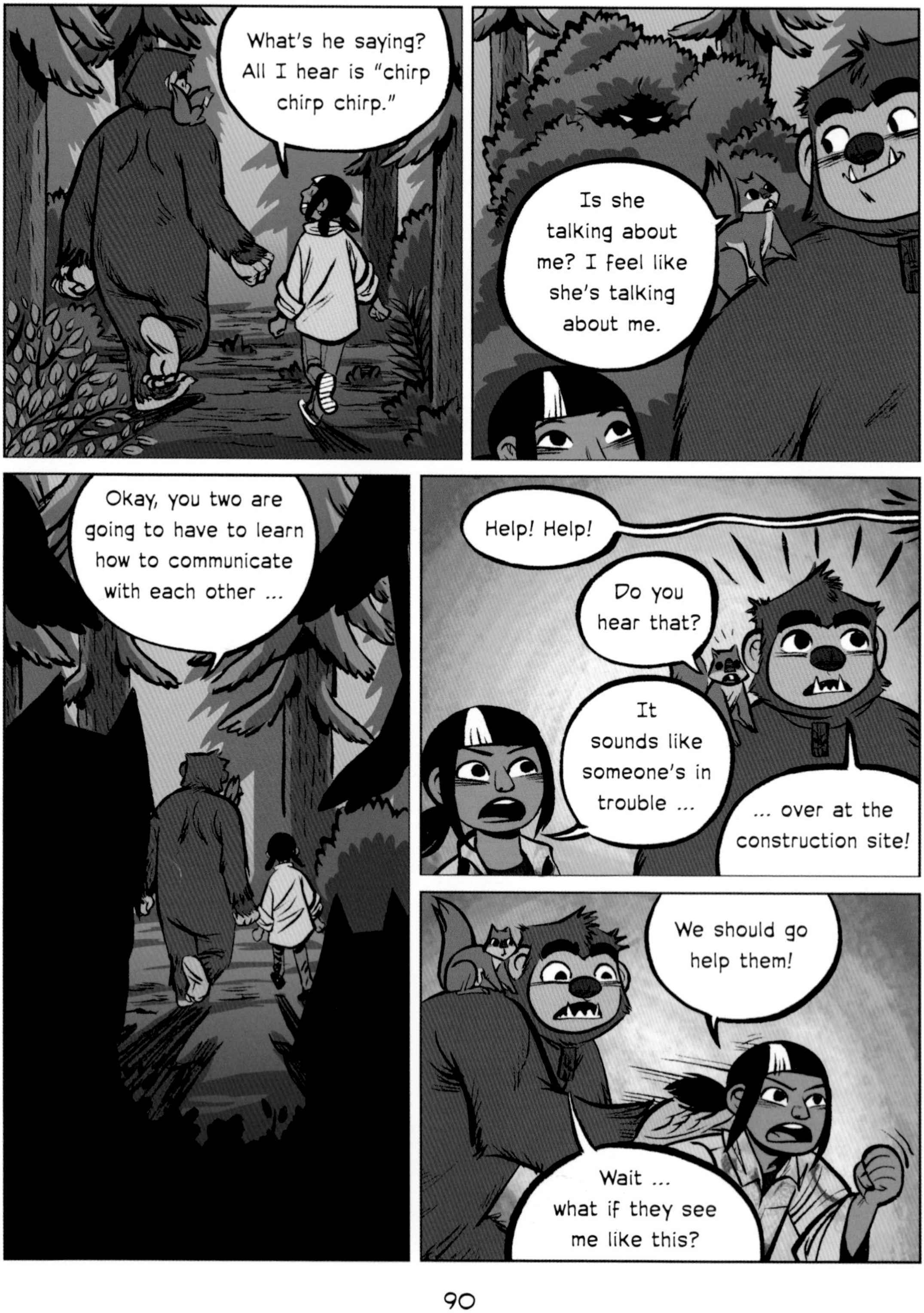

What's he saying? All I hear is "chirp chirp chirp."
Is she talking about me? I feel like she's talking about me.
Okay, you two are going to have to learn how to communicate with each other ...
Help! Help!
Do you hear that?
It sounds like someone's in trouble ...
... over at the construction site!
We should go help them!
Wait ... what if they see me like this?

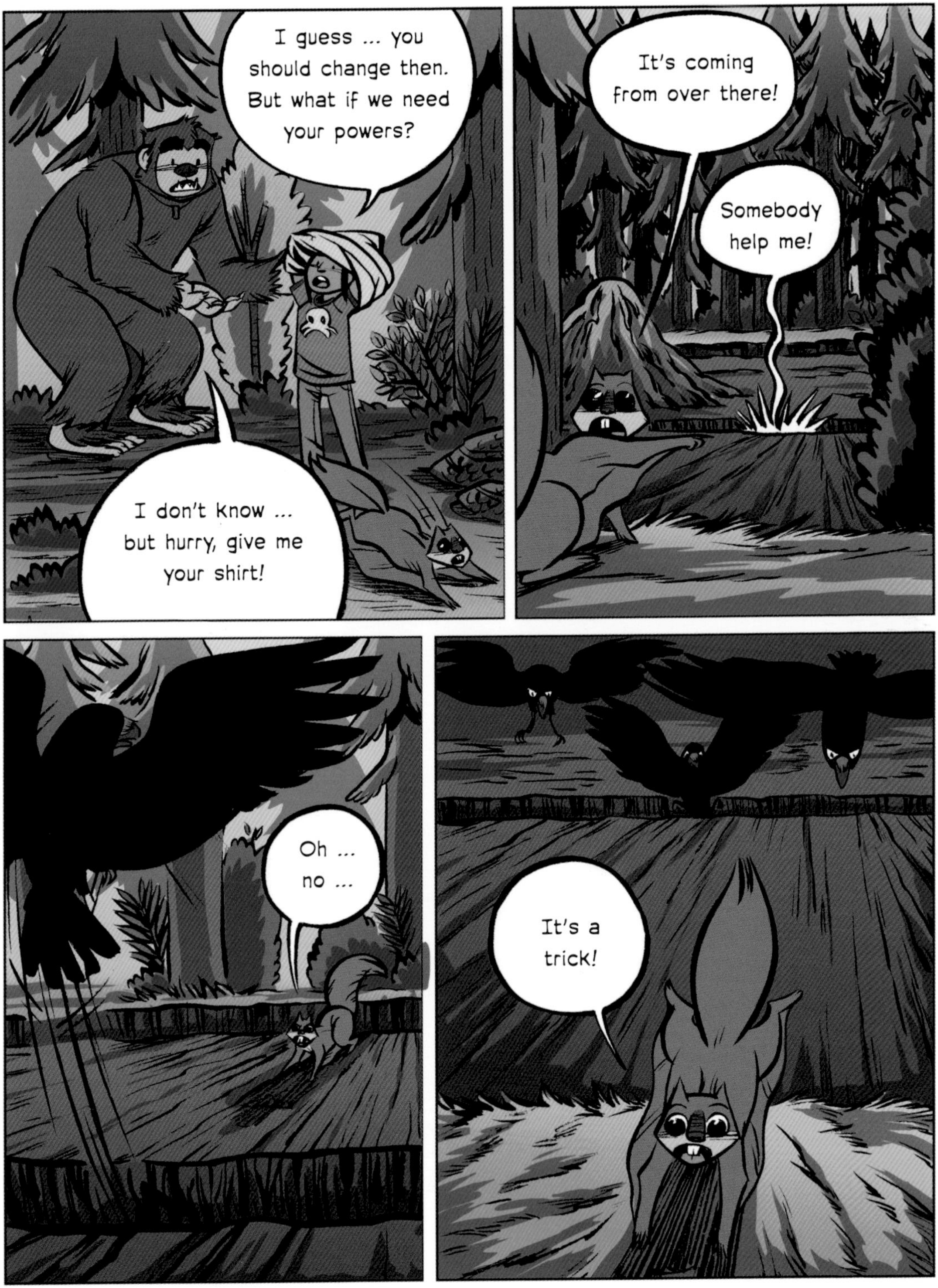
I guess ... you should change then. But what if we need your powers?
I don't know ... but hurry, give me your shirt!
It's coming from over there!
Somebody help me!
Oh ... no ...
It's a trick!

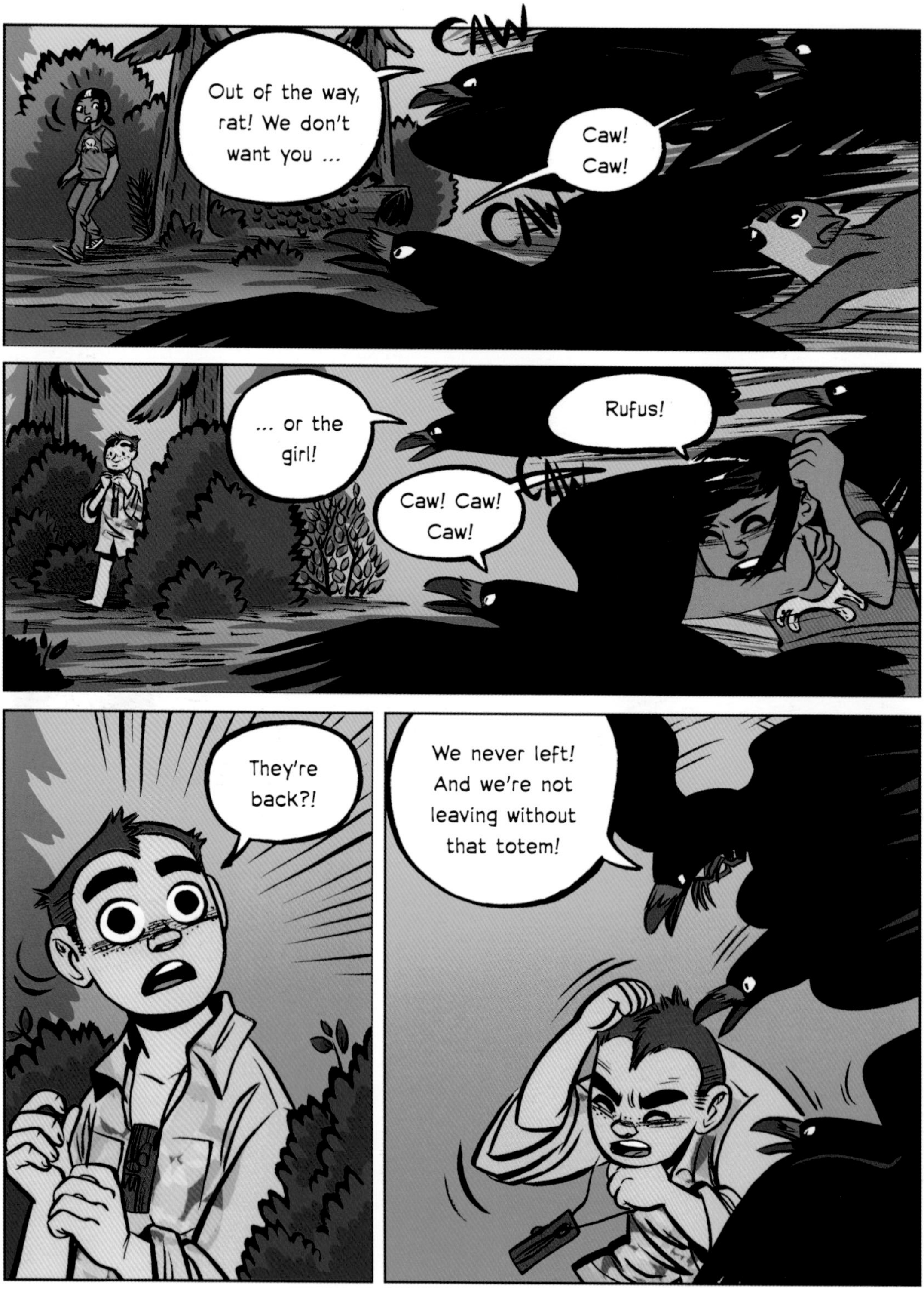
CAW
Out of the way, rat! We don't want you ...
Caw! Caw!
CAW
... or the girl!
Rufus!
Caw! Caw! Caw!
CAW
They're back?!
We never left! And we're not leaving without that totem!

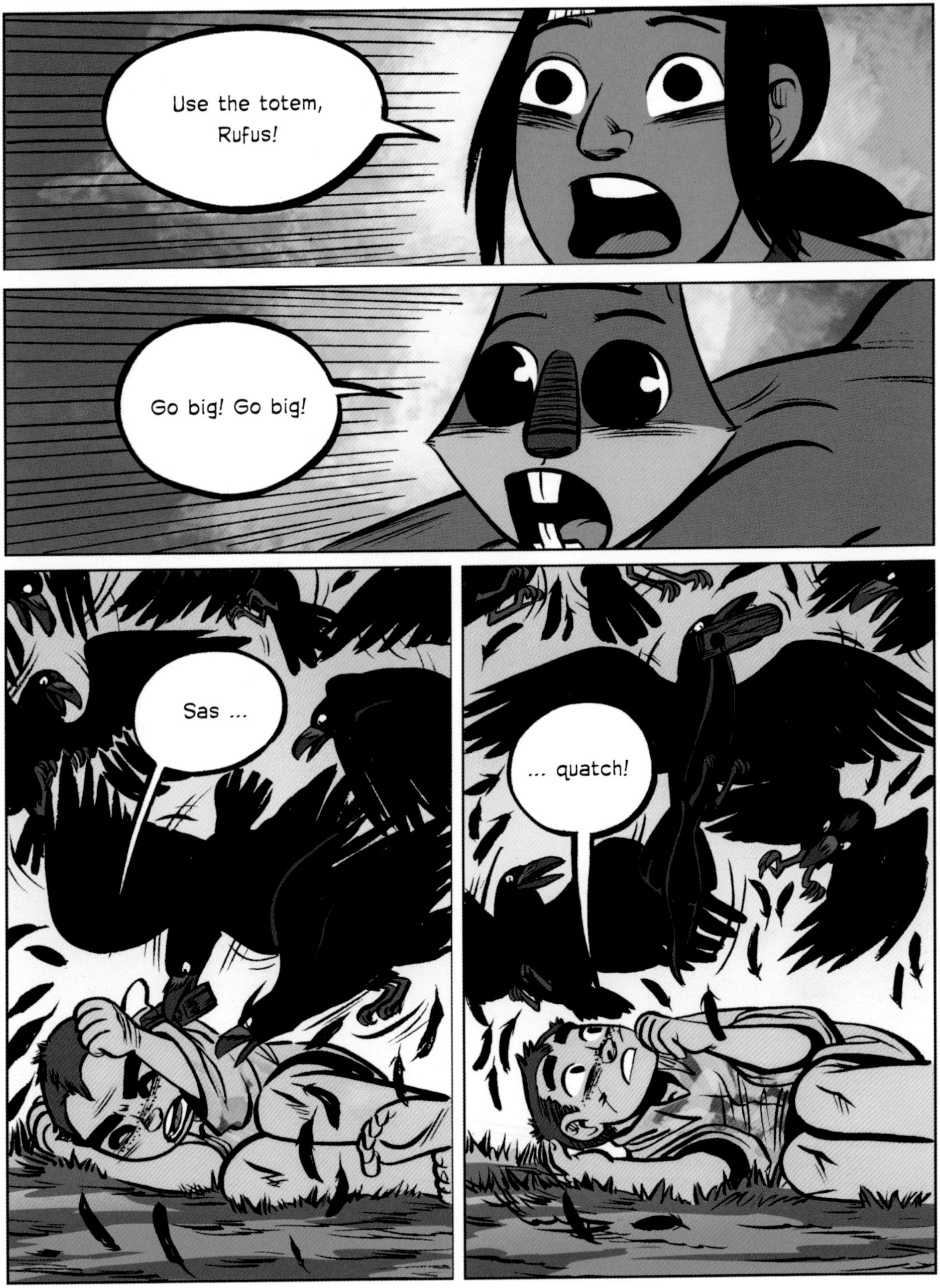
Use the totem, Rufus!
Go big! Go big!
Sas ...
... quatch!

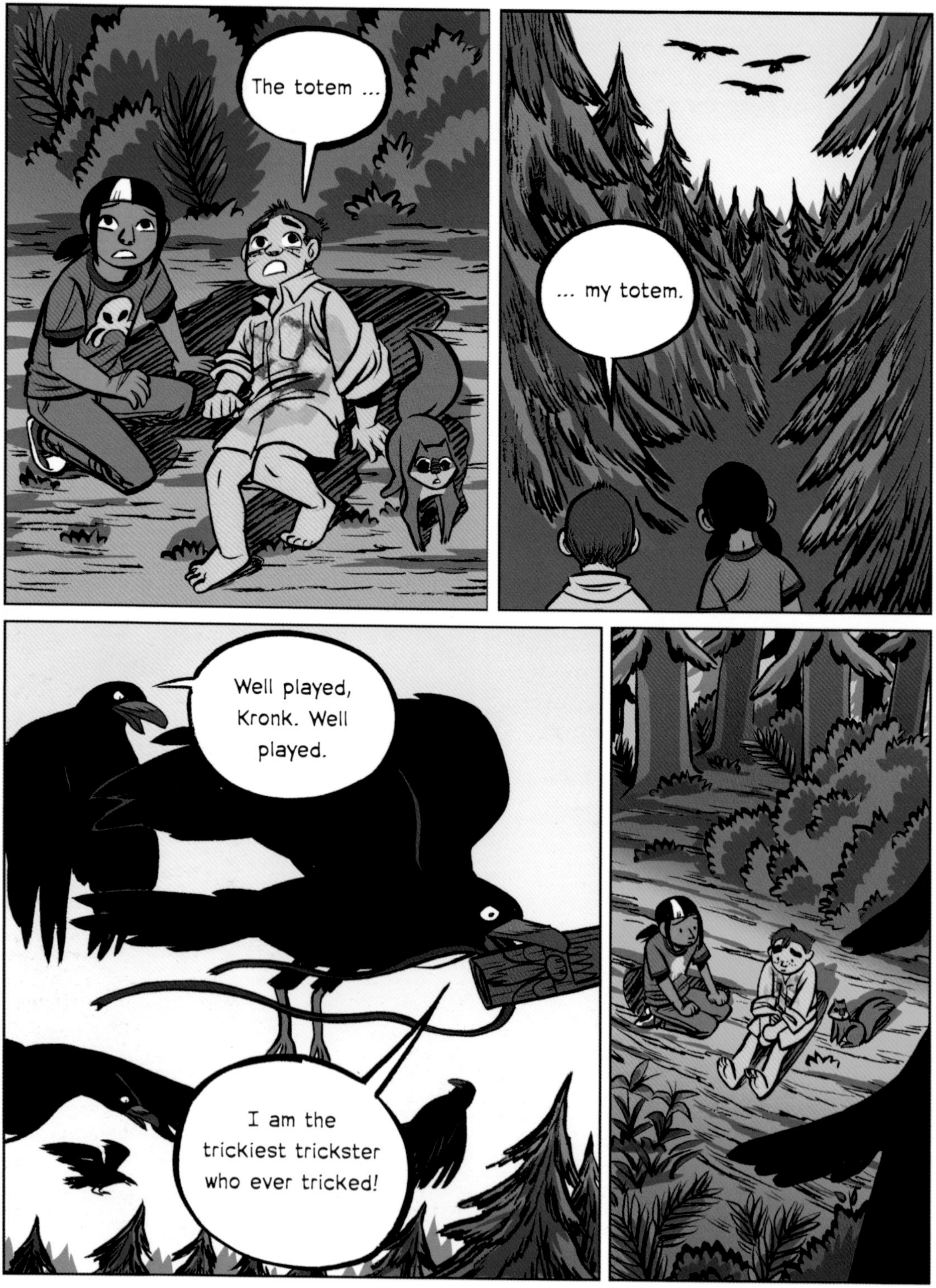
The totem ...
... my totem.
Well played, Kronk. Well played.
I am the trickiest trickster who ever tricked!

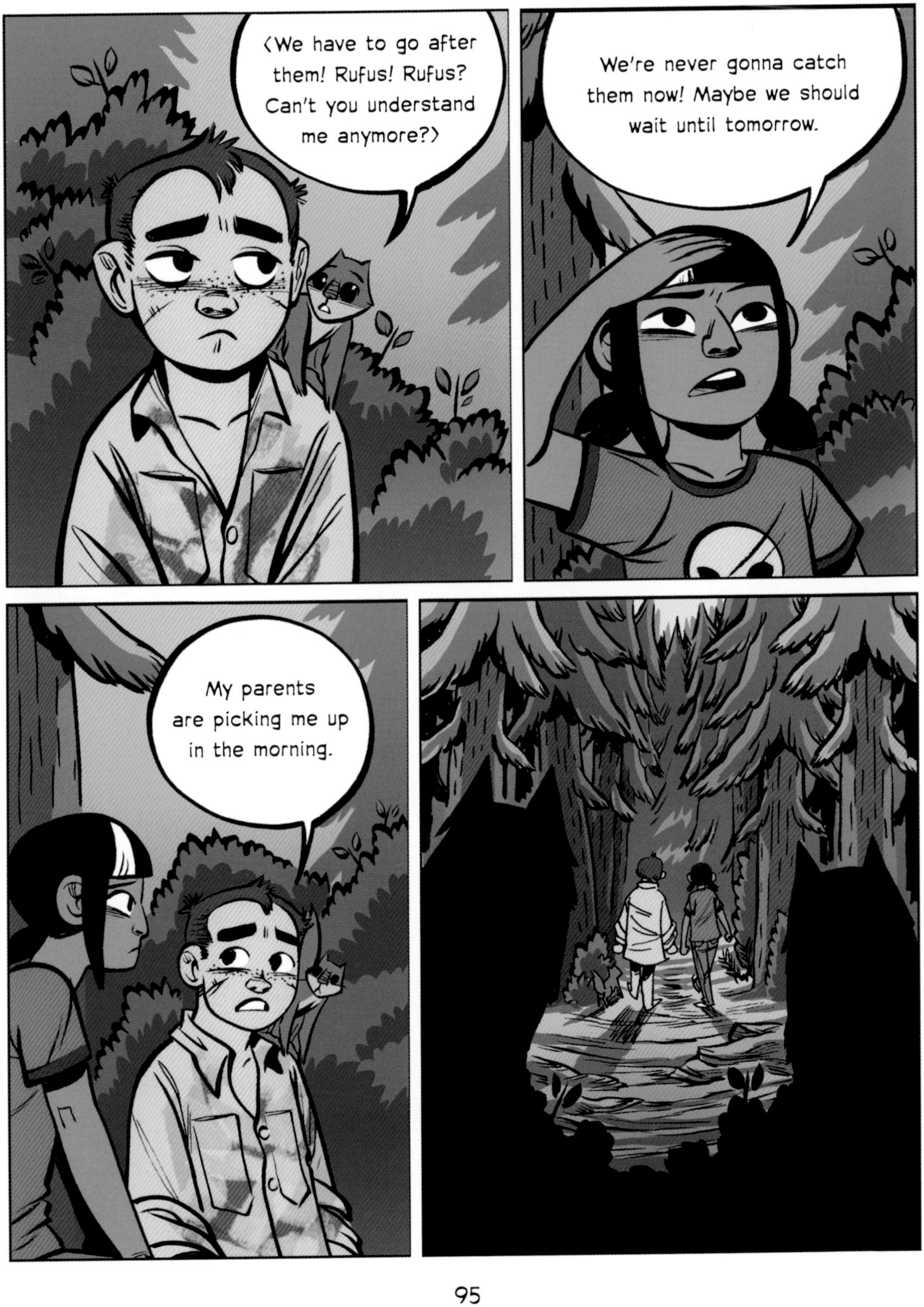
〈We have to go after them! Rufus! Rufus? Can't you understand me anymore?〉
We're never gonna catch them now! Maybe we should wait until tomorrow.
My parents are picking me up in the morning.

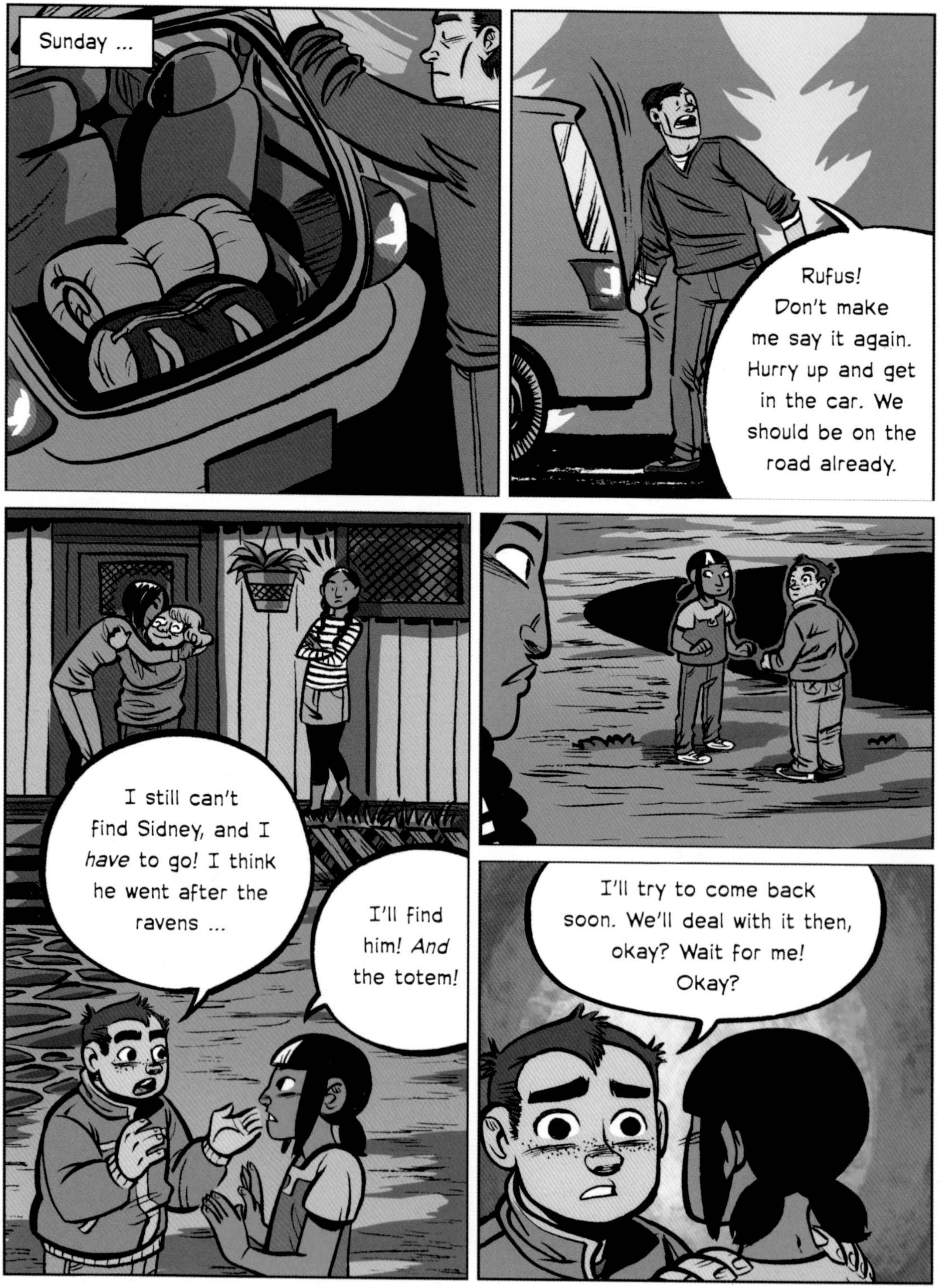

Sunday ...
Rufus! Don't make me say it again. Hurry up and get in the car. We should be on the road already.
I still can't find Sidney, and I *have* to go! I think he went after the ravens ...
I'll find him! *And* the totem!
I'll try to come back soon. We'll deal with it then, okay? Wait for me! Okay?

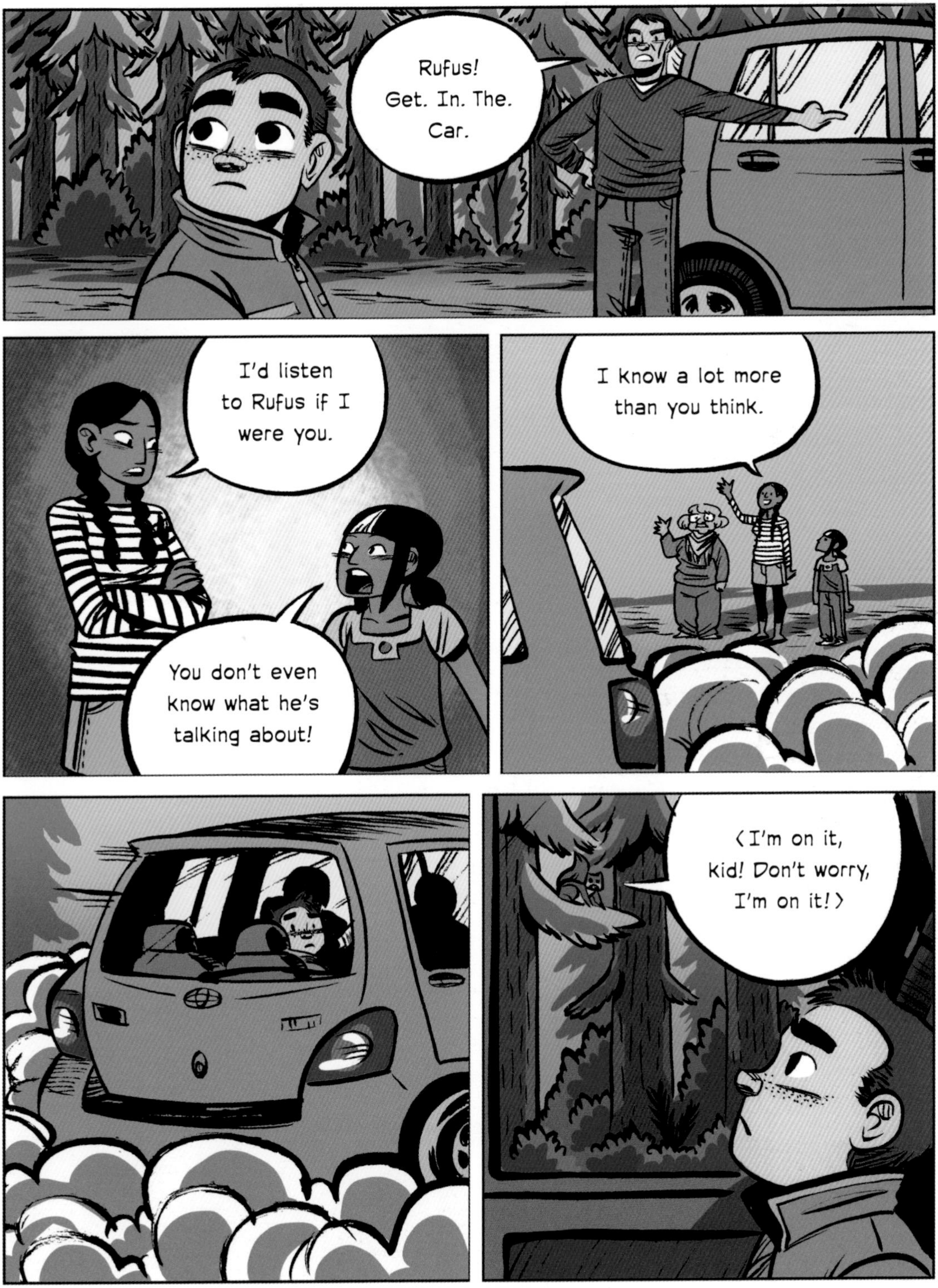
Rufus! Get. In. The. Car.
I'd listen to Rufus if I were you.
You don't even know what he's talking about!
I know a lot more than you think.
‹I'm on it, kid! Don't worry, I'm on it!›

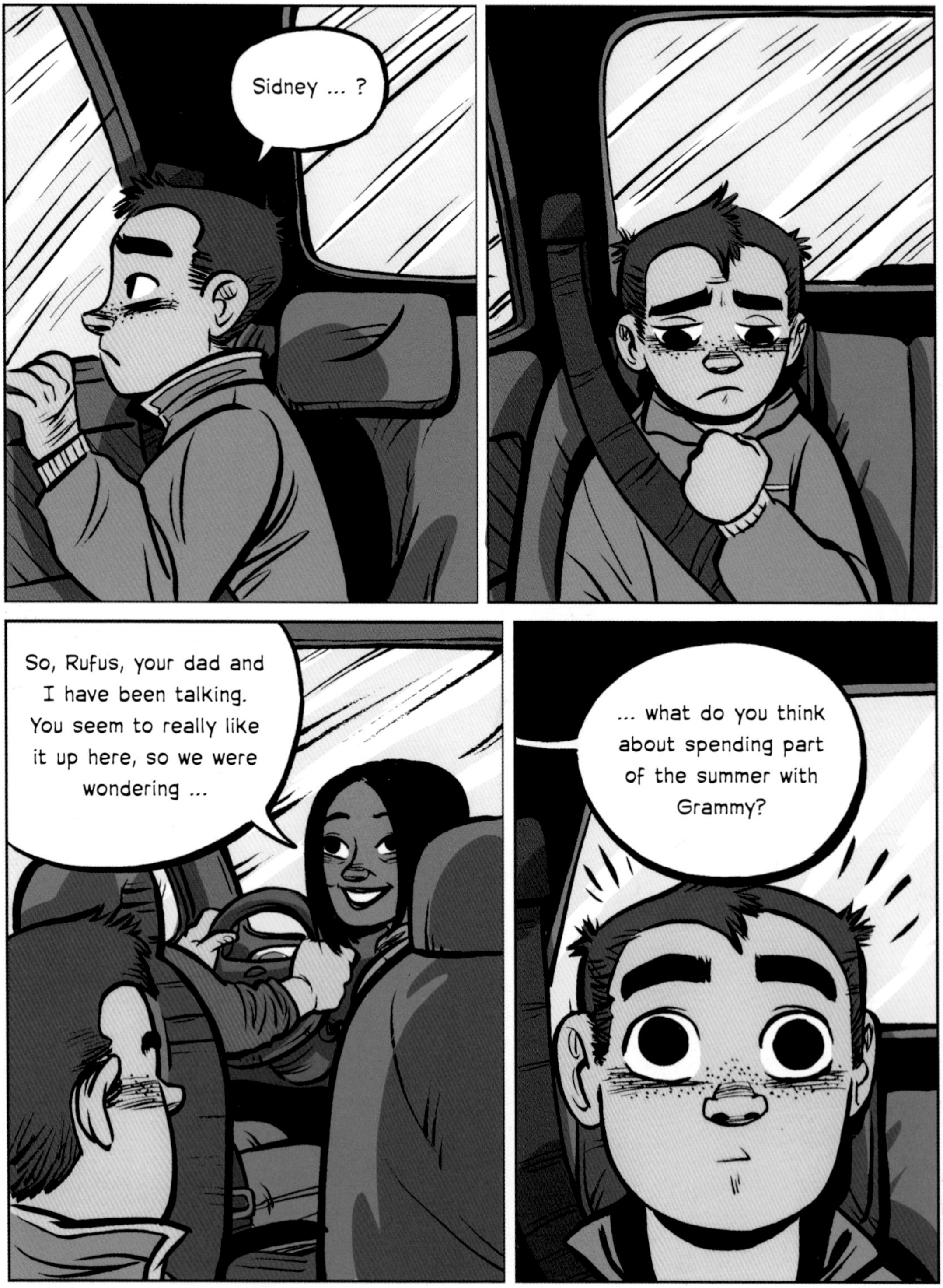
Sidney ... ?
So, Rufus, your dad and I have been talking. You seem to really like it up here, so we were wondering ...
... what do you think about spending part of the summer with Grammy?

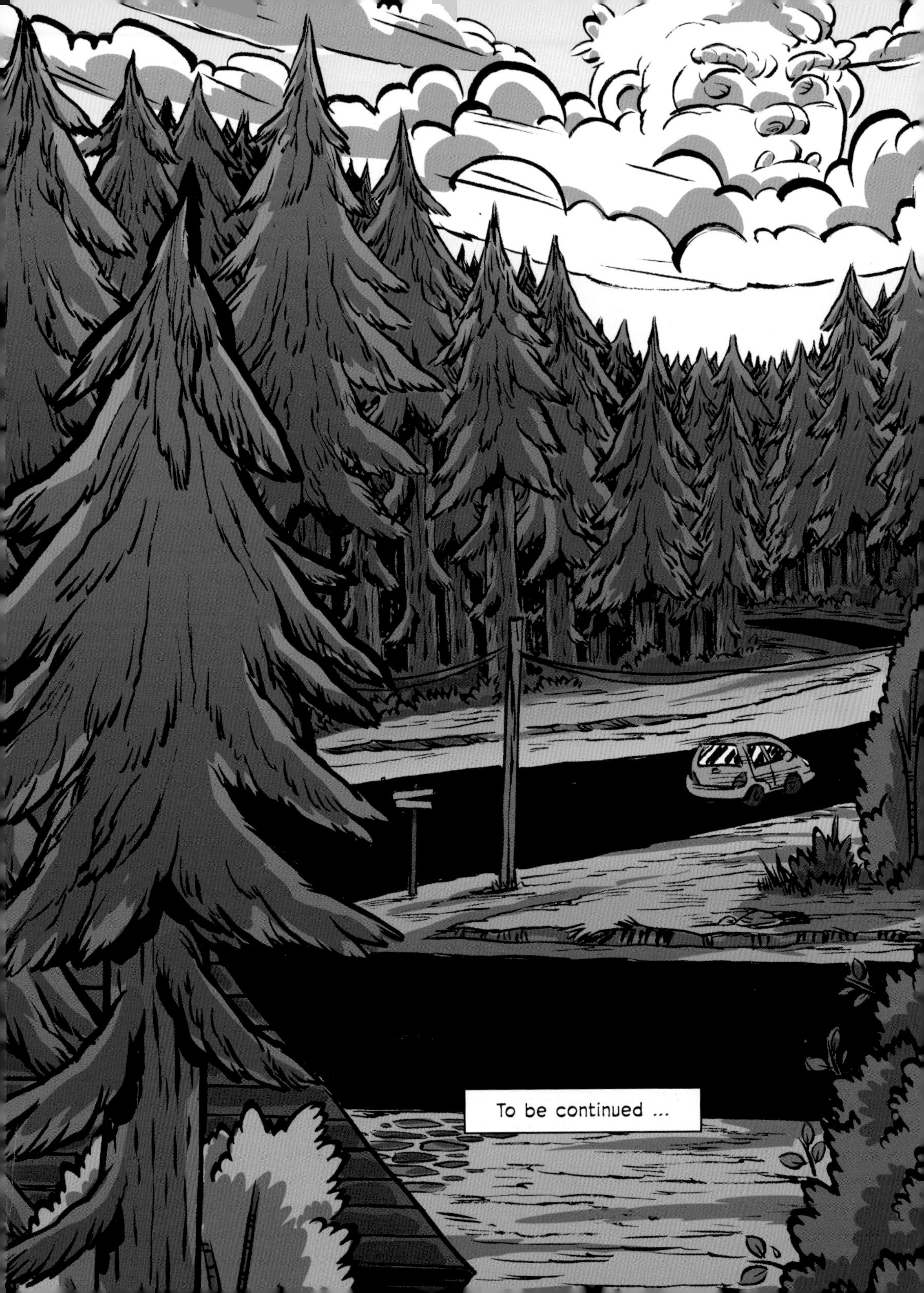
To be continued ...

DON'T MISS BOOK ONE IN THE BIGFOOT BOY SERIES

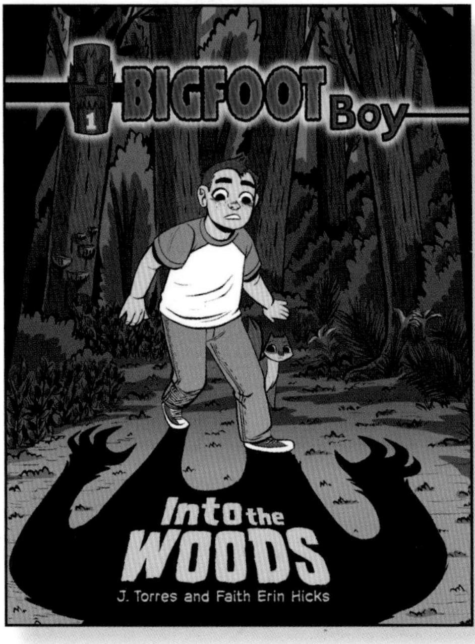

BIGFOOT Boy
1
Into the WOODS
J. Torres and Faith Erin Hicks

HC 978-1-55453-711-2
PB 978-1-55453-712-9

Praise for *Into the Woods*

★ "... magic, humor and just a hint of menace. ... This one gets everything just right. Be prepared for young Sasquatch fans roaring for more."

—*Kirkus Reviews,* starred review

"A solid introduction to a new adventure series, and young readers will clamor for a second volume."

—*Booklist*